Wendy Tipping is a self-published author who lives in Cairns, Queensland.

"*Love, Reignited*" is her debut novel and is part of a series of sweet romances set in the tropics of Queensland. It focuses on the men and women who work in emergency services, particularly police, firefighters and paramedics.

Wendy has worked in emergency communications for both the police and fire services over recent years and draws on her knowledge and experiences to create interesting and true-to-life stories.

Her other hobbies (when not busy at the keyboard) include camping, spending time with the family and pets, reading and conducting research for new ideas.

Connect via her website at https://wendytipping.com, on Facebook at https://facebook.com/wendy-tipping-author and Pinterest at Wendy-Tipping-Author.

Witchy Publishing
Mount Sheridan, Queensland

ISBN Print Version: 978-0-6487751-0-2

Visit author's website at:
https://www.wendytipping.com

LOVE, REIGNITED

Wendy Tipping

*To Mum
for everything*

*To Bradd
with love*

Chapter 1

At first, the constant buzzing didn't register in Evie's mind, but its persistence and increasing volume made her eyes snap open in frustration.

"For goodness' sake, what is that awful noise?" she muttered, rubbing shampoo from her eyes. She'd been enjoying herself, standing under the spray, thankful for its cooling effect on her overheated skin.

The water cascaded over her, sliding over the peaks and troughs of her slight figure. She reached up for the bottle of body wash, pumping some into her hand, lathering it over her upper chest and arms. The heady scent of vanilla and orange filled her nostrils and the sense of indulgence put her in an almost trance-like state, despite the intrusion of the noise.

The workout with Nicola had been full on, raising a sweat Evie couldn't wait to remove. Not that it took much to perspire these days, smack bang within the humidity and intense heat of the wet tropics, certainly a sharp contrast to Melbourne where she'd lived her whole life.

Until now.

Yet, she wasn't complaining. Workouts with personal trainers were meant to be exhilarating and Nicola sure knew how to push her to the max.

The *whoop whoop* sound continued, and Evie suspected this wouldn't bode well for her relaxing afternoon. Having only moved into the apartment complex, she didn't recall the on-site manager mention anything about a weekly alarm check. Thoughts of her new job entered her mind then, and her anxiety rose slightly.

She turned the taps off, unable to ignore the urgent screech of the alarm any longer. *Better check out what's going on.*

Maybe it's someone cooking toast or something, she mused. *I'm sure it will stop any minute now.* At least, that's what she told herself. Still, she felt uneasy, not knowing what was going on outside her door.

It still felt weird–this living alone.

Not really a situation of her own choosing, and hopefully not a long-term option.

Wish Ben was here. Or…, Evie shook her head in denial. *Don't go there. They can't help you with this. No one can. It's just you, girl. From now on. Toughen up.*

You'll be fine.

She grabbed a fluffy towel from the rack and started to hum, hoping that her action would tune out the sound and lessen her anxiety, yet both persisted, and she was left with no other option.

As her feet pattered across the cool tiles of the apartment floor, Evelyn Meriwether had little way of knowing that her afternoon was about to get interesting.

* * * * *

"Firecom Far North to 8-11 Bravo, fire call over."

Seconds slipped by as Station Officer Nathan Barrett scowled at the interruption from his portable radio.

Great timing, Firecom.

Having just started to lift over 230kg of incapacitated male flesh onto the stretcher, sweat started to bead his brow and run down his back as the heavy weight impacted his arms. He wasn't a wimp by any means, but this guy took every ounce of exertion from him and his entire body screamed under the load. And he was fit! God knows how the rest of the crew were feeling?

Nathan hated summer—mostly for this reason.

Without a doubt, January through March was the worst time of year to get these type of requests from the Ambulance Service. Being mid-February now, there wouldn't be a reprieve anytime soon. Unfortunately, this poor guy had fallen in the bathroom and wedged himself in tight.

The male had grunted he'd been stuck on his bathroom floor for around twenty-four hours after slipping, and the stench in the whole place wasn't inviting enough that Nathan and his crew felt inclined to stay for tea and scones.

There was a not so graceful dumping of the patient as the entire crew released their load onto the stretcher's frame. They all stood as one to ease the strain on their backs, Kenny wiping the sweat as it poured down his face.

Nathan couldn't help but smile at the sight as he reached for his portable.

"Firecom, this is 8-11 Bravo, go ahead," he responded, breathing heavily.

"8-11 Bravo. Request for you to attend a fire alarm at the Regency Apartments on Sheridan St. Are you available from your location, over?"

Nathan sized up the situation in front of him before replying.

"Firecom, we're still assisting the paramedic with moving this patient to the ambulance. Will be available in about three minutes, over." His prediction was likely an under-estimation, but his plan was to get out of here as soon as they could.

Incidents like this weren't out of the scope of the fire service these days but that didn't stop most of the crew complaining about it. Kenny always tried using his recurring back injury as an excuse to avoid the heavy stuff, demonstrated now as he held the guy's head at the top of the stretcher. The attending ambulance officer, Angie, was operating solo so there was no way she could have dealt with this situation alone.

"Okay guys, we're ready to go," she said, checking the IV drip was in place. She was no doubt keen to get her patient to the Cairns Base Hospital as quickly as possible. She'd told Nathan his blood pressure almost read off the scale, more than likely due to the combination of his weight and the stress of the fall.

"Let's take this slowly and lift on my count of three," Nathan instructed as he moved into position at the head of the stretcher. He noted Kenny's look of reluctance as he shuffled to the corner of the room but was waylaid by his senior officer.

"Kenny, you need to help us out for this one. We need all hands on deck. Can you grab the lead at the front end?" Nathan directed as he knelt down at the foot of the stretcher. He recognised Kenny's frown and could sympathise with the older firie yet needed everyone to pitch in.

Sure as hell not looking forward to this part, Nathan thought as he started the count.

* * * * *

Five minutes later, Nathan radioed through his team's availability to attend the alarm after depositing big boy into the ambulance.

Chances were high the alarm would prove to be false as per usual, otherwise they would have been told of more emergency calls coming through by now.

Nathan couldn't remember the last time he'd been to something substantial. These days the job was more mundane than exciting, dealing with the lift assists, alarms to premises, traffic accidents and school visits, not to mention lecturing wide eyed five-year-olds about being fire-aware.

Not exactly what he'd signed up for.

Fourteen years ago, as a young man of twenty, the recruitment drive had promised a life of excitement and stimulation. His mind had conjured up images of attending explosions, huge out-of-control fires and daring rescues. These days there was just as much paperwork as action.

Still, he wouldn't change it for anything. He had no plans to leave and still believed it was one of the best jobs around. He'd worked his way up the ranks and earned the respect of his team as their station officer.

A far cry from his early days as a carpenter's apprentice, slogging it out in the heat with a hammer and nail.

A lifetime ago.

For now, though, it was road speed to the centre of town.

"Okay, Oscar, let's get to Sheridan Street," Nathan directed the young rookie as he waved a goodbye to Angie as she sped off, ambulance sirens wailing.

"No problem, boss. Next stop, Regency Apartments," Oscar said, pulling into the busy end of day traffic. "Not great timing though, with everyone heading home. Doesn't look like we'll be back before..."

"Firecom to 8-11 Bravo, over," the pump radio cut in.

"Firecom, this is 8-11 Bravo, pass your message," Nathan responded, wondering what was coming.

The silence which greeted his request had Nathan concerned. Time delays were unusual, unless Comms were being swamped with jobs or dealing with other radio traffic from crews.

The radio crackled back to life.

"8-11 Bravo, standby for further info." Rylee was the radio operator today, her husky tones recognisable to him as opposed to Caroline's more chirpier, brighter tone. The younger and less experienced Rylee had been on his shift for a year now, and Nathan found her efficient if not a little immature.

He knew that Rylee had a thing for him, in the few times they'd met, even though he'd made it clear he wasn't interested. Wouldn't be interested for a long time - if ever - after Liv.

Don't even go there, mate, his inner voice urged. *Not today*.

His thoughts were broken once again by Rylee's more urgent tone.

"8-11 Bravo, we've received multiple triple 0 calls advising there is smoke now issuing from the location on Sheridan Street. They report persons are evacuating. We've dispatched police, ambulance and the power authority," Rylee said. "What's your ETA at the location?"

This latest information caused Nathan's heart rate to rise and adrenaline to run, ever so slightly. He showed no outward sign of stress or fear. It was still business as usual, as far as he was concerned.

Unlike some, Nathan's experience and calm demeanour ensured he didn't let himself get too flustered or stressed. It was this part of his personality his crew respected the most and looked up to.

"Firecom, our ETA is three minutes from Regency. Based on the information provided, can you upgrade response to a second alarm and contact the senior officer of the incident," Nathan requested.

Perhaps this may turn into something more interesting after all? he thought.

"Firecom to 8-11 Bravo, copy last, 1735," Rylee replied.

"Shit boss, looks like we have a goer. I can see smoke," Kenny advised, as the truck turned into Sheridan and made its way to the front of the building.

Nathan's mind started to tick over now that he had a potential fire situation on his hands.

"Okay guys, let's make sure we have our gear ready to go. We'll get to the fire panel first and speak to the manager. Kenny, once the second unit gets here, you and I will make up the Safety Team," he directed. "There'll be a crowd of people so hopefully the police will deal with that."

Oscar sounded the horn to clear a path to the apartment entrance, avoiding the group of onlookers standing around, most with mobiles in hand. A crew from a local news station were already setting up, the young female reporter straightening her hair and dress through the camera's lens.

Obviously, they'd heard the incident on the local scanner which they routinely monitored, and wanted a piece of the action.

Oscar parked the appliance and followed Nathan's lead, grabbing the thermal imaging camera, or TIC as it was known, which identified potential hot spots in the building. Will reached for the heavier Hooligan tool, used to break down doors to gain access if needed.

As the onlookers stared, the entire crew wondered if this job would prove as exciting as they hoped.

Chapter 2

Across town at Fire Communications Headquarters, Rylee McIntyre and her shift partner Caroline Kerr were in the final hour of their day. Rylee, as radio operator for the afternoon, got to hear firsthand the dulcet tones of Nathan Barrett's voice on the radio. As far as she was concerned, he made being on shift way more interesting.

She'd had a thing for him for a while now, ever since being introduced at last year's staff Christmas party. Not only was he one of the hottest firefighters in town, but he had a kind of macho that Rylee found more than sexy.

She'd tried more than once to advertise her interest, but he didn't seem keen. *His loss*, she lamented. She'd heard on the grapevine he'd been involved with a paramedic but thought maybe they'd broken up. Her slim hopes remained alive and she refused to give up just yet.

"I'll change this job to a structure fire from the alarm, Rylee," Caroline interrupted as she tapped away at the keyboard. "But I bet it's someone cooking again and burning the toast."

"Or steam from the shower. That's always popular," Rylee suggested. "People just don't get how sensitive they are."

The emergency line rang and Caroline reached to answer it. "Queensland Fire, where is the location of your emergency?" she prompted the caller.

"Ahhh… I'm Alan, the Manager calling from the Regency Apartments on Sheridan Street. You've probably received an alarm coming through for here." He raised his voice to speak above the high screech of the siren. "We're evacuating because of smoke coming from one apartment. I think it's on the Sixth Floor but I'm not sure what it is yet."

"Yes Alan, we're aware of that and have a crew on the way coming lights and sirens. Can you see any flames or is it just smoke from your location?"

"Um, I've been told there's smoke, but I haven't got up there. I'm only new here and I've been trying to check the fire panel first," Alan responded, a hesitant catch in his voice. The middle-aged male was discovering his new job was more stressful than he'd expected. First, there'd been the burst hot water system, then the head chef quitting, and now this!

Caroline reassured the manager as she ended the call. "Okay, that's fine. If you meet the crew on arrival and keep evacuating people, that would be great. I'll pass the information on to the crew."

"Rylee, there's more info on the job if you want to pass that over," she informed her partner as the phone rang once again.

Rylee nodded in acknowledgment. Some days, the workload was hectic yet others could be quiet. The advice they'd received about this incident so far gave both operators the impression it may take some time to complete, meaning a busy last hour to their shift.

"I'll be happier when those two new operators start here next week to help," Rylee remarked as Caroline nodded her head in agreement.

* * * * *

Alan's face reddened when he saw the fire truck pull up outside the front entrance. He wasn't prepared yet, having only just located the key to the fire panel behind reception. Arthur had offered him a brief rundown of how the damn thing operated last week but, not being tech savvy, Alan really had no clue of what he was looking at.

Hopefully, these guys could sort it out for him.

Wiping his brow, Alan walked towards the entrance and waited as Nathan and the crew entered the foyer.

"Excuse me, are you the Manager of the complex?" he was asked by the fireman holding a radio. The remaining three firefighters each carried different pieces of equipment in their hands, as the situation became more serious in Alan's mind.

His throat tightened. "Ummm, Yes Sir. I'm Alan Robard, the new manager here. A guest said there's smoke coming from about the fifth or sixth floors but I haven't got around to checking yet," Alan stuttered.

He was grateful when the firefighter took control. "If you can show me the fire panel, we'll see what zones have activated," and Alan dutifully led him to the reception area.

Nathan signalled his arrival back to Firecom. "This is 8-11 Bravo. We are code two, smoke issuing from the building. Have second attending appliance attend forward control point on ground level." This referred to the designated area for meet ups where he could liaise with other responding crews. "Fireground Channel is three. Standby for further sitrep," Nathan advised, whilst opening the glass panel providing access to the alarm system. A red light flashed next to Zone Two on Level Six meaning the alarm activation was coming from one of the apartments there.

"Is there anyone still upstairs at the moment?" Nathan turned to Alan, as the manager patted his head with what appeared to be a napkin of some sort. His large nose and balding crown dripped with liquid as he tried to regain composure.

It was more than obvious the frazzled manager wasn't too comfortable at the drama unfolding in his building.

"Um, I don't know. There are two permanent residents who live there and four apartments rented out to holidaymakers. I believe most of them are out but I'm still trying to get the numbers together."

"Okay, we'll head up there now. Just keep people moving out, take their details and keep a tally. When the next truck arrives, let the Senior Officer know where you're at. Where's the nearest stairwell?"

Alan pointed to a corner of the foyer showing the stairway entrance. "Yes, okay, no problem. I can do that," Alan squeaked, realising he sounded less than convincing.

At least the cavalry had arrived now–they'd know what to do!

* * * * *

Up on the sixth floor, Evie had almost reached the door when she heard a heavy knock. She clutched the towel firmly to her as it began to slip. She caught a whiff of what smelt like a burning electrical odour coming from outside her apartment door and she tensed.

A sense of panic crept into her mind as images of high-rise fires played out, yet she just as quickly dismissed them. *Surely, nothing like that could happen here?*

"Okay, okay, give me a sec," she called back as the tapping grew louder and more insistent. She folded the towel around herself, securing it as best she could, before patting her hair and grabbed at the heavy-set door, easing it open.

Expecting to see the large-nosed, balding Alan, she was more than startled when confronted by a fireman donned in full firefighting regalia.

Through the yellow hood, she had a glimpse of rich brown eyes which appeared similarly surprised by her appearance. It was at that moment she remembered all she was wearing was the towel-and nothing else. Her skin reddened and she grasped it a little tighter around her chest.

Great, she thought, hoping news of this wouldn't somehow get out to her new workmates before she'd even started the job.

"Miss, we have to evacuate everyone from this building. There could be a fire somewhere in the premises. Everyone has to leave-now." His voice sounded firm and authoritative, not likely open to negotiation, yet she couldn't help but ask.

"Um, officer, is it okay for me to change first? I'm not dressed to go outside. If I could just…"

"I'm sorry, we don't have time." It seemed the fireman wasn't the type to accept delays. "I still have another floor to check and we need to ensure that we account for all residents. You'll be fine. Chances are this will all be over soon." He put his arm out as a signal for her to leave but Evie stood resolute in the doorway, unable to believe he'd ignored her plea.

His tone became more serious as he shook his head. "I'd appreciate if you leave now using the stairs and make yourself known to the Manager so he can add you to the headcount. Hopefully, we can get this sorted as soon as possible and you can return to your apartment. Thanks for your co-operation."

He turned on his heels and his quick departure surprised Evie. She'd wanted to ask if he knew where the internal staircase was located as she'd had no reason to use it before now.

She moved forward slightly to call out to him, realising a second too late as the door shut behind her with a loud thud that she now had a more pressing issue to deal with.

* * * * *

Thanks for your co-operation! He grimaced to himself, replaying the words in his head. *What was that about?*

Nathan strode away, finding himself strangely unsettled in the attractive woman's presence.

He couldn't help but admire her determination and had tried hard to keep the smile from his face at the vision she'd presented. It wasn't the first time he'd seen a near-naked woman, but this one was more pleasing to the eye than some.

Standing at just below his chin, slight but not too slim, she'd held the flimsy towel to her body as her well-toned arms showed she either had good genes or worked out, or both.

Her hair, still damp from the shower she'd obviously just exited, hung about shoulder length, some droplets falling onto bare skin. Full lips had pouted at his request to leave and he noted they looked soft and entirely kissable. Light blue eyes, which had widened at his appearance, were the type a man could never tire of gazing into.

His quick observations had seen him distracted, and he'd turned away, not wanting to make more of a dick of himself than he thought he had.

It's not like he hadn't seen women in a state of undress before, even if she was only covered by a scrap of material. *Cute perk of the job*, he mused, as he made his way down the corridor to continue the door knock for other residents.

Once that task was done, he made a mental note to check on the mystery woman's welfare once he made it back downstairs.

All part of the service, he told himself with a smile.

Chapter 3

That same afternoon, at St Kilda Road police headquarters in Melbourne, Ben Herney gazed at the smiling woman in his phone's photo gallery. He lay fingers over her smile and once again felt the familiar ache in his gut. He'd taken the picture on their trip to the Sunshine Coast, and he realised how the blue sky and crashing surf paled compared to how beautiful she was.

Although the office was buzzing with police officers and other personnel going about their business, all Ben heard was the loud thump of his heart and his head started to pound in accompaniment.

Damn stupid Valentine's Day, he thought. That's what it was.

Trying to push tomorrow's over-rated festivities from his mind only made the separation from Evie feel more intense. More than it had in quite a while.

For what seemed like the hundredth time, he closed his eyes, rubbing his temple while playing out their last exchange as he pictured the pain reflected in her eyes when he'd told her he was ending it.

The look of disbelief and shock had paled her skin. Hating to see her in distress but ignoring the flood of tears, he'd tried to explain his reasons but they'd sounded as piss weak then as he felt now.

McDermott chose that moment to waylay his thoughts as he approached Ben's desk with his usual swagger.

"Hey Herney, have you finished those interviews with the Hardy witnesses yet? I want to put the brief together and I've got jack shit to give to Prosecutions."

Nothing like a polite request from a colleague to brighten your day!

"Yeah, I've just about finished." Ben put the phone in the drawer, slamming it shut. "My computer keeps freezing so I'm trying to get them printed." An outright lie. He hadn't bothered to transcribe anything from his notes yet but Barry wasn't to know that.

"Well make sure you get it done ASAP. I haven't got time to waste on this crap." The older detective waved to someone calling from the back of the office, with a "yeah coming" response before turning back to Ben. "I need you to help me set up an interview for the rape victim, Claire… whatever the hell her name is. So let's put this other one to bed, hey."

"That would be Claire Finch," Ben reminded his partner, whose tendency to disassociate himself from victims of crime annoyed the hell out of him. As if learning their names made them seem more real, not just a case number on a file. "Mate, no problem. I'll get it to you by the end of today."

Another lie. Typing wasn't one of his strongest assets so there was no way he could give McDermott what he wanted.

Ben didn't care much right now.

McDermott gave a final grunt and shuffled off. *Asshole*, Ben thought. The arrogant son of a bitch was one reason he felt as though his life was falling apart. He wanted his old life back - or at least the one he'd had with Evie. That, and their plans for the future. Plans that had blown away like the beach sand in the photo he'd taken.

"You can't have her and the career you want too, Herney. She's tainted and always will be. You need to make a choice." McDermott's words from months ago echoed in his mind and he grimaced at thinking how much he'd believed them to be true back then.

Ben wondered again, as he had so many times of late, if the job and his career was worth it.

If he hadn't made the biggest mistake of his life.

* * * * *

God, I don't believe this.

Evie turned around to find her apartment door closed with the front edge of the towel wedged firmly inside. A gentle tug proved useless and all but dashed her hopes of having it budge, as the material remained resolutely stuck.

She tried pulling again in the vain hope it would by some miracle dislodge itself but, nope, the damn thing wasn't moving.

She was trapped, with no way of escaping, unless she considered baring all and making a dash for, well …, nowhere in particular.

No use for it but to wait and hope that one of her neighbours would return. There were six units on this floor, half of them with permanent residents. Surely someone would be up soon. Either that or wait for this drama to be over but even then, she'd have to somehow get Alan to let her back inside with his master key.

Over five minutes later, and Evie's panic rose as no one materialised. She couldn't see or smell any smoke yet the noise of the alarm persisted. She turned her head, checking the entire length of the corridor yet it remained eerily empty.

Several large coloured prints lined its walls, promoting the tropical theme displayed throughout the complex. The dark blue hallway carpet dotted with seashells felt lush on her bare feet as the breeze of the air conditioner cooled her drying skin.

She shivered and rubbed her arms, but the towel started to slip, and she clasped it once again. Even though she was happy with her body image and worked hard to keep trim, she wasn't in the habit of making such public displays of herself.

Her mind began to imagine crazy scenarios-a group of teenagers entering the corridor, laughingly taking photos of her predicament and posting them on Facebook.

Heaven knows she'd endured enough unwanted publicity recently to find herself the target of any kind of public attention again.

That was why she'd left Melbourne to come to Cairns in the first place-to keep a low profile and find some way of forgetting and starting over. Yet, the transition to the single life was proving difficult, far more draining than she'd expected. If only she could…

Lost in her thoughts, she let out an audible squeak when she heard a voice from behind her, making her jump.

It was him again, and this time, he didn't look happy.

* * * * *

Nathan wasn't used to having civilians ignore his instructions, even if it was the hot woman on Level Six. He'd made a mental note to keep an eye out for her downstairs, and when she hadn't appeared, his concern grew. He could have sent Oscar or Will but at least it gave him another chance to place eyes on her again.

At present, his crew were donning their breathing apparatus, or BA as the firies called it, to check an apartment one level down, which the fire panel had identified as the source of the smoke. Good-old AI had confirmed a family of tourists were staying in the unit but was unsure if they were inside or not.

Realising she was still standing where he'd left her some ten minutes ago, Nathan approached.

"Miss, I'm not sure what the problem is but I need you downstairs *now*. There's the strong possibility of a fire somewhere in this building and I need to have all residents accounted for. Can you come with me, please?"

"Yes, well, Officer I'm trying but I can't leave right now. As you can see, I'm stuck." Evie said.

"What do you mean, you're stuck?" Nathan couldn't help but feel a smile threaten to appear. It was obvious she was embarrassed and he suddenly felt protective of her modesty.

"The bloody towel got caught in the door and it just slammed shut, if you must know. It won't move and I can't move either," she snapped but obviously regretted her tone immediately as she apologised. "Sorry. It's not your fault. I should have put the door stopper out or blocked it open, I guess."

She continued.

"Look, I'm sorry, I can't go anywhere, particularly downstairs, with no clothes on. I don't think the Manager or other residents will be impressed."

"I'm not too sure about that," Nathan replied. "Personally, I think it would make their day." A smile from her and his heart raced a little faster.

"Gee thanks, you're all heart."

"Here, take this and put it on," Nathan offered, placing the hand-held radio on the carpet and pulling off his heavy overcoat. "I know it may be hot but it'll protect your modesty at least."

He wasn't too happy having to go against procedure by removing his protective gear, but no other alternative came to mind. He'd have Oscar grab his spare from the truck as soon as he could.

Evie eyed the offering with a look of disdain, yet no doubt realised her options were limited.

"Look, sorry Miss, but you don't have a choice. It's this…," he said, holding up the yellow coat, "… or nothing. Either way, we're heading downstairs in thirty seconds."

Gritting her teeth, it was plain she had no comeback this time.

"Oh alright, for heaven's sake. Turn away then while I put it on." Evie kept one hand on the front of the towel to protect herself and held out the other to take the coat. Its weight must have surprised her as it dropped to the carpet before she could catch it.

"Dammit, it's heavier than it looks."

He bent to retrieve the coat. "No problem. They're made that way for protection, not designed to save damsels in distress. I've got it." She gave a throaty laugh in response.

"Is that what I am? A damsel in distress?"

"Maybe not so much in distress as a damsel in undress," he smiled, moving to place it around her. "Perhaps leave the towel on. Put this on top. That should preserve your modesty a bit."

He turned his back as she put the coat on, giving her a moment to adjust the fastenings.

He faced her again as she spoke. "Okay, let's go, Officer…," she started walking off, as he picked up his radio and followed behind.

"It's Station Officer Barrett. Nathan Barrett. And you are…?" he queried, noting the slim thighs poking out from underneath his turnout coat. *It sure looks better on her than it does on me.*

"I'm Evie. Just… Evie," she stood aside as he moved in front to open the stairwell door.

"Well, nice to meet you, just Evie. Shall we go?" he prompted as they made their way to the stairwell.

It seemed she wasn't too keen on sharing personal details yet that didn't put him off. Not in the slightest.

He was a determined man-and mystery woman definitely warranted a follow-up visit.

Chapter 4

Evie held her hands to her chest in a valiant attempt to appear invisible as she and Nathan entered the foyer of the building. There were what seemed to be swarms of firemen, paramedics and police on scene, yet she sensed no fear or panic among the crowd. There were no smoke or flames evident which had to be a good thing.

Hopefully, this whole ordeal would be over soon and she could escape back to her apartment.

"Hey boss, you picking up new recruits on your travels?" Oscar noticed his senior officer was down to his t-shirt and overalls while a hot-looking woman appeared, wearing his overcoat. Oscar offered a smile and a wink which had Nathan slinging a silent profanity back.

"Never mind, Oscar. Just run out to the truck and grab me the spare coat. And make it quick."

Taking Evie's arm, Nathan navigated a path through the crowd. "Why don't we go this way," he said, pointing to a covered patio area. "Make yourself known to Alan so he can mark you off his list and show you as accounted for."

Once outside, the high humidity hit her like a steam train, and the added weight of the coat had perspiration breaking out in almost every crevice. Evie sat on a wooden bench underneath several small palms as she waved a hand in front of her face trying to conjure up a breeze.

This was what Cairns was well known for-its sweat producing, frustration inducing, humidity. Short-term visitors often dismissed it as quaint and "not what they were used to back home", all part of what made the place a tropical paradise. But to the long-term and permanent residents, the relentless heat often proved uncomfortable and, at times, overwhelming. She'd been in town several months and still Evie hadn't acclimatised.

She turned to thank Nathan, but he'd already headed back inside. Feeling strangely bereft as his absence, she realised he had a job to do - the last thing he wanted or needed to worry about was some ditzy woman who'd locked herself out of her room with no clothes on.

She shook her head, chuckling at her stupidity. Tendrils of now dried hair hung limply around her face yet acted as a source of protection from curious eyes. Trying to remain inconspicuous, Evie was horrified to find herself the object of attention of a young girl of around seven, staring and pointing at her as her family gathered nearby.

"Mummy, is she a fireman too?" Evie cringed at hearing the girl's question yet couldn't blame her for being curious, dressed as she was.

Evie didn't catch the woman's response, rising to move away from the scene to save herself further embarrassment.

Still, she felt inclined to offer the girl a grin and wave in acknowledgement. In reply, the little girl returned her gesture, staring at Evie like she was some kind of superhero. It bought a smile to her face which soon disappeared as she spotted a news reporter chatting with a policeman, no doubt waiting to see if they had a newsworthy story on their hands.

Amazing how the media had the uncanny ability to appear at scenes of personal drama, pain or tragedy. Evie herself had a first-hand account as to just how soul destroying they could be in their relentlessness to chase a headline for the evening news.

No way was she prepared to get caught up in another drama.

Eyes downcast, Evie hurried from the area.

She spied Alan near the carpark entrance, holding a clip board to his chest. The poor guy looked out of his depth in his current role as the counter of heads, and Evie approached with a smile, reaching out to touch his arm. He jumped in surprise and the list fluttered to the ground.

"Sorry, I didn't mean to scare you," Evie apologised, bending to retrieve it.

"That's alright, you just gave me a fright." He looked at her with widening eyes, noting her outfit. "Why on earth are you wearing that, my dear?"

"God, don't ask." Evie tugged at the coat's collar. "I got locked out of my apartment when the alarm went off and one of the fireman lent me his coat. When this is over, could you let me back in, please?"

"Yes. No problem." He patted his wet brow once more with a hand towel. "I wish they'd hurry and find out what's wrong. There's no smoke or sight of any flames. Hopefully it's a false alarm and all this has been for nothing."

Evie tried to reassure him. "I'm sure you're right." She was soon proven correct. "Oh look. I think the head fireman is coming to speak to you now." She'd spied Nathan moving towards them and felt a flush return to her cheeks. *Stop it,* she told herself. *He's just doing his job.*

"Ah, Alan. Here you are. Been looking for you." Nathan avoided Evie's gaze. "We've given the all clear and everyone can return inside. Someone left a lithium battery plugged in for recharging in Unit 5304 and it overheated and started smoking. Lucky the alarms activated when they did because it could have ignited after a while."

Alan cheered at the news, as relief overtook his face. "Thanks Officer, for your help. Ahh,… and I'll get more training on the fire panel in case this happens again. Which hopefully, it won't," Alan held out his hand which the firefighter accepted.

"No problem. That would be a good idea."

Alan turned to Evie. "Just give me a minute and I can come upstairs with your room key," he said, scuttling off towards reception.

Now they were alone again, Evie shuffled her feet and took a step back, increasing the distance between them. It was getting way too hot, even though the sun had set some time ago, and she fanned her face.

"When Alan lets you in, could you drop the overcoat back down to me? I'll be clearing up with the team and leaving in about ten minutes," Nathan prompted.

Evie cleared her throat. "Sure, no problem, I'll be as quick as I can. And thanks. For the coat, and everything," she said, her hands awkward at her sides.

"All part of the service," he smiled, striding off before she could reply.

Soon after, as she made her way up to her apartment with Alan in tow, Evie prayed once more that word of her near-naked exploits didn't make it back to the new workmates she'd be meeting come Monday morning.

And Nathan Barrett?

Well, she'd put their brief encounter from her mind.

She definitely wasn't on the lookout for any romantic entanglements. Far from it.

She'd given up on the idea of happily ever after. That particular fairytale had proven to be fatally flawed.

From here on in, it was the single life for her.

Chapter 5

The following Monday had Evie's heart fluttering with first day nerves.

Standing at the office entrance, she once again tugged at the belt around her waist in a nervous adjustment before gathering the confidence to enter.

Fire Communications Headquarters, or Firecom as it was more commonly known, was located ten minutes north of the city centre in the suburb of Manunda. The neighbouring cemetery, its fence line high with weeds, was home to various birds and other wildlife and it wasn't unusual for the staff to be frightened half to death by the ear piercing shrieks of curlews which regularly wandered through the grounds.

The Fire Service shared facilities with the Ambulance Service, making for a busy environment as emergency vehicles were dispatched to incidents all hours of the day and night.

Well past its use-by date, the ageing complex was over thirty years old and lacked the spaciousness and appeal of some other, more modern, government agencies. Evie had been told at her first interview that promises of a new centre had been made but, as yet, a construction date hadn't been set.

She checked her pocket for the access pass Eileen had provided as she once again fought to keep her anxiety under control.

First days were always the worst!

The lingering fear that word of her embarrassment had spread also had her on edge. She'd agonised it over the weekend, trying to convince herself she was probably making a big issue out of nothing.

From what she'd seen, she felt confident that Nathan Barrett wasn't the gossiping kind. More than likely, one of his crew, particularly the cheeky looking Oscar, would love to tell a story or two.

Still, Evie reasoned, *she hadn't mentioned her last name to anyone at the incident and didn't think anyone at Firecom would check her address. Not enough to put two and two together, surely?*

Try as she might, she hadn't been able to put the events from her mind as thoughts of him had stayed with her over the weekend. Kind of hard to forget those sparkling brown eyes.

Forget him, Evie muttered under her breath as she swiped the card and walked inside.

There was no way, after how things had ended with Ben, she wanted to get tied up with anyone else.

Particularly with the stigma she carried.

* * * * *

Across town, at Cairns North Fire Station, Nathan was also thinking back to the alarm job of last week as he checked his gear, as was the routine when beginning a new shift tour.

Picking up his overcoat, he couldn't help but smile at memories of the woman who'd filled it out so nicely. He swore he could almost smell the lingering scent of vanilla or something like it on the collar.

You're going crazy, man, he thought. *Forget about it.* He shoved the coat back inside the truck and slammed the door.

Olivia had worn a perfume with a similar scent, once declaring she liked it because it reminded her of her long dead mother's baking. "As good a reason as any to choose a perfume," she'd responded to his bemused look.

Dammit.

He didn't want to dredge up old memories. Nathan hadn't thought of Livvie for a while but her image came to him now, almost as if she was standing in front of him. He let out a sigh as he ambled towards the office.

He had too much to do today than waste time down memory lane with his ex. *Still,* as his Dad had often reminded him, *"It's not always so easy to let go of the past, son, no matter how hard you try."*

And his father had known about past hurts, that was for sure.

Nathan still missed the old man, even though he'd been gone almost three years. He'd still been alive when Nathan and Olivia got together and he hadn't been keen on her from their first meeting.

"There's just something about her son. I don't know if she's right for you. Don't think she's the settling down type." His father's words had irritated him at the time but somehow stuck, often replaying in his dreams.

Had his father seen something in Olivia that he hadn't?

He'd thought, perhaps mistakenly, that they'd wanted the same things-kids, a house and holidays at the beach. Yet, her unwillingness to give him the commitment he'd craved proved to be a major reason for ending their relationship.

One of them at least.

It hadn't been pleasant. Ending a long-term commitment with a woman who'd been a big part of his life still left battle scars, no matter who was to blame.

Scars that had yet to heal completely.

Nathan deliberately shut the memories off, unwilling to let them spoil his day. "Oscar. Kenny. Will. Get your butts out here so we can get these checks done," Nathan yelled to the three firemen lounging around the staff kitchen watching the morning show.

He sounded gruff, he knew, but the untimely reminiscing left him feeling agitated and he wanted to shut it down.

Focusing on work was his main priority for now.

* * * * *

Pauline Meriwether pursed her lips slightly, applying her favourite shade of Revlon's Teak Rose lipstick as she peered at her reflection in the bathroom mirror.

Noting the greys that teased at the sides of her hairline, she raised a hand to investigate, turning her head this way and that, to inspect the despised follicles.

She shook her head in passive resistance, regarding the ravages of time and anxiety with a sigh of resignation.

The grey hair, the wrinkles around her eyes, the heart palpitations and continual sensation of nausea had all materialised in the last year or so. She not only looked older, she felt it too.

She longed for her old life. Back to the time before the lies, the separations and scandal that had torn her once close family apart.

Now, here she was. Alone in the house where they'd all been so happy.

Alone with her memories.

And her guilt.

Shrugging off the moment of melancholy, she switched off the light and returned to her bedroom to collect her handbag before leaving.

She spied the photo of Eric and herself on the bedstand, taken on their twenty-fifth wedding anniversary. She smiled as she recalled the romantic cruise they'd taken that year to Hawaii, rekindling the spark that had somehow dimmed over the years of raising children and working hard. But it had never diminished-not really. Not to this day.

Eric was the love of her life, she'd known it from their very first meeting, and he'd proved to be just as faithful to her. More than any woman could hope for.

She'd been so lucky.

Produced two amazing children who made them both so proud. Evie and Cameron had both matured into wonderful adults and she was more than grateful to have them in her life.

They'd worked hard to pay for their home in Caulfield, one of Melbourne's more well-to-do suburbs.

Seen her husband build an enviable career that saw him respected by his peers and friends alike.

Yet she'd risked everything—because she was bored.

Bored and feeling as if she'd done nothing else worthwhile. Not for herself, anyway.

Not until…

The outings had made her feel alive, if only for a little while. For some stupid reason, the sense of rebellion, of risk, had been the biggest draw card.

And the biggest downfall.

Now, she was alone with nothing but memories.

And he was paying the worst possible price.

Chapter 6

"You're way more advanced than any of the other recruits we've had before," Rylee said as she sat with Evie at the work console. An experienced operator at age twenty-three, she'd been assigned to act as Evie's mentor for the next two weeks, and appeared impressed by what she'd seen of the recruit so far.

"Gee, thanks. It's a lot harder in reality than it was at training in Brisbane," Evie replied. "It's so different between what they teach to what it's like in real life Comms."

"Yeah, well, each Centre has its own regional procedures, so it's hard to cover everything in six weeks I guess."

"At least the training these days is more thorough than ours was," Caroline commented from the next desk. "We only had one week and then, bam, you're straight on the job. But I guess there's more to learn now. It was nearly seven years ago when I joined up."

"I think they put a lot more focus on learning the software than actually becoming familiar with the local areas," Evie said. She was quickly beginning to think the six weeks of intense learning was nothing compared to what she'd experienced so far on her first day. It was all slightly overwhelming yet she wasn't complaining.

She'd been looking for an opportunity to make a move and when she'd seen the job advertisement for communications officers in the Far North, it had caught her eye. One application letter and a phone call later was followed up with a whistle-stop flight to Brisbane to undertake further testing. The next thing she knew, Evie had trained and graduated into a new career and a new life. Although she'd had several placement options, Cairns had seemed like the ideal choice to Evie after hearing positive reports about the place from others. Long sunny days, a laid-back lifestyle and the fact it was far from home had given her the impetus to take a leap of faith into the unknown.

This was exactly the challenge she'd had been hoping for when she'd left Melbourne. Something to keep her mind occupied. As far as she was aware, both Ben and her father had no idea where she was and Evie was more than happy to keep in that way.

Not that Dad could visit soon, anyway.

Pushing him from her thoughts, Evie tuned back into Rylee's instructions. She'd learned that the role of emergency communications operator was one which demanded the ability to stay cool, calm and collected at all times. Being the first point of contact for the public in stressful situations often meant there would be some nasty situations to deal with. Yet with the help of her more experienced workmates, Evie felt confident she'd pick up the ropes in time.

Both women appeared friendly and eager to help with her constant questions. Rylee and Caroline seemed to get on well together and operated effectively as the team designated to work A Shift, of which Evie was now a member.

She had a good teacher in Rylee. Although younger than her by about six years, she'd been willing to let Evie find her way, demonstrating how things worked and offering suggestions. She'd even put Evie on as the radio operator for a time, to gain confidence in turning out crews to several routine incidents in the city area.

Her first emergency 000 call had been minor, yet still nerve wracking enough to set her heart pacing. "Queensland Fire, what's the location of your emergency?" Evie had repeated the spiel taught during her drills. Easy enough under training conditions but in the real world, it somehow became scary and more real.

"Oh, hello. It's not really an emergency," a female replied, "but I've locked my dog in the car. I think he jumped on the door lock and the key's inside."

Rylee, who was listening in on the call, smiled and raised her brows. "We get these all the time," she whispered to Evie whose mind had suddenly gone blank.

What the hell do I do with this call? Evie thought. She fought off her panic, taking a breath to consider her response.

"Where are you, Maam?" she queried. The woman's detailed description of her location gave Evie time to create the incident via an electronic job card, her fingers flying deftly over the keyboard as the woman spoke.

A crew was despatched a short time later, the dog retrieved and placed back in the arms of his happy owner.

First job a success.

"How's it going so far," Eileen Monahan asked as she walked out of her office into the main work area, a mere five or so steps. Almost everyone referred to the Centre as the "broom closet", with its desks, computers, cupboards and chairs colliding with each other in a desperate fight for space. Three main workstations comprised five computer screens each, displaying various programs for the efficient receipt, running and evaluation of incidents. To the non-initiated, it looked daunting and confusing.

A glass sliding door was all that separated the Manager's office from the main operating area and Eileen regularly popped her head in to check how the day was progressing.

Evie was undeterred by the set up, having worked in a similar environment for the police force in Melbourne prior to her leaving. There, starting out as a data entry operator, she'd progressed to the level of supervisor. It was there, in the corridors at work, she'd first met Ben where he'd been stationed as a Constable.

He'd struck up a conversation and she'd been drawn to his quick wit and dedication to the job. He'd been smitten immediately, he'd admitted to her later.

Before long, they started dating and after several years, had started to talk about building plans for their future. They'd been well on the way before…

"Evie? Earth to Evie."

She was brought back to the present by Caroline's chuckle as she realised three sets of eyes were presently focused on her.

"Sorry, I was miles away. What was that you said, Eileen?"

"I just mentioned I'm trying to arrange for you to attend a fire station tomorrow, so you can ride with a crew and get a feel for the local area. I'm not sure whether it will be Redlynch, Edmonton or Cairns North yet but I'll let you know."

Evie's eyes sparkled with the prospect of getting in on some action. "That's great Eileen, thanks. So long as I don't have to operate one of the fire hoses. They're so heavy and I'd probably make an idiot of myself."

Evie thought back to when the recruits had participated in real fire scenarios which had included extinguishing a car fire. They'd worn breathing apparatus, all the requisite gear and experienced the intensity and threat of a live fire. Evie hadn't realised how cumbersome some equipment was and had been glad to take it off when the exercise was over.

It wasn't something she was keen to repeat, yet she now had a greater appreciation and awareness of what it was like for fire crews on the job. She also now knew that fighting fires was only part of the role. There were calls to rescue people from car accidents, attend vertical and water rescues often involving falls down cliffs, or saving people from rising water, just to name a few.

"No, no, you won't be doing anything other than observing," Eileen said. "Hopefully, it'll be busy and you'll get to see a variety of incidents. I know that Suzanne helped in the rescue of a dog from a drain. She thought it was terrific." Eileen referred to the second recruit, Suzanne Ingalls, who'd shared a room with Evie during their residence in Brisbane. Sue had since been allocated to work C Shift.

The unmistakable ring tone of the emergency phone interrupted their conversation and Eileen wandered back to her office.

"You can take this one," Rylee indicated to Evie, nodding her head in encouragement. Her heart started to pound, but she pressed the receiver and spoke confidently into her headset.

"Queensland Fire, where is the location of your emergency?

* * * * *

"Evelyn, could you come in here a minute please," Eileen stepped out later that afternoon.

"Sure, coming," Evie said, wondering if this was to be good or bad news.

From what the girls had mentioned of their boss, Eileen had worked her way up to managerial level over the years, starting as an operator just as they were now. She'd been in the Service almost thirty years and aged in her late fifties was possibly not too far off retirement. Eileen was childless and spent a good deal of time painting landscapes, several of which dotted the office walls.

Eileen looked up from where she sat, addressing Evie as she stood close by. "I've organised that station visit for you tomorrow. It'll be at Cairns North which is on McCooke Street. Yo can check with Rylee or Caroline for directions on how to get there."

"That's great. Thanks. What time should I arrive?" Evie asked.

"Around eight, in time for shift changeover. You'll be riding along with A Shift as they will be your regular crew. It's run by Station Officer Nathan Barrett. He's very nice and should look after you."

"Great. I can't wait." Evie smiled through gritted teeth.

Chapter 7

"Hey boss, look who's here!" Kenny said, walking into Nathan's office where he'd been checking through endless emails all morning, most from senior management. Starting new tours usually saw his time consumed in this way. Frustrated by the administrative side of the job, as he was now, Nathan was glad for the distraction.

He looked up and grinned. "Moira, nice of you to visit. Haven't seen you for a while." Nathan stood, holding out his hand as she clasped it in both of hers. A woman of senior years stood before him, a huge smile upon her face.

Moira had been attending the Station for close to five years now, having turned up out of the blue one day with trays of food. As a result, she'd become a firm favourite.

She took the chair Nathan motioned for her to sit on, placing a hand on his arm as she did so. "I know, Nathan. It's been slack of me. I've been out-of-town visiting friends, but I felt neglectful of you boys here and decided it was high time to come back home."

"To celebrate my return…," she continued, "… I've cooked up a storm and brought in a mud cake and two trays of zucchini slice which I know everyone loves. Or at least, they tell me they do," she said, raising her brows. Kenny nodded from where he remained standing in the doorway.

Looks like a lovesick puppy, Nathan thought. "We appreciate everything you do for us, Moira. You know you're not obliged to feed us, but we definitely won't be saying no."

"Well, it's my pleasure. It's my way of giving something back to you all for the wonderful job you do in the community."

People like Moira made Nathan's job worthwhile. It meant a lot that some members of the public were charitable, and Moira was a great example.

She'd once made mention that her son was a firefighter interstate and didn't see him much as they'd had a falling out. It seemed she now filled the void by volunteering her cooking skills, no doubt her way of contributing something in her senior years.

At close to seventy years of age, Moira remained an attractive woman, her face only lightly tinged with wrinkles which became more prominent when she smiled. Her smooth skin and defined cheekbones gave Nathan the impression she must have broken a few hearts in her day, but she'd once mentioned to him she was happily single and enjoyed her independence.

Kenny Harris hadn't taken that news too well, being totally smitten with her, yet fearful to take things any further. At age sixty-four, he was one year off retirement, facing the prospect of loneliness in the years ahead unless he took the next step.

"Just ask her out, mate," Nathan had suggested to his older colleague, but the stubborn bastard had so far refused to make a move.

His loss, Nathan mused, escorting Moira to the kitchen, as she enthusiastically took the chance to catch up with the rest of the crew.

* * * * *

Moira was well aware of Kenny's attentiveness, standing as he was in the doorway with a lost look on his face. She couldn't deny his attraction to her was a timely boost to her ego. He was friendly enough, and she felt certain it wouldn't take much encouragement on her part to strike up a connection between them.

The years had proven to be less than successful where she and men were concerned. No matter how hard she tried to keep them, it appeared long-term commitments weren't for her.

"Do you want to catch up with the rest of the boys, Moira? I'm sure they'd like to thank you for the goodies."

Nathan broke her chain of thought. "That would be lovely, Nathan, thanks." She absently fingered the gold locket hanging around her neck.

The old-style pendant design of red rosebud and leaves lay raised above pale yellowish petals. The filigree border and scallop shaped clasp hinted at a style of a bygone era which had been handed down to her from her grandmother. It was the only piece of jewellery Moira never took off. Touching the locket often took her back in time to days long since gone, regardless of where she was.

Returning to the present, she glanced around the Station. It gladdened her heart that she could contribute something worthwhile and bring some happiness to others, even if it was only to fill the bellies of a hardworking crew. Yet, that wasn't her only motivation.

Since returning to Cairns a little over five years ago, she'd come to realise how appealing and easy life was here.

Not much had changed since her younger days, yet her inner transformation had been significant. She was different now, less selfish. She wanted to contribute more—be a part of something.

Yet it may be too little, too late.

Some wounds were just too deep to heal.

* * * * *

As Evie chatted to her mother later that evening, she felt a sense of trepidation at what tomorrow would bring.

Keenly interested in her first day in the job, Evie was quick to reassure Pauline, "Yes, Mum, everyone seems nice and friendly," and for the umpteenth time, "Yes," she was still fine living alone.

Evie's departure from Melbourne had meant her mother now lived alone but after Ben's dumping six weeks before their wedding, Evie had needed to escape as quickly as she could. Her one comforting thought on leaving was the fact her brother, Cam, and his wife Lizzie lived close to Pauline and with their baby's birth imminent, her mother would be kept busy with her first grandchild's arrival.

The last few years had been tough for her mother-the aftermath of her dad's spectacular fall from grace and the media circus which had followed tearing at the fabric of the whole family.

Yet, Pauline had steadfastly refused to give up on her husband, visiting him every week at Loddon Prison to make sure he was coping. A former detective, his incarceration hadn't made for an easy transition on the inside. Luckily for him, he was housed in a safer area, away from any former antagonists who may have held a grudge against him.

From all accounts, her father seemed to be managing well. Evie refused to visit, not seeing him since the last day of the trial, when all hell had broken loose in the Supreme Court. She and Pauline had wept as the court officers had led a stoney-faced Eric Meriwether away.

The media considered that as a definite sign he felt little remorse for his actions.

They'd swarmed around the family like bees to a honey jar, the sordid details saturating the news in the weeks that followed until interest waned and the bees were attracted to another flower.

Evie blamed her father for it all.

Ben's about face and their wedding being called off. Cameron's architectural business taking a financial hit and losing clients. Not to mention her mother being left to face it all alone.

Evie had come to the realisation she wasn't likely to have a proper romantic relationship ever again. At least, not for a long time, anyway.

The stigma of her father's fraud had stuck to her family name like shit to a blanket. It made her angry just thinking about it.

Ben had been proof of that. "I just can't take the risk, with my career and all." His words still had the ability to sting, even now.

"Are you still there, dear?" her mother's voice startled Evie from her thoughts.

"Yes, sorry, I'm still here. What did you say about the new neighbours?"

Chapter 8

Nathan had to admit he'd forgotten all about Eileen's call and the impending visit with the new Comms recruit until Oscar tapped on the office door. "Boss, there's someone here from Firecom to see you."

Dammit, he thought. This wasn't ideal. He still had to complete and send off the monthly costings to Head Office. Now he'd have to play tour guide for the shift. And he'd forgotten her name. Pain in the ass.

His scowl soon turned into a smile as he recognised the woman walking inside.

"Well, hello. We meet again," he grinned, holding out his hand in an official gesture of welcome.

Evie—that was it. How could he have forgotten her?

Moving towards him, she had no choice but to take his hand, Oscar standing behind her with a goofy smirk on his face.

"Hi again," she said in return. "Thanks for letting me visit. I hope I won't cramp your style or anything by my tagging along but it will be helpful to get to know how everything works with you guys."

"No problem, Evie. We're happy to have you." Accepting her slight hand, he noted her firm grip, holding on for a few seconds before letting go.

"If you'll just give me a sec, I'll join you in the tearoom with the others." He addressed the young fireman. "Oscar, can you take Evie across and introduce her to the crew? I've just got to send off this email and I'll be over.

Nathan turned to face her. "Later on, I'll give you a personal tour of the place. You can leave your things in the office if you like," he noted the items she carried and pointed at her jacket. "I'm sure that one's a better fit," he said, remembering the oversized fluro version of several days ago and just how well it had emphasised her slim legs.

Evie's face reddened yet she refused to take the bait. "Thanks". Her voice sounded croaky, which had her clearing her throat.

"Let's go then." Oscar offered Nathan a slight wink and nodded towards her.

As they left his office, Nathan determined to finish his work quickly which would free him up to spend time with the mysterious Evie.

* * * * *

It was immediately obvious Oscar remembered her from the alarm fiasco and Evie's face turned a slighter darker shade of beetroot as he led her into the vehicle bay.

She skirted around the large red truck known as Alpha, all doors open in anticipation of a callout. These were the most common fire trucks seen driving around town with sirens blazing.

Parked next to it was a larger version, known as Lima. This vehicle was responded to technical and more specialised rescues. It carried equipment such as stretchers, ropes, angle grinder, splash suits, hazardous materials kits and gas detection monitors, and was operated by two crew rather than the standard four of the Alpha.

Evie turned to Oscar. "This truck is huge," she said. "We got to see a similar one down in Brisbane and given a run through of what it's used for." She hoped her chatter would distract him from bringing up their previous meeting. Thankfully, he seemed happy enough to join in with her conversation.

"Yep, it is pretty awesome. I'm not a Level Two yet but I'm going to do the course so I can operate it and get to some of the trickier jobs," he said. "I've only been in the job about eight months and the boss reckons I need more experience before I apply."

Oscar pointed towards the largest vehicle in the fleet at the rear of the Station's courtyard. "The India is really cool too. That's the one out back with the extension ladder that we use on high-rise buildings. You might get lucky and be taken up in the basket one day. It's fun, but not if you're afraid of heights."

"Sounds amazing," she said, hoping that the opportunity wouldn't present itself today. No matter how safe Oscar proclaimed it to be, she'd rather leave that particular feat to the experts.

Making their way across the concrete, Evie noticing the fire station was larger than it looked from the outside. She'd learned from Rylee that the facility also housed the vehicle workshop, Hazmat and training areas and was quite an extensive complex, even though it was beginning to show its age.

"So, is it true that you guys spend your nightshifts watching movies and sleeping?" she said, knowing full well her comment was likely to get a rise out of the young man. He seemed amiable, if not a little innocent, in his demeanour but was obviously more than capable at his job. The intensive training of cadets Evie had witnessed down south had been enough to convince her that firefighting wasn't a job for the lighthearted.

He seemed blissfully unaffected by her jibe. "Yeah, if we're lucky, we do. But just don't tell anyone otherwise everyone will apply to get in," he smiled.

"I promise I won't say a word. I mean, who wouldn't want to work four days a week and get four off-sounds like a dream job to me."

"Sure is. Wouldn't change it for anything," he proclaimed, opening the door to the staff room and ushered her inside.

Upon entering, she noticed one of the crew members from the alarm incident, an older man, but didn't recognise the other two. One was cradling his cereal bowl, eyes transfixed on the local morning news. The other was playing with his phone, oblivious to their entry.

"Hey guys, this is Evie," her guide announced. "She's just started at Firecom and will ride with us today, so we have to be on our best behaviour, right?" Evie stood nervously behind him, aware she was likely disrupting their morning routine with her arrival. In fact, she would probably cramp their style for the entire day, but it wasn't really by choice.

"Hi, I'm Kenny," the older fireman held out his hand as Evie stepped forward. "And believe nothing that comes out of that guy's mouth," he greeted, pointing at the cereal guy who shook his head in response.

"You're soooo funny, Harris. A real comedian." The male stood and accepted her hand. "Just ignore the old geezer, Evie. He's a few years short of retirement and starting to lose the plot." I'm Will and that's Barney. He works in training," he pointed to Mr Rude with the phone.

"Hi," was the muffled response from the balding Barney, his attention transfixed as he briefly glanced up.

Evie smiled and moved to sit at the table. "Hope you guys don't mind me hanging out with you today and that there's room in the truck." Evie's attempt at breaking the ice seemed to be working as her concerns appeared unfounded. The others, apart from Oscar, didn't seem to have recognised her at all.

"No probs. You can sit in the back next to me," Kenny said. "I'm sure you'll enjoy seeing how exciting our job can be," he said, raising white bushy eyebrows as the others shook their heads in unison. "No really. Most likely we'll just cruise along the Esplanade and order coff… "

He was interrupted by the flashing of a red light above Barney's head and the simultaneous ringing of a loud buzzer coming from the loading bay. The station doors started raising as Caroline's voice was clearly heard over the PA system.

"Station 11, 8-11 Bravo, turnout to an alarm activation, Cairns Convention Centre, Wharf Street. Access keys are twenty-one. Acknowledge."

"That's us, Evie. Let's get going," Oscar prompted as the others pushed their chairs back and sauntered from the room.

Evie followed their lead, noting that Nathan had also exited his office, collecting the job printout which had been automatically generated by the Firecom operators.

Evie stood beside the truck, like a duck out of water, not knowing what to do or how to even get in the darn thing.

"Let me help you up," Nathan appeared at her side as she hesitated at the rear door. "It can be tricky to enter."

Evie struggled for a foothold as he placed a hand at her elbow, prompting her to move. A spark of static electricity surged between them and she jolted at the unexpected contact. Judging by his sudden laugh, he'd felt it too.

"Uh, thanks," she said, catching the slightest scent of musk from his aftershave. It was one of those manly, woody aromas, just the right fit for a man of action. Her knees almost buckled as she stepped up, landing beside Kenny with a thud.

Nathan took his position in the front passenger seat next to Oscar, and picked up the portable radio from its cradle.

"Firecom, this is 8-11 Bravo. Proceeding Code three-zero to the alarm at the Convention Centre. Secure doors to station."

Evie made a grab for her seatbelt as the appliance trundled its way onto Brown Street. She sat back and realised she had an excellent view of her saviour of the other day.

She couldn't help the shiver of excitement that coursed through her.

Chapter 9

"Evie seems pleasant." Barney was known as a man of few words and his parting comment as he walked towards the exit had Nathan raising his eyebrows.

"Yeah, I'm sure she'll be great. Nice to get some new blood." Nathan agreed with his colleague's assessment and elevated it to the next level. *More than nice*, he thought. Something about Evie had him impressed.

Perhaps it was her keenness to learn about the job and all it involved. She'd asked lots of questions at the traffic crash when they'd cut that guy from the wreck.

Yeah, that must be it.

Or possibly it was her friendly and cheery demeanour, keeping the mood light as they drove around town. There'd been quite a few laughs coming from the rear seat and it surprised him how quickly she'd fitted in with the crew.

Or maybe it was her killer body, and the fact he felt the desire to get to know her better.

Bingo. Hit it on the head genius!

The hard part would be getting her number without becoming obvious.

He looked up then, and the fates had him smiling when he spied her jacket where'd she placed it on the office chair earlier that morning.

Seems like he'd found the perfect excuse, after all.

* * * * *

Evie's mind was preoccupied as she drove along Mulgrave Road towards her apartment. She couldn't get the hunky station officer out of her mind. The other guys were nice enough, but there was something about Nathan Barrett that set her heart to racing whenever she looked at him.

Shit.

This isn't supposed to happen.

Not after the Ben debacle.

She'd been impressed when Nathan took control at the road crash. He'd reminded her of her father in some ways, a confident man with strong leadership qualities.

At first, the few jobs they attended had been routine and unexciting. Kenny had suggested a tour of the town to fill in time even though she was already familiar with a lot of it.

As they'd driven along the Esplanade, the crew had provided an amusing running commentary, mainly directed at the weird and wonderful people out enjoying the day. The area was busy with tourists, many bathing at the lagoon or taking a yoga class on its grassy banks. With the crystal blue ocean as a backdrop and a bright blue-sky beckoning, it had seemed the perfect way to spend a day at work.

They'd visited the Marina where boats and ships of all sizes were moored. It was a hive of activity as people thronged around, waiting to board the numerous charter boats sailing to the outer isles. Located so closely to the Barrier Reef, Green and Fitzroy Islands, Cairns was a holiday mecca and had tourism operators clapping their hands in delight.

The sudden interruption of the pump radio had changed the demeanour of the crew as Caroline's message advised of a motorist who'd collided with a traffic light and was possibly trapped inside the vehicle.

On arrival, a scene of organised chaos greeted them. Ambulance officers, police and the obligatory bystanders all jostled for position; the latter most trying to take photos on phones held high above their heads. The single vehicle had managed to block the busy intersection, making it difficult for their appliance to get close yet Oscar somehow managed to gain access nearby.

Once parked, the crew sprang into action, Nathan leaping out of his seat before Evie had even unbuckled her belt. He instructed her on what to do as he handed her a yellow fluoro coloured lightweight jacket, complete with Queensland Fire Service insignias. "Evie, put this on so others will know you're with us," he'd said. "Stay near the truck and out of harm's way. That way, you can see what's going on."

His attention shifted from her as he weighed up the situation and how his crew would best approach it.

"Kenny, get ready to grab the hydraulic, just in case. I'll speak to the Ambos to see what they've got. Oscar, grab some cones to put around the perimeter," he'd pointed out while marching towards the paramedics crouched down at the driver's door.

One looked up, a blonde-haired female sporting a short bob, giving him a wink and a coy smile which had Nathan stopping in his tracks.

"Well, look who's here," Evie had heard her say, a slight accent in her voice. "Didn't you know I was back in town?"

Nathan offered a muffled reply which Evie missed but from his stance and stern look, the pair were definitely acquainted.

Nathan's less than amenable greeting seemed out of character from the little she'd seen of him so far.

Evie had been intrigued, wondering who the mystery woman was, while the attending personnel went about the business of freeing the single casualty.

As the male was stretchered from his wrecked vehicle to the waiting ambulance, Evie continued to wonder about the connection between Nathan and the mystery paramedic.

Soon after the ambulance doors closed, the blonde had put her hand on Nathan's arm and moved in closer to speak with him. It appeared their exchange was heated as he stormed off shortly after, leaving the woman shaking her head before returning to the ambulance and driving off, sirens sounding.

If body language was anything to go by, it was more than obvious there was some kind of history between the pair which suddenly hit Evie with pangs of jealousy.

Something she had no right to feel.

Whatever their connection was, Nathan's attitude hadn't improved by the time he returned to the waiting crew. "What the hell are you guys doing? Get this equipment packed up and check to make sure there's no leaking fuel."

There were no cheeky comebacks this time as the three men complied with Nathan's orders, no doubt keen to avoid any further disapproval.

Evie had shuffled on her feet as he approached her, running his hands through dark hair.

"Ahh, Evie." The frown disappeared and a smile took its place. "Sorry to leave you standing here for so long in this heat. The extrication took longer than expected. It looks like he'll be fine, though. A few fractures but nothing too serious." His face was tinged with sweat, either through exertion or due to the interaction with the blonde, she couldn't be certain.

"That's fine. I knew you'd have to do your job. You're not here to keep me entertained," she offered with a smile, hoping to ease the tension a little.

It appeared to work.

His smile widened as her heart fluttered once more in her chest. He fit so perfectly the image of what she imagined a hero was-super sexy, affirmative and caring. From what she'd seen so far, he seemed well liked by his workmates and respected by his peers.

A prime catch for anyone, she thought, as she pulled into the carpark entrance at her apartment complex and turned off the engine.

Too bad she wasn't on the market.

This annoying attraction that had taken over her thoughts was just that–stupid daydreams about heroes and sexy firefighters with killer smiles.

Just let it go, Evie.

Her chest tightened as she admitted that nothing good would come from daydreams. She couldn't let it.

If anyone ever realised the connection with her father…

The story had been broadcast on several national channels so who knew?

It just didn't bear thinking about.

* * * * *

Pained eyes stared back at the blonde-haired woman as she ran tired fingers through the tangled mess. The crack in the mirror distorted her image but couldn't disguise the anguish in her eyes, and she turned away in disgust.

Olivia's distaste for her own reflection was growing day by day and as she often did nowadays, reached for the medicine cabinet. Peering inside, her anxiety grew as she pushed away several bottles, not finding the Benzos she needed.

Did I use them all?

Her memory was sketchy these days yet she was certain she'd swiped some from work last week. Most ambulances kept a small supply of Benzodiazepines on standby for anxiety or epilepsy patients, and she'd been careful not to take too many to set off any alarm bells. Not enough to be noticed, anyway.

Now they were nowhere to be found.

Shit. I need them, she thought, as her heart rate increased. They helped to ease the tension that followed most shifts these days. The stress of dealing with the sick, injured, overweight or downright abusive patients was taking its toll, yet Olivia still managed to find a measure of satisfaction in a job that was often thankless yet gratifying.

It was the one thing that gave her life some purpose. Yet, even that lifeline was becoming tainted day by day.

The face of the violent female ice addict they'd attended to last week appeared in her mind once again. Her venomous words had stayed in Olivia's head ever since. "Get away from me, you filthy whore. Don't touch me. You're nothing but filth, bitch!"

Olivia had copped abuse before, plenty of it, over the years. It shouldn't get to her and usually it didn't. But this woman's words had stuck.

Filthy whore. You're nothing but filth.

Exactly what her father had said to her, all those years ago.

Thanks to that recent encounter, the dreams had started again—nightmares she'd dealt with since childhood which she'd never really been able to erase from her psyche.

He featured in each—he always did.

The man she should have trusted the most. Her father. The one man who'd defiled her trust in the most despicable of ways. Him and Uncle Hans…

These days, it took the pills and alcohol to make the memories fade. But even their ability to dull her recollections was lessening.

She worried about that.

She'd kept her little secret for years. Even Nathan hadn't been aware as her addictions had grown. She'd covered her shame for quite a while before she began losing the ability to cope. Slowly, as she grew to need the pills more and more, their effects had become more noticeable and he'd grown suspicious.

God.

It was hard seeing him again today.

She'd been surprised at her own reaction, feeling a deep sense of loss where once she'd felt lucky to be free again.

The loneliness seemed harder to deal with these days.

She'd never told him about the abuse inflicted by her father and uncle. Couldn't bear to see the pity and shame on his face.

Still, he'd known that something wasn't right with her. He'd tried to help, even suggested counselling, but she'd driven him away, setting herself on a path of self-destruction she couldn't seem to stop.

Nathan's desire for a permanent commitment, which included having kids, had scared the hell out of her. She could never be the person he wanted. She was trash, end of story. Everyone had always said so.

When she'd slept with Mike, and Nathan had walked in, the look on his face had made her realise he'd reached his limits. She'd pushed him too far. But she couldn't help herself.

She'd been relieved to no longer have to pretend she was someone she wasn't.

Accepting the transfer to Rockhampton had given her time to reflect on what she'd given up. His laughter and stupid jokes, his great cooking, not to mention the sex, which she'd always enjoyed.

She'd thought it best to break all ties and try to forget. Unfortunately, it hadn't worked. Not really. Something had pulled her back to Cairns. Back to where she'd settled after leaving Germany.

Seeing Nathan today had thrown her for a loop she hadn't expected. Was he the real reason she'd come back?

If she was honest with herself, it had devastated her at losing the one person who'd cared. He'd been the one she could rely on, someone who understood the pressures of her job and could talk to after a bad shift. She'd been content with the way things were but knew from what he'd said over time that he wanted more. A commitment for their future.

She hadn't been able to give it.

Maybe he missed her?

Just a little.

She padded over to the couch and lifted the pillows in the hope she'd find a pill bottle. She spied one stuck at the very back of the sofa and grabbed it, almost skipping towards the kitchen with glee.

Minutes later, as she sat back with a scotch and two pills in hand, she pulled out the tattered photo of Nathan from her wallet and touched his face lightly. *I miss you Barrett*, she thought. *More than I thought I would.*

Maybe it wasn't too late, though.

Maybe he'd take her back.

Chapter 10

It was several hours into their day at Firecom before Rylee began digging for details on Evie's station visit. Evie had been impressed by Rylee's restraint but knew it wouldn't last.

It wasn't long before it dawned on Evie that her young co-worker was more than a little keen on Nathan although, apparently, her feelings hadn't been reciprocated by him.

Deciding to test her theory, Evie couldn't help but ask, 'You think Nathan is cute?"

"Yeah, he sure is hot," Rylee said with enthusiasm in her voice. "I've seen him at a few of the socials and Christmas parties but I think he was hooked up with a paramedic. I heard they broke up though. Or that's what Ricky told me. I may still have a chance, eh?"

Evie's ears pricked up as the image of the mystery blonde popped into her mind. It was definitely a paramedic that Nathan had talked to at the accident scene and she wondered if this was the ex-girlfriend Rylee referred to.

Not wanting to torture herself with her thoughts any longer, Evie resolutely decided to focus on her work, putting Nathan from her mind.

For now, at least.

"So, how many rural brigades do we have in the Region?" she asked Rylee and they spent the next hour discussing the procedures for despatching volunteers to fire outbreaks.

Later in the morning, Evie was interrupted by Caroline waving a hand to grab her attention.

"Evie, call for you. Think it's the Station Officer from Cairns North," her co-worker advised. Evie's heart raced a little faster.

"Uh, thanks." She wiped her hands on her pants as she picked up the receiver.

"Hello. Evie here."

"Evie, hi. It's Nathan from Cairns Station." *As if she could forget that voice!* "I'm calling about your jacket. You left it here yesterday. I was wondering what you'd like me to do with it." Nathan said.

"Oh, I'm sorry. I hadn't even realised I'd forgotten it," she said. "I can drop by and collect it, I guess. My lunch break is coming up soon."

"That'll be fine, if it's not too inconvenient. We should be here unless we get a callout," he said.

"Yeah, we'll try our best to keep the emergencies to a minimum. I'll see you in an hour or so."

Evie checked the clock, noting it was about ninety minutes until her designated break.

Enough time to calm the staccato rhythm of her heart as it jumped in anticipation of seeing him again.

* * * * *

"Right. See you then." Nathan hung up from the call with Evie, only to find Oscar standing in the doorway with his perpetual goofy look up on his face, like an overgrown kid who found a joke in everything.

"Are you going to ask her out, boss?" Oscar was way too intuitive for his own good.

"Shut up, Oscar. I'm just doing the right thing, telling her about her jacket. I have no other reason to see her again, thanks very much."

"Yeah, right," the young male whistled as he sauntered off.

Nathan swivelled back to his computer, spying her jacket as it hung on the door hook, and smiled

* * * * *

Evie hadn't expected to be returning to the fire station so soon and hoped she could dash in and grab the jacket without encountering Nathan Barrett, no matter how sexy he was.

Stop it! she told herself, as she pressed the buzzer at the entrance.

He probably doesn't have the slightest interest in me anyway and is just being nice.

Her thoughts were interrupted as the door opened and a woman in fire service uniform exited. "Oh, thanks," Evie said, before stepping inside.

There was no one at front reception so Evie walked to the office she'd visited the day before. Nathan stood facing the rear wall pacing, a mobile held to his ear. "I can't talk now. And I don't want you calling me again." He appeared agitated, if the slamming of the phone on the desk was anything to go by. As he turned around, he noted her arrival and gestured for her to come in, his agitation appearing to lessen as he focused on her with a killer smile.

"Sorry 'bout that." He pocketed the phone and motioned for her to sit.

Judging from what she'd just witnessed, Evie thought it best not to prolong the visit or encourage further conversation, so remained standing. "I'm sorry but I can't hang around long. We hardly get time for breaks at Comms," she offered by explanation. The less time she spent around the attractive fireman the better. Save any potential heartache later on.

Unfortunately, it seemed he hadn't got the same memo.

"I understand. Here's your jacket, anyway," he held it out, and she stepped forward.

As she accepted it, he continued. "I was thinking. You're new in Cairns and probably haven't seen much of it yet. I thought I could take you to some of the sights. The Daintree Rainforest is heritage protected and spectacular, and the

Kuranda Railway is amazing too. It snakes its way up into the mountains and the falls at Barron River are impressive this time of year after the rains."

"Um, thanks but I'm going sightseeing in a few days with Rylee and her brother. They've promised to take me on the train. Thanks for the offer anyway."

She felt like an ungrateful bitch but figured it was better to stop him in his tracks before he got his hopes up. There was no way there could be anything between them-no matter how she ached to feel a man's touch again, or make plans, only to have them crash and burn. Any normal guy would run a mile once they found out about the scandal she had the potential to bring on.

Thankfully, so far, it seemed no one recognised her from the news or tabloids, but all it would take would be one person and the drama would start all over again. The media hounds had been unbearable, and the trolls who'd caused her to close her Facebook account were almost as bad-their nasty slurs abusing her and the family becoming too much to handle.

Not an episode of her life she was keen to repeat soon.

As a result, she'd felt both betrayed by her father, who she thought she'd known, and condemned by those she didn't.

Nathan, however, didn't seem to have a clue about her identity or seem at all put off by her rejection.

He sweetened his offer. "I bet Rylee or her brother don't know the real Far North like I do. No offence but she's an outsider like you and has only been here for a few years. I'm a born and bred North Queenslander and can offer you a tour experience like no other." The dimple in his chin became prominent when he smiled, and she couldn't help the devastating impact he had on her senses, as her stomach performed flip flops while she stood in silence.

"Come on." He pushed his sales pitch even harder. "What have you got to lose? I promise you'll have fun. My tours come complete with a money back satisfaction guarantee."

She laughed at his persistence. "Sounds tempting. But are you sure you want to? Don't you have a girlfriend who'll get jealous or something." Evie regretted the comment as soon as it left her lips, hating that it sounded like one of those petty females trying to pry details from him in a desperate dig for information.

The smile left his face. "No. There's no one in my life right now to worry about. Hasn't been for some time."

She was sorry to bring about the pained look in his eyes at the reminder of past hurts, yet she thought back to what Rylee had said.

The blonde paramedic, perhaps?

His smile returned. "And anyway, it's just one friend taking another friend out for the day. No pressure at all, I promise."

"Well, if you're sure…"

"Just pick a day and time and I'll be there."

Chapter 11

Sunday dawned bright and sunny, and a canopy of trees in countless hues of green stretched leafy arms towards them as Evie and Nathan marveled at the view from the Skyrail cable car.

Evie stood by his side as Nathan pointed out the city of Cairns as it lay before them. The peaks and troughs of its valleys, mangroves and rivers dotted the landscape and offered a unique view of the city, one she'd not yet experienced.

"This is amazing," she said, and he felt pleased at her obvious enjoyment. Seeing the light in her eyes and her almost child-like wonder at the scene had Nathan thankful he'd made a good choice for their date.

Earlier, the rail journey to the township of Kuranda on the steam train highlighted the beauty and majesty of the Barron River Falls in full flow, a light spray misting their faces as they'd stood at the halfway vantage point. Evie had taken several pics on her phone to capture the moment, "To send to Mum," she'd told him.

He gazed upon her now yet she refused to maintain eye contact for long, perhaps fearing things may get too personal, too soon. It was clear she was keeping him at a distance, he just had to find out the reason why.

As he'd taken her hand while walking around the marketplace, the contact had made his skin come alive. He was sure she'd felt it too and he'd been reluctant to let go but had no choice, handing her the latte they'd ordered from the refreshment stall.

"So, what do you think of Cairns so far? I bet it's a far cry from the big city." Nathan had asked, wanting to learn more about the woman that had him intrigued. Not since Livvie had he been interested in even trying to get close to anyone, but he was growing tired of being alone, of not having someone to make plans with or build something tangible for the future.

"I'm enjoying it so far. It seems to be a great place to live, and work. Lucky for me, I saw the ad for the Comms job at just the right time."

He nodded, taking a sip of his coffee as they'd ambled through the village. "So, what prompted the move? I'd think that wouldn't be easy, giving up everything familiar, your family and friends?"

He knew he was digging for clues but wanted to learn more about the pained look in her eyes. What should have been full of light and spark sometimes clouded over with a faraway look of sorrow.

He wondered what, or who, had put it there.

"I guess I felt the time was right for a change," she'd said. "I'd got into a rut and needed to get away. This seemed as good a place as any that offered a change of scene. Anyway, enough about boring old me." She'd finished her coffee and moved to place the cup in a bin. "Tell me more about the exciting life of a fireman. I haven't known too many before," she put the focus back onto him and he'd been happy to oblige.

Now, as they continued their descent through the trees, Nathan resolved to not give up just yet.

Time enough for discovering more about the mysteries of Evelyn Meriwether.

* * * * *

Several days later, Nathan was still on her mind as Evie sought to distract herself with an early morning run with Nicola. It wasn't long before she seriously began to doubt the wisdom of her decision.

"Wow, you said this workout would raise a sweat, and you weren't kidding," Evie said, her chest heaving as she stood with hands on hips. *It's six-thirty in the morning. It shouldn't be this hot, this early,* she thought, although it was good to get the blood pumping.

"I told you it would raise your heart rate. That's what you pay me for, right?" Nicola DeVere stood in front of Evie, looking every inch the fitness fanatic, sporting rock hard abs and with only a slight glimmer of sweat on her porcelain features. "It'll set you up to have a good day at work, anyway."

They'd been jogging the Red Arrow, a popular track smack bang in the middle of Cairns, at a steady pace for forty minutes. For Evie, the going had been a challenge, having to contend with jungle-like vines, sandflies and a steady flow of fitness junkies out to get their daily fix.

Still, it was a change of scene from their regular gym program. Its location offered an impressive view of the area which included untamed bushland contrasted by occasional glimpses of the main runway at Cairns Airport. Several times during their run, the sound of engines roaring and lifting high into the air had interrupted the otherwise stillness of the track.

Nicola prompted Evie to move to the side of the path as she was almost bowled over by a guy running head down, wearing a backpack. "Whoa, this place gets busy," Evie said, dodging out of the way just in time to avoid the collision.

"Yeah, it can get crazy sometimes. It's really popular with the locals. There's also the Blue, Yellow and Green tracks we can try out some other time but for now, this should help get your body acclimatised a little to the heat and humidity. We can tackle the others another time. You'll feel your it in your legs tomorrow though."

Evie's brows drew together, not altogether cheered at the prospect of a sore and aching body. "Great. Just what I need." She gave her legs a light slap. "But, honestly, it's good to be exercising again." Evie was glad to have found a trainer like Nicola who pushed her hard, was demanding but not to the extreme. Since hooking up, the women had taken a genuine liking to each other and formed a friendship beyond trainer and client.

Nicola had shown Evie around town and the two had met up for coffee several times. She was becoming a much needed friend for Evie, a nice change from the loneliness of the last few months. The few girlfriends she'd had in Melbourne had all but dumped her when the scandal broke, and now, only a couple kept in touch through social media.

The relationships Evie were forging with her new workmates were still in the early stages and would take time to build, yet with Nicola, she experienced a sense of kinship she hadn't felt for years.

Evie's breath had almost returned to normal, and the pair began to walk towards the carpark, when interrupted by a male voice.

"Well, hello again. Of all the places to meet up…," Nathan pulled up mid-stride as Evie's eyes widened in recognition.

"Nathan." Evie said, noting sweat pouring off his face and body, drenching his t-shirt and shorts which were cut away to emphasise his tanned and fit physique. Her face turned beetroot red as she appreciated the eye candy. "Looks like you're having fun too." A slight sense of guilt hit her that she'd avoided any contact since their date two days ago, uncertain what was happening between them.

"Yeah, well. Whatever it talks to stay in shape, I guess." He glanced at Nicola and smiled in acknowledgement. "Sorry, didn't mean to ignore you." He rubbed sweaty hands on his shorts before offering his hand to her. "I'm Nathan, one of Evie's workmates."

"Hi. I'm Nicola, Evie's trainer." She shook his hand. "I've just had the pleasure of introducing Evie to the joys of working out in the heat and I don't think she was too impressed."

"Yeah, I can sympathise. It's not too forgiving this time of year." Nathan glanced back towards Evie, who was feeling more than self-conscious now, dressed as she was in her workout gear. He smiled as she swatted at a bug that landed on her calf.

Nicola noticed Nathan's pre-occupation with her client, as she feigned a sudden interest in her watch, making a gesture to leave. "Oops, gotta run. I have another client to meet so I'd better get going. Nathan, nice to meet you. Evie…," Nicola touched her lightly on the shoulder, "… you can text me when you want another session," she said, as she disappeared down the path with a wave and a smile.

"She seems nice," Nathan acknowledged Nicola's departure with a return wave.

"Yeah, she is. She's been great, showing me around town a little. We've been shopping and lunching as well."

"That's nice. What more could a girl want?" he said. "Speaking of showing you around…," he said, rubbing his chin, "… how about I take you out again? I really enjoyed the other day."

Evie nodded. "Yeah, I had a great day too, Nathan. It was fun." She felt even more like disappearing into a hole for not replying to his texts.

He didn't seem put off. "I've got a few places in mind you might really like. I may not be too keen on the shopping thing, though."

His smile was enough to send her heart into a spin.

God - why do things have to get so complicated?

Evie wrestled with her emotions, her mind in turmoil whether to accept now and take the plunge-or kill this growing attraction in the bud while she still could.

He stood in silence, waiting for her response, and Evie experienced a thought of inevitability as her heart took control of her head before she could process what was happening.

"Sure, I'd like that. You can call me tonight if you're free and we'll decide then. It might be a bit difficult to talk at work."

"Yeah, I get that. No problem. I'll call you later tonight." He checked his watch and pointed towards his car, touching her arm slightly. "Better hit the showers before Firecom hassles me with jobs," he gave a wink, leaving her at a jog, eventually disappearing from sight.

Evie laughed at his parting joke, standing for a minute while her heart rate settled, wondering what she'd just agreed to.

* * * * *

Later that evening at his rental house in Edge Hill, memories of Evie brought a smile to Nathan's face as he contemplated where he could take her next.

Happily, she'd at least been agreeable to the idea even if he'd needed to push a little. Fortunate for him they'd run into each other at the Red Arrow this morning; seemed the Universe definitely had his back! Still, for whatever reason, it seemed Evie wanted to keep him at a distance, and he'd be damned if he knew why.

They'd definitely enjoyed each other's company the other day, of that he was sure, as they'd chatted abut the things they had in common. From what he could tell, early indications had him believing they were more than compatible.

They both liked Aussie Rules Football (a definite tick), eighties music and Chinese food. So far, so good.

Yet, it was her unique traits he was most attracted to.

Her natural scent, the way she carried herself with an air of confidence whilst possessing a certain fragility that kept him guessing. She could hold her own in conversation and made him laugh several times with her stories as she'd described her experiences as a communications recruit.

All this left him thinking Evie Meriwether was someone he could grow to care about. A lot.

There was something lurking in the background and it frustrated the hell out of him. Most likely, it was an ex-boyfriend, or ex-husband maybe, which made her wary of getting involved with anyone else. Understandable. He knew only too well how the sting of a failed relationship could hurt for a long time.

Dammit, but he didn't want to end his day thinking about Olivia.

The "ice queen" from Berlin who'd caught his attention from the first time they'd met. For over three years, they'd continued down a rocky road, the rare happy memories overshadowed by her dark moods and growing addictions. To prescription meds. To alcohol. And to other men.

It wasn't until he'd caught her downing pills one day he'd even realised she'd had a problem. Often highly strung and possessing a temper anyway, Nathan had put her worsening behaviour down to Olivia's German roots and the occasional bout of hormones.

"They're to calm me down after work," she'd responded once to his worried look. "I can't do this job any other way, alright".

He hadn't bought into her excuse. "That's bullshit. Plenty of us working in the field get stressed out, but we don't all drown our sorrows in pills." He'd tried to suggest solutions. "If you're not coping Liv, we should see someone. You know the Service offers…"

"No, no. It's not that bad," she'd said, attempting to diffuse his concern. "I don't need to talk to a shrink. Not ever, okay! Management would find out and I'd lose everything. I'll be fine, I promise," she'd said, and he'd not mentioned it again.

Nathan hadn't been convinced by her attempts to fob him off. He'd been sure her troubles lay somewhere buried in her past, something she'd steadfastly refused to talk about. "Why bother? It's over," she'd once said, as he'd sought to discover the truth. But she'd shut him out—unwilling to open old wounds she kept locked away.

No matter how understanding or attentive he'd been over the months that followed, Olivia's behaviour had worsened, almost as if she was on a deliberate path of self-destruction. The tension in their relationship had grown yet without a willingness on her part to change, Nathan felt there wasn't a lot more he could have done.

He'd persevered and made excuses for her behaviour, hoping somehow she'd settle down and change her mind about starting a family with him, but in his heart he'd known that wasn't likely to happen.

The final straw came one day when he'd arrived home to find her in bed with one of her workmates, their telltale green paramedic uniforms lying crumpled on the floor where they'd been dropped in the height of passion.

He'd told her to go, and she hadn't put up much of a fight. That was over nine months ago, and he hadn't seen or heard from her since, until she'd appeared at the crash scene the other day. She'd followed up by calling him at work, asking if they could meet up for a talk over coffee.

Coffee? What the hell was that about?

He'd told her he doubted it.

He wasn't keen on revisiting old hurts.

He thought briefly of his mother, and the pain she'd caused with her infidelities. She'd done the same thing— cheated on the man who had given her all he had to give, yet apparently wasn't enough.

What was it with the Barrett men and women? Are we cursed to never have long-term relationships or what?

Dismissing both women from his thoughts, he put his focus on more positive ones. He'd made his peace with the past, and as far as he was concerned, there was no altering it.

When it came to romance, Nathan hoped his luck was about to change.

He lifted his phone, searching his contacts for Evie's number. It rang for several seconds before her breathy voice came on the line.

* * * * *

"Hi. I've just finished eating, so great timing, Evie said, answering Nathan's call even though she'd been both eager, and terrified, as she waited for the phone to ring.

"Good to hear. I wasn't sure how early you got to bed before starting your day shifts. I usually hit the sack before ten myself," he said. "Even though there's only two days , they can still take it out of you, that's for sure.

"Yeah, I'm finding that out," Evie admitted, still not 100% used to the routine of the ten-hour days and fourteen-hour nights. "I suppose I'll get used to it eventually."

"Well, it can take time. Has its benefits though. The days off are a bonus, especially living in a place like this. Speaking of which…," he said, deciding to jump right in. "… how about I take you somewhere special on Saturday morning? I'm not saying where-it's a surprise."

She paused as she fought her uncertainty. "Um, I'm not sure, Nathan. I know we had fun and everything, but I don't know if we should do this–going out and working together, I mean." She hadn't worked up the courage to deliver a straight out *No* to his request.

The risk was high that he'd find out who she was; that he'd discover the story of her father and the disgrace he'd brought to the family. She couldn't go through that pain again.

His voice came back, calm and resolute. "Well, technically, we don't work together. I mean, we *do* work for the same organisation but I'm not your boss. We usually only talk on the radio when you get to tell me where to go."

"Yeah, well I like that part," she smiled.

He laughed at her cheeky comeback before continuing.

"Look, Evie. I'm not sure what your relationship history is but there's no pressure from me, I promise. Just an offer to show you the sights and if you're lucky, you might get to taste my speciality home-made lasagne. How's that for a deal?"

He was wearing her down, bit by bit, yet it felt…. right. Dammit!

"Sounds too good to be true. Give me a little while to think about it, Nathan. I just can't let my life get too complicated again. I'm sorry if that sounds vague, but it's all I can offer right now."

"Good enough for me. I won't hassle again, I promise. You can call or text me if you like when you decide," he said. "I already mentioned it Evie but, for the record, I had fun the other day."

His reassurance made her feel less guilty at her uncertainty.

"So did I Nathan, I really did. It was a great day. I'll be in touch," she said, as she quickly hit the button to end the call. She hated hurting his feelings, but there was no other choice she could make right now.

Her phone beeped with a text not ten seconds later and as she looked down to check, her smile widened as she saw the image of a large plate of what looked like lasagne with the caption "Best Home-Made Lasagne in Cairns!"

She was still laughing as she set her alarm for the morning, punching the pillow as she lay down.

"Gee, he's persistent," she muttered as the phone rang once more. It seemed like her plans for an early night had been scuttled.

"Yes, I know it looks impressive, but I still need time to decide," she answered.

Her smile all but disappeared as she heard the low tone of a voice well too familiar.

"I'm don't know what's impressive, but that's not why I called.

Evie, it's me, Ben. We need to talk."

Chapter 12

Evie's mood hadn't improved as she sat down as the radio operator the following morning.

As if her mind wasn't stressed out enough with having to learn vehicle calls signs, radio channels and communication protocols, she now had Ben's call front and centre of her thoughts, to completely fry her concentration.

Damn him, she cursed, as she tried to concentrate on whatever the hell it was that Rylee was instructing. Evie had worked hard to put the debacle of their ill-fated wedding behind her, yet hearing his voice again, after months of nothing, had thrown her for a loop.

As far as she was concerned, he was a weak excuse for a man, no better than all the other so-called "friends" who'd deserted the family when the scandal broke.

She replayed the call in her mind, hearing his words as if seated next to her.

"Evie, I think I may have made a big mistake. About us, I mean," he'd said, not sounding himself. At first, she presumed he may have been drunk or worked a long shift. Different to the confident man she'd spent the better part of five years with.

"Ben, what are you calling me for? I thought we'd said everything that needed to be said. You're not a part of my life anymore. I'm going to…"

"Listen for a second, please." He'd paused, and she'd gripped the phone in clenched fingers. "No, Evie, please don't hang up. I know I've been a bastard with what I've done but I,…" he said. "Well, I miss you. I miss what we had and can't believe I was such a dick."

She gave an exaggerated laugh.

"Well, you've got that part right." She couldn't bring herself to speak, her voice cracking as she heard his desperate appeal. Her resolve weakened. No matter how many times she'd cursed him, he'd still been the man she'd been planning to marry. Not so easily dispatched to the rubbish dump.

"Look, I know I deserve to be called whatever you want. I don't blame you. But I haven't been able to stop thinking about you. When I found out from Pauline that you'd left, well…, I couldn't believe it. That I'd been the reason you had to leave town."

"It wasn't just about you, Ben, so don't flatter yourself." Evie recognised the snippety tone in her voice, hating the fact he brought out the worst in her. *What was it about failed relationships that turned once happy people into vindictive, bitter and twisted wrecks?*

"How's the job, anyway? I bet you're well on the way to becoming Senior Detective or Inspector by now, seeing as that's your biggest aim in life?" Evie couldn't keep the sarcasm from her voice, wanting to end the conversation before she completely lost it.

"Don't remind me about that. Look,… I thought the job was everything you know, but now with you gone, I can see that's a crock of shit. I'm missing you being in my life. Evie, this is crazy." She sensed his frustration as his words became more insistent. "I can't talk to you like this over the phone. I want to see you so we can talk things through."

She'd been lost for words, rubbing tired eyes, trying to comprehend what he was implying–that he'd made a mistake?

"I think we've said all that we had to. I just…"

"I'm not talking about going over things, Evie. I want us to get back together. I really miss you and…"

"Ben, I know you're still hurting but I can't do it." She raised her voice. "I can't. I've dealt with all the crap, the fallout and now I've moved on." Nathan's face popped into her mind and she regretted the fact that he'd likely only end up a nice fantasy. *I mean, who'd take on the daughter of a criminal - a criminal who was once a cop?* "You need to do the same."

"Evie, you don't mean that. Babe, you can't. If you just…"

She'd disconnected before he could continue, throwing the phone across the bed, where it landed with a soft thud.

Dammit Ben, she'd cursed under her breath. Just leave me the hell alone!

"Evie, did you hear that radio message just then? Rylee interrupted her reverie.

Evie shook her head, lost in memories. "What? No, sorry. Who was it calling?"

"Never mind. I got it," Rylee said. "Just checkin' you're okay."

"I'm fine. Silly daydreams," Evie said, determined to remain focused for the rest of the shift.

She'd deal with the Ben issue later on, although she feared it wouldn't be the last she heard from him.

* * * * *

"So, bro', what's this I hear about some hot new chick working at Firecom?"

Sweat ran down Mason Bligh's face as he passed the hammer to his mate. They'd been working on the frame for several hours now and the midday sun was starting to bite.

Constructing the home on the block he'd purchased on the Atherton Tablelands was taking longer than expected, but Nathan wasn't in any hurry. He'd rather spend time to get it the way he wanted rather than rushing or paying other tradesmen to do it. The fact he and Mason had carpentry experience made this the perfect opportunity to keep up their skills, and gave him something to occupy his mind on his days off.

He took a gulp of water, grinning at his best friend.

"Whatever you've heard, it's all crap." Nathan raised the hammer and resumed the task, refusing to take the bait his friend planted. He knew it was next to impossible to keep secrets at work, yet it never failed to amaze him how quickly gossip spread.

"Young Oscar told me this crazy but very amusing story about a certain woman locked out of her apartment. Then, allegedly…," Mason continued with obvious relish, "… that very same woman appeared on your Station's doorstep days later and had you smiling from ear to ear."

"Goddam Oscar has a big mouth," Nathan muttered, missing the nail and smashing his thumb with an intensity which had him swearing several profanities.

"Yeah, well, it's about time you got back on the horse, mate. You wait any longer to hook up with someone and settle down, you'll be living in this house all on your lonesome. Only having the dog to keep you company…," Mason gestured towards Cooper, Nathan's black and white collie, "… won't keep you warm at night."

Nathan didn't both responding as he turned to inspect his throbbing thumb. Privately, he agreed what Mason said made sense. His friend had seen him through the ugly break-up with Livvie and Nathan trusted him enough to know that his buddy always had his back and only meant well.

They'd met at around age sixteen when both started as apprentices to old Al, the cranky owner of the main carpentry shop in Ayr. Upon finishing their trade, Mason quickly grew frustrated with the poor pay as a junior and decided to apply to the fire service instead, like his father before him. It was on his friend's recommendation and cajoling that had prompted Nathan to join several years later.

Mason, being the more ambitious of the two, had since worked his way up the ladder to the rank of Inspector, whereas Nathan was content having attained the position of Station Officer. He preferred to stay on the trucks and be part of the action rather than taking on a pen-pusher role at Headquarters.

Still, Nathan couldn't deny the incentive of a greater pay packet could one day see him reconsidering his priorities.

"Everything all right over there?" he could hear Mason chuckle as he bent to retrieve the dropped hammer.

"Right as rain, mate," Nathan said, standing back to inspect his handiwork.

Apparently, his friend wasn't finished with offering his relationship expertise. "Yeah, well, seriously you need to get a move on and find a pretty lady to settle down with. Speaking from experience, life's a lot better when there's someone to share a beer with at the end of the day."

"Wow, what an incentive from the expert," Nathan said, unable to deny the truth of his friend's words. Life *was* better when shared. That was mostly the reason he was building his dream home.

All he needed was the right girl.

Perhaps he'd already found her.

An image of Evie popped into his head, and Nathan wondered whether she'd be the one. *Early days mate*, he though. His attraction to her couldn't be ignored. Even though she hadn't responded to his texts or answered his calls, he'd backed off to give her some space. It was possible that whatever was haunting her was the reason, but he hoped she would see her way through to giving him a chance.

Nathan stood under the wooden frame of what was to become the front entrance, hands on hips and contemplated the view. Rolling hills, scattered trees and a distinct lack of nearby neighbours had appealed to him the first time he'd seen the acreage for sale. It was the ideal setting to raise a family, with enough local amenities close-by to satisfy the needs of any discerning wife.

With a little luck, he'd have his answer soon.

Chapter 13

Thoughts of her conversation with Ben lingered as Evie sat in the front seat of Nathan's four wheel drive. She'd questioned more than once whether she'd made the right choice by agreeing to go out with him again. In the end, it had been his "just friends" argument that had her convinced not to panic.

At least, not yet.

After Ben's call three nights ago, Evie's reluctance to commit to another date with Nathan had become more problematic. It left her confused about what to do. She hated the thought of leaving Nathan hanging with no explanation at all. As far as Ben was concerned, she didn't really care.

Finally, she'd decided to take the plunge. Scary as hell, though.

Like jumping off a cliff with no way of knowing what lay at the bottom.

When she'd called Nathan yesterday, and he'd replied with that smooth-as-honey voice, her mind was made up.

"I know where we can go. I'm sure you'd like it," he'd said, refusing to divulge anymore. "It means an early start though so we'll have to be up with the birds."

"That's fine, as long as I'm not skydiving out of a plane or bungey jumping," she said, not keen on being scared half to death.

"No, no, you'll be perfectly safe. You'll love it, I promise. And if you're really good, there may be a picnic lunch included in the package as well."

They set off up the Kuranda Range, a winding, picturesque roadway leading to the Tablelands district. A touch after five-thirty in the morning, her view was partly obscured by the night sky, yet every so often she caught glimpses of large mossy trees, some overhanging the roadway, which formed a tunnel of green for much of its length. In full daylight, the occasional glimpse of the distant ocean made it one of the most scenic driving routes in the region.

Feeling the chill of the early morning, Evie secured the rug he'd offered over her knees, turning her eyes slightly toward him with a smile.

He really is handsome, she thought, mortified to suddenly feel her face blush, a trait she'd deplored since her teenage years. Hoping Nathan hadn't noticed, she turned to face the rear seat, putting her hand out to pat the collie sitting obediently, his face resting on the opened window.

"Your dog is well behaved. How long have you had him?"

"Ah, let me think. I got Cooper at about eight months old, six years ago. He'd been dumped at the animal shelter and we were attending a charity day to raise money for volunteer firefighters. I saw him in one pen and we took to each other pretty quickly. He's a great dog, really smart." He swivelled his neck to address Cooper who gave a quick bark in acknowledgement and Nathan laughed. "Good boy."

He slowed the vehicle as he pulled into the Henry Ross lookout which overlooked the entire valley, and gestured for Evie to exit. "I know the sun's not up yet but you may like a look at the valley." He undid his seatbelt and opened the driver door. "Coops, you stay inside buddy," he instructed his four-legged friend who'd poked his head back out the window to sniff the surrounds.

"Wow, this is amazing," Evie said, laying eyes upon the impressive vista below. Through the morning mist, meandering creeks were visible amidst sprawling thick foliage, reminding her of the Dandenongs back in Melbourne.

Yet here, coupled with the intensity of cloud and sky, it seemed grander somehow, more open and immense.

Nathan echoed her observations. "It's an awesome view from up here. I love to come up when I can. Even though it's not that far from Cairns, it has a real country feel and openness to it. You'll see what I mean when we get further up. "

He placed his hand in the small of her back, and she felt heat there as he continued to point out more landmarks. Evie tried to ignore the thrilling sensation, snapping a couple of pics from her phone but not really sure what images she'd captured, as her mind remained preoccupied on his soft touch.

Several minutes later, they returned to the warmth of the vehicle and Evie gave Cooper another friendly pat. She loved animals, dogs in particular, and regretted having to leave her silky terrier, Bailey, with her mother. From all accounts, he was coping well enough without her and was now a comfort to Pauline living alone in the house.

They exited the range after negotiating another series of bends, emerging onto a straighter section of road.

They drove in silence for several more minutes, Evie content to soak up the scenery, before speaking. "So, are you going to tell me what's going on yet?" she said, trying to dig for clues. Unfortunately, Nathan wasn't budging, only shrugging in response. It was obvious he enjoyed keeping her in suspense.

Whatever the outing, Evie was more than certain they weren't about to share bacon and eggs in a cosy café somewhere.

Soon after, Nathan pulled off the bitumen onto a dirt road where a large sign read "Hot Air–This Way," and Evie spied several vehicles and a large basket in the distance. Reality shot in that her fears were about to be realised.

She turned to Nathan who was grinning in obvious anticipation and excitement.

His, "Looks like we've found your surprise," had her mouth forming an "O" yet her voice remained silent.

"Cat got your tongue, Evie?" He must have sensed her unease. "Look, it's okay. I've gone up a few times now and there were no issues. You can trust me, you know. I'm a fireman, after all!"

"What about Cooper?" she attempted a feeble argument, hoping to somehow avoid the inevitable. "We can't leave him alone."

"Relax, Evie. He'll sit and wait it out with the ground crew. They said it would be fine."

She gulped, realising her protestations were futile.

Her fate was now in his hands.

* * * * *

A little over two hours later and Evie had to admit that floating metres above the ground was both exhilarating, and petrifying.

After they'd arrived at the take-off site, they'd been joined by another couple, Mark and Taylor, and under direction from their guide, the effervescent Tony, all helped to inflate the balloon in readiness for the flight.

Ascending in the early morning mist with the sun rising overhead, Evie conceded the experience was one of the most exciting things she'd done. The silence was entrancing as they hovered high above the treetops, broken only by the mooing of grazing cows, as the basket cruised over fields of green and yellow. Nathan took her hand in a gesture of support which she'd gratefully accepted.

He'd smiled at her with those drop-dead looks of his and her legs almost gave way. *Don't even go there Evie.* The battle between her intellect and heart threatened to take over once again, and she almost pulled from his grasp at the sensation of overwhelm.

Tony's voice interrupted the moment as he radioed his colleagues on the ground to confirm the landing site. He moved to release the parachute valve, allowing air to escape from the top of the balloon as they slowly began their descent to the paddock below.

They'd been briefed before take-off and all passengers readied themselves as the basket landed with a soft thud. The ground crew ran around, grabbing at the ropes, pulling to stop it being dragged along and potentially injuring someone.

When the momentum stopped, Evie gave a silent thanks to the Universe at having survived her adventure, as Nathan moved to help her from the basket.

Alas, Tony had other ideas and quickly overtaking him, stepped forward to lift Evie out. "All part of the service, pretty lady," he'd said, failing to notice the scowl on Nathan's face, as her feet touched the ground.

"Hope you enjoyed the ride." Tony took Evie's hand and raised it to his lips in a dramatic gesture. Before she had time to respond, he ran back to the waiting crew and soon drove off, leaving a trail of dust in his wake.

From the look upon Nathan's face, he was glad for their guide's departure. "Well, that was fun. Did you enjoy yourself up there?"

"It was awesome. Thanks so much for taking me Nathan, even if I was petrified at first." The sound of his name on her lips was becoming a familiar one, yet only raised her anxiety level about what on earth she'd gotten herself into.

He seemed too good to be true. Maybe she'd read the signals wrong. *I mean, who'd want someone like her with the family's chequered history?* The incident with Cameron, then her father. *Idiot*, she thought. Evie had to keep reminding herself that Nathan knew next to nothing of her past. But there was no hiding it forever.

What the hell am I thinking? No one would take on a woman with a past like mine.

It wasn't just about the last few years, either. Scandals had a way of following her family around.

She could see them now–her so-called "friends" from Year Nine, Hayley as well. So much for being Evie's bestie. Loyal through thick and thin.

Yeah, right.

Everything had been fine in Evie's world. That was until her older brother Cameron had chased the most popular girl in school.

Melissa McCourt. She'd never forget that name.

The blonde haired, blue eyed bimbo who'd dazzled her brother, if not half the males in Year Twelve, with her flirtatious ways and giggly smile. Evie had warned Cameron not to mess with someone who'd obviously "done the rounds" but he'd seemed oblivious to his sister's concerns.

Besides, Melissa was keen on him.

At first.

They'd been dating for about four weeks and Cameron was the cheeriest that Evie remembered. He'd gone from being just "one of the guys" to the "luckiest guy in school". He'd scored the top prize.

That was until the night the police came knocking at two in the morning.

Dad had been interstate attending a trial so there was no one, apart from her half-dazed mother, capable of dealing with the fact her brother was being led from the house in handcuffs, accused of assaulting "poor" Melissa.

The girl's statement to the police alleged that earlier in the evening, Cameron had visited her home, at her invitation, when things got out of hand. Melissa claimed he'd assaulted her which Evie had found impossible to believe. Her brother was someone she trusted implicitly. Cameron, in his defence, stated he had been at Melissa's place but left before midnight after she plead sick with a headache.

Evie and her mother were in shock and weren't much use to poor Cam, as he was led away by the police. Pauline could only offer a faint "I'll call your father, Cameron. He'll know what to do," in response.

Although the incident had occurred in the days before social media, it didn't take long for word to spread about the events of that night.

Evie's attendance at school the following day proved to be one of the worst of her young life. Virtually all her friends and classmates turned their backs or pointed at her, calling her the sister of "that creep." Hayley had refused to sit with her in class, despite Evie's pleas of Cameron's innocence.

"How am I to know, Vee, if you're telling the truth or not? Maybe even you don't know." Her friend's excuse was lame. "Sorry. I just can't risk being seen with you right now."

Almost overnight, Evie was being judged solely on her relationship to Cameron and school life went from being something she'd enjoyed to a nightmare of blank stares, cold shoulders and accusations.

She began to dread having to attend classes and even at home, Evie couldn't escape the stigma. One time, a rock was thrown through her bedroom window as a youth yelled out, "You all belong in jail," running off laughing which left her in tears.

Her parents had demanded the school principal come up with a workable solution yet that proved fruitless, as it became clear his allegiance remained with Melissa's version of events.

After almost a month of ongoing torment, her parents decided to enrol Evie at a nearby public school where her notoriety wasn't so well known.

When Melissa finally admitted to her lie, exonerating Cameron of any wrongdoing, it came too little, too late for Evie. The girl admitted she'd ditched Cameron that night to take up with another boy who was also competing to win her affections. Apparently, he'd become a little too keen.

The bruises and cut lip Melissa had suffered had forced her hand at making some kind of excuse. The fact she'd blamed Cameron, and not the mayor's son, wasn't revealed until her confession.

The police and courts were left to deal with the ensuing mess while Evie and Cameron attempted to get on with their lives. Even though she patched things up for a time with

Hayley and some other friends, those relationships were never quite the same again.

Years later, when history repeated and her father brought shame upon the family once again, Evie and the others had been left to pick up the pieces.

"Evie. Are you okay?" Nathan's concerned voice had Evie drag herself back to the present, having lost herself in her memories.

"What? Oh, I'm sorry, just miles away," she offered in resignation, her gaze fixed on the grey clouds hanging low in the distance.

Nathan remained silent as her took her hand in his, offering a gentle squeeze in support. Evie fought hard to keep the tears from falling as they began the return trip down the Range, droplets of rain pattering the windscreen.

The sun had well and truly disappeared from her day.

Chapter 14

The ferocious heat rising from the concrete had Evie's heels sticking to the surface as she walked along the Marina precinct. The area was busy with its usual mix of backpackers, seniors practising tai chi and tourists on the hunt for their next trinket.

Although she'd been here several months now, Evie cursed at the intensity of the midday sun, raising her armpits in frustration. Feeling sticky, hot and bothered was all part of living in the tropics, she knew, but she'd not really believed it until now. *These summer months were hell*!

Cameron had warned her about choosing to settle in the hot climes, having holidayed in Cairns several times in the past. Yet, Evie was stubborn in her choice, picking the location mostly for its long distance from Melbourne. She'd wanted to get as far away from the city as possible. *And besides, what could be so bad about living in a paradise that boasted some of the world's most spectacular tropical rainforests and coral reefs?*

Yet, these past months had tested Evie's resolve, and more than once she'd contemplated packing her bags and heading home.

Back to what was familiar.

But that would be giving in.

Something she refused to do.

Evie felt a pinch on her little toe and hoped a blister wasn't about to form as she continued on. *Bloody hell.* Choosing to walk from her apartment was a decision she was coming to regret.

She spied the restaurant ahead and quickened her pace. The sooner she arrived, the sooner she'd be out of this damned heat.

It didn't take long to spot Nicola sitting at a balcony table, waving for Evie to join her. Grateful to rest her aching feet, Evie plonked into her seat before fanning a hand in front of her face.

"God, I'm glad I found you. Don't reckon I could have lasted much longer in this heat," she said, wiping at the sweat trickling her hairline.

Her friend laughed, passing Evie a glass of water. "I know, right. This season's been a killer. Here, take this," as her companion gratefully accepted the offering.

Meeting Nicola had been a godsend in Evie's eyes. Not only was she an excellent motivator and instructor, but was turning out to be one of her best friends as well.

Evie hadn't realised how much she'd missed having female company and someone to talk to until she arrived in town, knowing absolutely no-one. The local gym staff had recommended Nicola as one of their most popular trainers and from their first session, the two women had hit it off. They were similar in many ways and had much in common.

Aged thirty-one and a fitness junkie, Nicola was an ex-model who hailed from Sydney, and for the last three years, had made Cairns her home. Like Evie, she'd left her busy life behind for the quieter, less stressful city in the Far North. Also, like Evie, Nicola presented as an introvert who'd worked hard to forge her own way, establishing a strong list of loyal clients who raved about her services.

She spoke little of her family or former life, and Evie respected that, not being keen herself on telling too much of her own past. She'd told Nicola of her broken engagement but not the reason behind it. No doubt, her friend had a history she'd prefer to put behind her, as well.

Having cooled down enough to gather her composure, Evie perused the menu and considered her choices.

Nicola leaned back, raising a glass to her lips. "So, tell me. I've being dying to ask. What's the story with the cute guy we met at the Arrow? He seemed interested in you, that's for sure," Nicola said, sipping her juice. "And please don't tell me he's not on the market. That would just be devastating."

Evie had suspected her friend would raise the subject of Nathan after their meeting. After all, it was only natural she wouldn't soon forget the hot looking male she'd been introduced to.

"Nathan's a firie who works on my shift." Evie felt the heat return to her face and used the menu to fan herself. "We've met a few times through work and he seems nice but I'm not pushing anything."

Nicola sat up straighter. "Why not? Give a little push, I mean? You've got nothing to lose. And anyway…," she held a hand up to summon the waitress to their table, "… you know you don't want to be alone forever. Even after what's happened, I know you enough already to see you need someone to love in your life. Maybe this guy's the one, eh?"

Evie was grateful for the distraction of the waitress who appeared at the table. "Maybe. We'll see." The backpacker spoke with a European accent and it soon became clear she had difficulty with the English language, as it was several minutes before she was able to understand their order.

"Gee, that was a struggle," Evie laughed and Nicola nodded in agreement.

"I never thought ordering a salad could be so hard. But backpackers need to make money somewhere I guess. Hopefully, she'll get to improve her language skills!"

Evie gazed sideways, noting the tables full with the bustling lunch time crowd, the noise level having increased in the short time since she'd arrived. "I'm sure she will. It's busy in here now."

Nicola nodded. "It's a popular place. Anyway…," she continued, "… getting back to what I was saying, you should give the guy a chance. From what I saw the other day, I think he really likes you. Don't stop believing that something might happen." Her friend's genuine tone had Evie nodding her head in agreement. "You're a great girl. Who wouldn't want to spend time with you?"

"Actually…," Evie took a sip of her water before continuing, "I have to fess up. We have been out a couple of times. He even took me hot air ballooning which was a nice surprise. I'm not sure about jumping into something, though. It's confusing-you know?"

Nicola offered a smile in response, just as the backpacker returned, precariously balancing two plates in her hands.

As she began tasting her chicken avocado salad, Evie once again pictured Nathan's face in her mind.

After her mini-meltdown following the trip back from their balloon ride, would he even both with her anymore?

Only time would tell.

* * * * *

"Queensland Fire, what is the location of your emergency?" Evie repeated the spiel becoming second-nature to her, as she gradually eased into her new role.

Often considered a thankless job, working within Emergency Communications was a role requiring a certain amount of grit, yet Evie relished the challenge at pushing herself. The sometimes stressful nature of calls, shift work and long hours 'wasn't everyone's cup of tea', as Caroline had once told her. She was right.

Evie hadn't expected the workload to be as diverse as it was. Not only was there the call-taking and operation of radios to learn, but the need to become familiar with the entire region in a geographical sense which sometimes tested her commitment. *Hell, she even had trouble programming addresses into her Navman at times, so she needed to be on top of her game!* She wasn't stupid by any means but the fact that she wasn't a local to the area put her at a distinct disadvantage.

Evie realised it may take longer than expected to become as proficient as the others at the position.

Today, she was operating as the solo call-taker on phones for the first time with Rylee on radio while at times, Eileen walked in to check things were running smoothly.

She stood by Evie's desk now, listening until the call was concluded, then addressed both women. "Just to let you know. A media crew is coming in here tomorrow to do a story on the Fire Service and how we operate. There should be three of them so it'll be cramped, but it should only take about an hour. We might even be on tomorrow night's news."

"Wow, that's cool," Rylee stood and stretched. "About time we got some attention in here. I'll be sure to put on my shiny buttons." Eileen simply smiled and sauntered back into her office.

Rylee glanced at her workmate. "Hey, why so glum? They can film me if that's what you're worried about. I don't mind getting some extra attention. Who knows—I might become famous, and trust me, in Cairns, that wouldn't be too hard."

"What? Uh, no, I'm just not that into having a lot of attention. I'd rather stay in the background."

"Sure. Don't worry about it." Rylee resumed her seat as the radio crackled to life. "Firecom to 9-12 Alpha, repeat your message," she focused back on the job, the subject of their conversation soon forgotten by the young operator.

Evie couldn't forget so easily.

Her mind darted back in time, reminding her how much she despised the tacky journalists who reported the news-

'Top cop brings further shame to Victoria Police,'
'Family of disgraced cop plans overseas holiday,'

The headlines screamed in her mind as she recalled the relentless attack that had continued for weeks. She'd almost been fearful of leaving the house yet had gone about her life as best she could.

The announcement from Eileen had the potential to derail her life. Again.

It appeared Evie's days of attracting media attention weren't as far behind her as she'd hoped.

* * * * *

Across town, Nathan's concentration was broken by his friend.

"Hey bro, are you working on the house this weekend?" Mason walked into Nathan's office, taking a seat at the desk. "I'm at a loose end and can help you out, if you need. Or we can go over a certain job application, perhaps?" he said, placing fingers to his lips, hinting at a secret.

Nathan put down his phone after checking for messages, turning to face his friend. He'd been hoping to receive a text from Evie but so far, nothing.

Had he upset her?

He was thinking either he was trying to hard or she just wasn't interested. Yet their day at the Tablelands had gone well and the fact she hadn't ditched him told him he wasn't off the mark.

So why the silence?

"Mate, I'm not sure yet. It depends…"

"Does this have something to do with a certain Firecom operator, perhaps?" Mason grinned. "Is she higher on the priority list now? Taking up all your spare time?"

"Yeah, no, it's fine. I'm still focused on the house, don't worry. It's on track to be done by mid-year, right about the time my lease is up for renewal. The timing will be perfect then to get the electrical installation done, too." Nathan pushed back in his chair and raised one leg onto the other, hands behind his head. "I'm not that sure she's interested, anyway. Have to wait and see. It's not like I'm in any hurry."

"For romance, or the house?"

They both smiled.

"Well, time's movin' on mate and you're not getting any younger. I'm sure anyone would be better for your mental health than the crazy bitch you had before. Did yourself a favour, getting her out of your life." Mason could be straight in your face and speak the truth as he saw it, no matter how much it hurt to hear. That's part of why he and Nathan got on so well. None of the usual subtleties-just straight down the line, was Mason.

"Well, that's great advice coming from the king of permanent relationships." His mocking tone had Mason shrugging his shoulders in acceptance. His relationships, or liaisons, rarely lasted longer than a few months. He'd claimed that was the way he liked it but Nathan was unconvinced. "She wasn't that bad. Had a few issues, that's all."

"A few issues, alright." Mason sounded incredulous as he raised his brows. "Screwing around on your partner isn't something I'd forget so easily. You amaze me sometimes, man, how forgiving you can be." He leaned back. "And for the record-it's my choice to play the field, so I'm speaking from experience here." Nathan chuckled in response. "You, on the other hand, want the whole wife/kids/house scenario which is why it was never gonna work with the ex."

Nathan had to agree.

"Mate, I've said it before. It's just not worth getting into the whole bitterness thing. Takes up too much energy. Dad spent over thirty years grieving after Mum took off and look where it got him." His father had been devastated when his wife left, vowing never to give his heart to a woman again. Something he'd later regretted, he'd told Nathan on his deathbed.

Mason stood as his mobile started ringing. "Shit, gotta take this. Let me know when you go back up the hill for more work on the dream home," and walked out with a backward wave.

Nathan thought on what his friend had said about not wasting time.

It was true. Well into his thirties, he'd often thought about having kids one day. Just had to find the right woman to do it with.

If this thing with Evie wasn't going anywhere, he'd have to consider jumping back onto the dating scene, not exactly an exciting prospect. He shrugged to himself and left his office, deciding to check on what his crew were doing.

Obviously not a lot, Nathan noted, spying Kenny chatting to Moira. He didn't mind, but this particular fireman was easily distracted, and their visitor seemed to have won the old fella's heart.

"Hey Kenny, have you checked those hose reels yet?" he said, stifling a laugh as he noted the sudden redness passing across the older man's face.

"Uh, boss. Didn't see you there," he said, offering Moira a quick wink as he shuffled forward. "Haven't got to them yet. But look who's here again." He smiled with lovesick eyes at the object of his affection and Nathan wondered if Moira realised she'd attracted herself a potential suitor. Or a new pet!

Love-struck spoke again. "I was just asking Moira if she'd like to come to the quiz night next week. We're low on numbers and I thought she might enjoy it." Kenny was a master at diverting attention off anything work related if given the chance.

"Hi again, Moira. Hope this old codger's not hassling you too much," Nathan asked as he approached. "You know you can say no if it's not your kind of thing." He knew from experience the social club events could bore outsiders sometimes.

Kenny reached into his pocket, pulling out a crumpled up flyer on the event. "Here you go, Moira. This has all the details of where it's being held and the time. I can pick you up, if you like."

"That would be lovely, Kenny. Thank you." She accepted the wrinkled paper with a smile, folding it before placing it in her bag. "Will you be going too, Nathan?"

"I'll see. I might have to work an overtime shift that night." The white lie sprang to mind. He wasn't keen on attending work functions-a lot of small talk about the job bored him.

A light went off in his brain, sparking a new idea. *If Evie was there, he may just reconsider.*

Kenny jumped when the turnout bells began sounding, accompanied by the PA announcing their next job. "Oops, gotta go." The rest of the crew materialised, collecting their turnout gear before climbing into the truck.

"Bye Moira. See you next time," Nathan grabbed the job printout as he checked its details.

"Ah yes, bye. I'll call you," Kenny said as he launched himself into the rear seat. "Thanks for the food."

"No problem. Happy to help. I'll speak to you later on."

Moira stood watching, giving a wave as the truck activated its siren and headed out of the engine bay until it disappeared down the street.

It was several minutes before she moved and made her way towards the exit door.

Chapter 15

Evie kept her head down as Eileen welcomed the media crew the following morning. She'd had her fill of being in the public eye and didn't need to bring any more attention to herself.

Just keep a low profile and it'll be over soon.

Yet, it seemed the Universe didn't want to play that game as Eileen stopped in front of her desk, performing the obligatory introductions.

"Everyone, this is Evie, our newest recruit…," Eileen said, failing to notice her recruit's forced smile through gritted teeth.

"… and that's Rylee…," Eileen pointed to the excited girl, grinning with a much greater exuberance. "Out the back is Caroline, who's the third operator today." Caroline stuck her head around the corner with a "Hello" and a wave. The media contingent nodded in acknowledgement, unable to manoeuvre much in the cramped space.

"They'll all be glad to help you with any questions you have and can decide who wants to be filmed if you need an operator for the story," Eileen said.

"Thanks very much Eileen. I'm sure it'll be great," a young male responded. "We promise not to get in the way too much". He turned to face the operators. "I'm Geoff and this is Elle, who's filling in for our community reporter on leave. Elle reports on crime stuff but has agreed to help us out today, which is great." He touched the woman's shoulder, giving her a smile and Evie wondered if they had a thing going, judging by their familiarity. Geoff coughed and refocused on the introductions. "The guy on the camera is Ethan," he indicated to the other male with a sideways glance.

"I'm keen to learn a lot about what you guys do," Elle said, smiling with perfect teeth as she perused the room. Something about the confident reporter set Evie on edge yet she remained silent.

Geoff took a moment to survey the limited space his crew had to work in before giving them direction. "Basically, the story focus is to show viewers what Firecom does and how emergency calls are actioned. We've done similar stories with the police and ambos but not with the Fire Service, I believe. We might shoot some vision of you girls working first and then decide on the voice-over and what content we want to put in later."

Eileen agreed with his assessment. "I'm sure the Commissioner will be happy with any positive stories and I'm confident you'll do a good job," Eileen said before bidding a hasty retreat, leaving her employees with the group.

"Thanks Eileen," Geoff said, moving into the centre of the room, now markedly smaller with the additional bodies.

"This place is small, isn't it?" Elle observed. "Not the best working environment, eh?"

"Yeah, tell us about it. We're supposed to be getting a new centre at some point but who knows when that'll be," Rylee chimed in.

"Well, maybe we can play that up a bit and get some publicity going for you," Geoff said.

Elle had been staring at Evie for a moment before asking, "Have I met you somewhere before? I swear your face looks familiar." Evie groaned in silent panic.

Shit. This can't be happening, she thought. *I've only been in town a few months–I don't want to move again.*

"Uh, no." She attempted to dilute Elle's sudden interest in her. "I don't think so. I haven't been here that long. In Cairns, I mean."

Damn reporters. Why can't they keep out of everyone's business?

The reporter persevered, like a dog with a bone, not prepared to let go until she figured it out. "I'm good with faces and I swear I've seen you somewhere. I haven't interviewed you somewhere else, have I?"

Evie considered the less she was in the crew's presence, the less chance she had of being recognised. She turned away. "No. I'm sure we've never met before." *The sooner this is over, the better.*

"Where do you want me to set up, Geoff," cameraman Ethan interrupted, no doubt impatient and keen to begin work, and so began assembling his equipment.

"Let's get you set up to film Evie and…," the ringing of the emergency line interrupted Geoff's instructions.

"Sorry, gotta get this," Evie jumped on the call, even though that wasn't her morning role. Rylee looked confused and stood to whisper to Elle.

"That's an emergency call. Evie will take as much detail as she can and pass the job through to me or Caro for dispatching of the crew," she said by explanation.

Both Elle and Geoff listened while the girls dealt with what turned out to be a minor fuel leak.

"What other type of calls do you get?" Geoff began taking notes as Rylee spent the next few minutes explaining their role. She was at ease dealing with public relations commitments and more than happy to give them the insight they needed.

"I might take a break for a minute if that's okay," Evie said, removing her headset and standing.

She didn't make it far as Elle's memory had her clicking her fingers.

"I know where I've seen you before. It's just come to me. Evie. Evelyn Meriwether. I saw you and your family on the 7.30 Report or the Project," two of the more popular current affairs programs appearing on national television.

"Wasn't that your father, Eric Meriwether and the other two that went to prison?"

Chapter 16

All eyes fell upon her as Evie took a breath while a silent scream sounded in her head.

Rylee's eyes went round with curiosity and Geoff cleared his throat, uncharacteristically lost for words. Caroline poked her head in from Eileen's office, wondering why the room had gone silent. The camera guy stood next to Elle, his mouth agape. All waited in expectation of her response.

No sense in trying to hide now.

Evie stood. "Ahh, yes, it was. But it's not something I want to talk about. I don't have contact with him anymore."

"Yeah–I get that. It must have been horrible-a real shock for the family," Elle said.

Like she cared!

"It was." Evie pushed back her chair and made her way to the door, grabbing for the handle. "I'll be back in a sec."

Caroline's "Is everything alright?" echoed behind her as she left the room, running down the hallway towards the exit door. Finding it difficult to breathe, she gulped in air while a sob rose from her chest.

How long would this nightmare last?

Evie felt herself tense with anger as thoughts of her father had heat filling her face. It was alright for him–he could hide himself away in a jail cell while she, her mother and Cam had to relive the shame every day.

Damn him to hell.

"Hey Evie, are you okay?" Caroline's voice of concern saw her workmate turn and smile tentatively.

"I'll be fine." She took the tissue Caroline held out, wiping a tear from her face. She sniffed and offered a meek laugh. "It was bound to come out, I guess."

"Well, it's nobody's business, I reckon," her workmate said, placing a supportive arm around her shoulders. "You don't have to spill any details, so don't stress. We're all pretty laid back here, and I'm sure you weren't a part of anything bad. You're too nice for that. I mean, you don't even swear at the crews for God's sake."

Evie chuckled, appreciating Caroline's light-hearted comments. She hardly knew her well enough, yet here she was, defending her character, prepared to accept her in spite of the scandal.

What a nice change that was.

"Thanks Caro, that means a lot. It's something I don't want to get into right now. In fact, I'm trying hard to forget it ever happened."

"I bet." Caroline gestured to the office door. "Let's get back in, shall we? Knowing Rylee, she's probably taken over filming and put herself front and centre of the story. It'll end up being more about her trying to get on tv and score a date rather than focusing on what we do here."

Evie felt some relief as she followed Caroline back into the Centre, Geoff motioning for silence with fingers across his lips as Ethan filmed Rylee at her console. Caroline had been right-the effervescent Rylee seemed quite at home in the limelight and Evie, for one, was happy to keep in that way.

Caroline indicated for Evie to escape to Eileen's office, leaving the film crew alone, and she obliged. "Why don't you sit out here for a while and I'll take your console, she offered.

"Thanks," Evie said, sliding into the seat. This was not turning out to be one of her better days.

* * * * *

Across town, Nathan also felt stressed out, yet for a different reason altogether.

It wasn't like him to be tied up in knots over a woman. Particularly when he wasn't certain if his interest was reciprocated and it was all a big waste of his time.

Yet he couldn't give up hope-not yet.

He had to do something.

Nathan hated communicating by text message, believing it totally impersonal, but knew it would be hard for Evie to receive calls during work hours.

So here goes!

"Hi. Just checking if you're keen on going to the social club quiz tomorrow? I can pick you up around 7. Let me know. Nathan."

He hit the 'send' button, hoping for a positive response. He hadn't seen or heard from Evie in about three days and he'd not been able to focus his mind at work, which was more than frustrating. He needed to be sure—one way or the other—otherwise he'd go crazy!

Here he was, a grown man, hanging onto his mobile as he waited to hear the *ding* of a reply yet fearing the possibility she might turn him down.

He was turning into a soppy, lovesick teenager, and thoughts of Kenny moping over Moira came to mind, bringing a wry smile to his face.

Join the club buddy, he thought.

There sure were no guarantees in the game of love.

* * * * *

"Oh, my god. You really are famous." Rylee's exclamation had Evie cringing later that morning. The news team had gone after filming the women going about their routine, Geoff confirming that Elle would provide the voice-over during editing to describe the work they performed.

After the crew's departure, Rylee couldn't help herself, having to check out the story on line after Elle had spilled the beans. Evie conceded she most likely would have done the same thing yet in a more tactful manner than her young counterpart.

Damn you Google, she fumed, as Rylee recited the facts, all of which Evie knew by heart.

"It says your dad and the other two coppers were apparently taking cash from drug raids and other crimes. Wow, that must have been really full on-going to Court and all."

Understatement of the year.

"Not the most pleasant time of my life, that's for sure," Evie said.

"There sure are a lot of stories on the net about it. He must be really…"

"Rylee, I think Evie's probably heard enough about her father for today," Caroline interjected. "Have you done that draft procedure for the handovers that Eileen wanted, yet? She'll be mad if you haven't."

Evie sent silent thanks to her workmate for the diversion as Rylee grabbed at the pile of papers on her desk.

"I'm about half-finished and still chasing up some other info," came her flustered response.

Evie's phone pinged, and she picked it up, expecting it was Nicola wanting to confirm their next training session.

She smiled yet felt slightly terrified as she noticed Nathan's name appear.

On reading his invitation, uncertainty overtook her once again.

She'd heard about the quiz night from the girls but had remained non-committal about going.

Now, however, her motivation had changed.

What the hell, she though. *At least I can enjoy his company while it lasts?*

In fact, he was the biggest draw card. She was hopeless at quizzes and trivia nights and would normally avoid them like the plague.

She tapped out a response before she had time to change her mind.

Chapter 17

Saturday evening and Evie's heart was light as Nathan bent to register their attendance at the front desk of the Brothers Leagues Club, the venue for tonight's event.

She noticed him laugh as he received the complimentary mocktail and multi-coloured party hat, complete with tinsel and sparkles, handed out to everyone attending.

If his looks were anything to go by, she guessed he wouldn't be donning the headgear anytime soon.

She glanced around the room, waving in recognition when spying her workmates seated at a round table. She couldn't help but laugh, noting Rylee was the only one brave enough to wear the tacky headdress. The girl was obviously comfortable attracting attention to herself.

"Hey, Evie, Nathan…," Rylee stood, waving them over with enthusiasm. "Come and join our table," "Did you two guys come together?"

It was inevitable someone would notice their entry, and several pairs of eyes fell upon them.

"Ah, Nathan offered to pick me up after his shift," Evie said, attempting to downplay the attention. Nathan touched the small of her back, directing her to one of the spare seats. "He lives nearby, so it made sense."

Rylee wore a confused expression. "But I thought Nathan lived at…"

"That was nice of him," Jason Betts, an operator from B Shift interrupted Rylee's observation. "I wish I'd get an offer like that." He winked at Nathan, bringing a redness to the Station Officer's face as he sat next to Evie.

Jason's penchant for teasing and practical jokes made him a fun member of the Firecom team to be around and had him well liked by everyone.

"Jase, leave the poor guy alone." Caroline punched his shoulder, Nathan's unease evident. It wasn't the first time Jason's forthright manner was confronting to those who didn't know him well.

"Only kidding. Sorry, Nathan. Didn't mean to offend. Quite the opposite, actually." He picked up his drink and raised it with a grin.

"None taken." Nathan downplayed the exchange, turning to speak to Evie, but his words were lost as Kenny, MC for the event, waved from a nearby table.

Evie observed an older woman sitting next to him and turned to Nathan. "I thought Kenny was a confirmed bachelor. At least, that's what he claimed that day I rode on the fire truck."

"Oh, he's quite taken with Moira, our Kenny," Nathan said. "Has been for quite a while but the old bugger's been too scared to ask her out until now. She visits the Station now and then, bringing food for everyone. Remind me to introduce you two later."

The lights dimmed and several whoops filled the air as Kenny moved to the centre of the room, microphone in hand, to begin proceedings.

The night proved to be enjoyable, the quiz questions focusing on sport, entertainment and the local area, which made it easy for everyone to join in. Kenny was in his element as host, if not at times slightly distracted as his eyes wandered towards the woman seated at his table.

He wasn't the only one feeling flustered that evening.

Although in a room full of people, Evie keenly felt Nathan's presence nearby. On one occasion, his hand brushed hers as he handed her a pencil for the scoresheet, and another time, his breath touched her ear ever so slightly as he offered to buy her a drink.

It became difficult to ignore the curious stares from around the table, particularly from Rylee, and as Nathan excused himself to go to the bar, she jumped at the chance to dig for more details.

"Evie, you sneaky devil. Are you and the Station Officer an item?" the younger girl asked. "I've been trying to get him to notice me for months and you've snagged him within five minutes of being here." Her tone was slurred, and Evie wondered how many drinks she'd had.

Evie tried to downplay their association. "It's not like that Rylee. We're just friends, that's all. I hardly know the guy. And I'm not looking for any kind of relationship right now."

"It's okay. I'm just teasing." Rylee gave Caroline a nudge next to her, spilling a glass of red wine in the process which started to drip onto the floor. "If he's keen, go for it." Rylee replied, not noticing the liquid staining the cloth until Caroline grabbed for some napkins in an attempt to stem the flow. "Oh shit, did I do that?" she said. "Damn red wine goes straight to my head every time."

Caroline raised her eyes to Evie and shrugged, as Evie took it as the perfect opportunity to escape. "I'm off to the ladies. Be back soon." Things were becoming a bit too intense and Rylee's intoxication would no doubt leave her open to face more questions and innuendo.

Evie all but bumped into Nathan as he stepped back, two drinks in hand. "Whoa there, nearly gotcha," he exclaimed. "Not running off already, I hope?"

"No, just trying to escape Rylee's fishing for gossip. I'm thinking she's had a little too much to drink."

"I'm not surprised. She is a party girl, after all. It's what she does. I'm guessing she's digging for dirt about us arriving together?"

Evie nodded. "She's a little upset that you don't seem keen on taking her out."

"Well, she'll have to get over it I guess. She's a bit over the top for my taste. I prefer women who don't draw too much attention to themselves. Someone more like you, actually."

Evie offered a slight smile, not knowing what to say. All she wanted was to escape and leave the stares behind.

He must have picked up on her vibe, his, "The quiz is all but over. Do you want to leave and go somewhere? Get some air?" coming as music to her ears.

"Sure, I'd love to. I'll grab my bag and say my goodbyes," she said, returning to their table.

Her quick getaway was thwarted as Rylee noticed Evie collecting her things. "Hey, you guys aren't leaving so soon, are ya?" She giggled as she burped, putting a hand to her mouth. "Oops, sorry," as she continued to laugh. "The fun's just getting started, and we missed you."

"Sorry guys. It's been a good night but I'm a bit tired after work. Nathan's offered to drop me home. I'll see you on shift tomorrow night," she said, addressing Caroline who, being the designated driver for the evening, had the *pleasure* of taking Rylee home. Evie hoped for her friend's sake that Rylee made it without throwing up in the car.

"Hey, Evie, did you tell your sexy man of yours about being famous and on the news yet? It's not every day that…"

"What's this about being famous?" Nathan said as he returned to the table, just in time to hear Rylee's comment.

Evie turned a bright shade of red. "It's nothing. Don't worry about it. Rylee's just a little tipsy. Let's leave now, shall we?" she stammered, grabbing his arm and leading him away. "Goodnight everyone."

Evie couldn't get out of there quickly enough.

The cat was well and truly out of the bag if his questioning look was anything to go by!

Rylee had been right about one thing though.

Nathan deserved to know the truth-about who she was and the shameful secret she kept.

It would be all or nothing as she braced herself for his rejection.

Nathan didn't notice the silent tear on her face as they left, hand in hand.

* * * * *

By the time they arrived at his car, Evie had composed herself enough to agree to Nathan's suggestion they go for a stroll along the Esplanade.

The venue was popular with locals and tourists, taking advantage of the warm night balmy air which smelt of salt and sand. The pathway remained busy with foot traffic even though it was well into the evening.

The tide was out, exposing the mud flats located several metres below the pathway. Two seagulls squawked over a delicacy thrown somewhere from above while some distance away, a group of pelicans lay nesting with long beaks settling on their chests.

The pair walked slowly, her attention focused on holding the ice-cream cone Nathan insisted she try from the Cold Rock Cafe. "It's the best in town," he claimed and she '*had to have one*.' The chocolate chips melted on her tongue as she struggled to stop the treat succumbing to the heat of the evening. She laughed as she noticed he seemed to be having the same dilemma.

"Here, let me. You have some chocolate on your chin." He gently wiped her face with a finger and his touch brought even more heat to her skin which had nothing to do with the temperature in the night air.

His hand cupped her face for a moment before he drew himself back, focusing on the cone which was dripping profusely. "Here. Grab one of these," he offered her a napkin, and they both set about wiping their hands while finishing the treat.

"Why don't we sit over here," he gestured to a bench seat facing the ocean, the twinkling lights of the marina beacons flashing red and green in the distance. They sat in silence, taking in the setting before them.

"Evie, I…"

"I just wanted to thank…"

She tried to pre-empt his speech, sensing he was about to get deep and meaningful, something she wasn't ready for. But in a macabre sense, she realised she wanted–*no, needed*-to hear what he had to say.

"Sorry, I didn't mean to jump in. You go first," she said, looking at him with a sideways glance before returning her gaze to the sea.

"That's alright. I was just going to say how much I enjoy being with you and that I'd like to see you again. I realise you may have been hurt in the past by someone and that's probably the reason you moved up here."

Evie experienced a sense of panic he'd hit so close to the mark and looked down at her feet. The familiar ache in her chest returned and her palms sweated up as she gripped the wooden seat, yet couldn't bring herself to speak.

"Trust me. I understand," he said. "You don't have to go into details about it if you're not ready. Just take your time. I sure as hell understand what it's like to have your heart smashed by someone."

Evie stifled back a sob as her mind flashed back to the memory of her trying on the ivory silk wedding gown. She'd swirled around like a little girl, not wanting to take it off, giddy with excitement as her mother had nodded her approval. She'd felt like a princess.

The dress hadn't seen the light of day since, yet for some crazy reason, Evie couldn't get rid of it. Just another haunting reminder of a day that had destroyed her heart.

"Evie. Are you alright?" Nathan's concerned voice jolted her back into the present and she grabbed his hand without thinking.

"What, sorry. My mind was wandering, but I heard what you said."

The sensation of his fingers entwined with hers, the warmth they generated, reminded her how much she missed the sensation of a man's touch . She and Ben had enjoyed a healthy intimacy, yet she'd not realised until this moment how she craved it still.

Nathan was slowly melting the ice that had taken hold of her heart and she felt like she was on a roller coaster ride she had no way of stopping.

Her mother's words came to her as she'd sobbed after Ben's betrayal. "I know you *will* find love again, Evie. You may not believe it now, but it will happen. You're too wonderful a person to live life alone."

She'd rejected her parent's words at the time, promising herself she'd never take the same risk again.

Yet here she was, being offered a chance to feel cherished once again.

Dare she take it?

Would Nathan still be interested once I tell him the truth?

Who knew?

Maybe it was time to let go of her fear and find out.

"I would like to keep seeing you Nathan, yes." She gripped both of his hands in hers and noticed his eyes light with anticipation.

"But there are things from my past you need to know about before you decide. Then we'll see what happens next."

"Whenever you're ready, I'll be listening," his reassuring reply as he touched her face, giving her confidence as she took a breath and began talking.

Chapter 18

What an asshole that Ben guy must be, Nathan thought later as he lay back in bed. Must be a real loser to let a girl like Evie get away, for the sake of his reputation.

He would never put a job before a woman, no way in hell.

He'd only dropped Evie off a short while ago, a little after two. Up until then, they spent time in a local cafe, downing several coffees while he allowed her time to share her story over the next few hours.

He'd let her do most of the talking, telling of a past which obviously still weighed heavily on her mind.

Nathan learned she'd not only been dumped by her fiance, but also been betrayed by her father-a double whammy anyone would struggle to cope with. No wonder she'd run like a frightened deer in the spotlight when the media hounds showed up.

Now, as he picked up a photo of his dad on his dresser, Nathan felt the familiar ache of loss in his chest that never seemed to go away. Three years and he still missed the old bugger–his knack for telling stories and offering advice to his only son–whether he'd wanted it or not.

Over the years, Nathan had learned so much from his father and was proud of the man who'd single-handedly raised his six-year-old son after his wife's desertion. Nathan knew it hadn't been easy-his father working full time at the railway earning a modest wage and managing their home. Their struggles had served to teach Nathan a lot about what respect and responsibility meant, and what it was to be a man.

For that, he'd be forever grateful.

As far as the woman who'd deserted them was concerned, Nathan felt nothing. An empty void had replaced the love she'd once offered him as a young child, yet no real bitterness lay in its stead, just a lingering sadness at what might have been.

Both he and his father had neither seen nor heard from her again, as they'd made their way together through the years, forging the strong bond that had only been severed upon Jack's passing.

Nathan placed the photo back on the nightstand and lay down, the warm night air making it pleasant enough to sleep without covers.

It had been an exhausting day but at least it had ended on a positive note. He sensed he'd made good progress in his relationship with Evie.

After hearing her story, he'd assured her that nothing she'd told him made him want to turn tail and run. In fact, for him, the opposite was true.

Knowing she was a genuine person with a real past, and not some girl untouched by life's twists and turns, made her even more attractive, in his eyes at least.

Having lived through unbearable hurt and a broken heart made her fledgling feelings for him even more genuine.

He'd taken her home after she'd stifled a yawn mid-sentence, realising she must have been as tired as he felt.

Not wanting to push his luck too hard too early, he'd bent to kiss her cheek before taking her hands, making a promise to call her the next day. She'd thanked him and closed the door.

His eyes closed as he drifted off, his last thoughts of what tomorrow would bring.

* * * * *

Not able to sleep, Evie sat outside on her small balcony overlooking the Esplanade where she'd walked with Nathan earlier that evening, the almost-full moon high overhead as it lit up the street below.

Thoughts of the night and the ease with which she'd been able to talk with Nathan ran through her mind. She replayed every word, every reaction from him, until her head started to pound.

Have I done the right thing? she asked herself, stressing if she'd been too hasty in spilling her guts.

After all, she hadn't known him long.

Yet, his nearness and the scent of his sexy aftershave almost had her quivering at the knees and she'd been helpless to resist his encouragement to share her story.

Finally being able to have an honest conversation with someone made her heart feel lighter somehow, like a massive rock had been lifted from her shoulders.

Even more amazing, after all the sordid details were laid bare, Nathan had been so accepting, showing an awareness in him that most other guys didn't have.

At least, none that she knew of.

There were no gasps of shock, no looks of disgust or pity. Instead, he'd stayed silent and given her the chance to lay bare the ugly facts.

She told him of her past relationship with Ben, where'd they'd met and the fact he'd been her first real love. "It was great at the start, when he'd made Senior Connie… ahh Constable," she explained at Nathan's bemused look.

"Back then, the job was still routine and when he came home, he wouldn't talk about it much," she said.

"After a few years, he started becoming keener on moving up the ladder, so he applied for detective school and was accepted." Evie recalled how excited and proud she'd been for Ben, happy his career was moving ahead, "…enough to provide them with a solid foundation for the future," he'd said.

She hadn't begrudged him the time spent away on courses or the endless hours of study at home when he'd paid her little attention. Evie had filled the lonely nights watching tv or attending extra sessions at the gym.

"When he finished the training and started working in the Crime Investigation Unit, he was rapt and took to it like a duck to water," she'd continued.

"His partner, Barry McDermott, was an older guy who'd been in the job a long time. He didn't seem to like me too much—called me '*girly*' and looked at me like I was a piece of dirt, not good enough somehow. Or maybe he didn't like it that I was the daughter of one of his senior officers. I think he resented the fact that Ben had a partner, and a settled life when all he seemed to live for was the job."

"When the shit hit the fan about my father, I'm sure it was Barry who encouraged Ben to end it with me, for the sake of his career. Ben never admitted it, but I don't imagine he would have done it if he hadn't been pushed."

"The guy's piss weak, if you ask me. If he'd loved you, he would have been more supportive, not dumping you as a liability to his career." Nathan said, touching her arm in a gesture of support.

Evie smiled, his concern giving her the encouragement to continue, even though the pain and embarrassment was still raw, like it had happened only yesterday.

"And your father? How's your contact with him now? I'm guessing not that great."

Evie's brows drew together, and she ran a hand over her eyes. For months now, she hadn't been willing to bring herself to think of him, let alone make any attempt to communicate.

The reminder of his betrayal to herself, her mother and everyone they knew, still hit her in the gut every time she thought of it.

"That's another part of the story, Nathan, but I just can't right now. It's too hard. Maybe later."

"It's okay. We don't have to learn everything there is to know about each other in one night."

"For now, I will say that I sure as hell don't care about what your father did or that he's in jail?" he said. "If anyone believes that you're anything at all like him, then they're just… well, I think you know what I mean," he'd offered with a smile. "Anyone with half a brain can tell that you're an amazing woman."

His words echoed in her mind now and the sense of relief Evie felt had been palpable. Even though they still had a lot to discover about each other, the fact she'd been ready to open up to him at all was a miracle.

She smiled at the realisation now and sipped her tea, which had cooled in the breeze. For the first time in ages, she felt a real sense of hope for what lay ahead.

A future that may see her find love again.

* * * * *

Several days later, Ben's gaze was drawn outside the tiny window to the glittering vista below and he craned his neck to get a better view.

At over 35,000 feet, the Barrier Reef looked spectacular from on high. Highlighting multi-coloured coral, the calm blue and green water lapped around small islands while several large boats, no doubt crammed full of eager tourists, bopped up and down in the current.

All too soon the view disappeared from sight as the plane made its final descent into Cairns Airport, the cabin crew making one last pass through the aircraft collecting rubbish.

I hope this isn't a huge mistake, Ben mused, rubbing tired eyes, thinking of the mess he'd left with McDermott. The fact the Finch trial was due to start in just three days weighed on his mind, yet he felt little remorse at leaving. The guy almost blew a fuse when Ben told him he was heading out of town on an emergency.

He'd sure weathered a spray from McDermott as he walked out of the office that night. Yet, Ben had ignored his tirade. Lately, he was more concerned with thoughts of what he'd done and how much he'd hurt Evie than work files and impending deadlines.

The phone call to her over two weeks ago hadn't gone well, but was pretty much what he'd expected. After her rejection, he'd tried to put her from his thoughts yet he couldn't let it go.

Hell, as far as she was concerned, he was no doubt a chapter in her history she preferred to forget. She'd made that plain enough. A once happy relationship that had ended all too badly. Not that he'd planned it that way. Never in a million years.

If that damn prick Eric hadn't…, Ben sighed, immediately pushing blame from his mind. Eric had always treated him well-just stuffed up big time on this occasion.

The elderly lady in the seat next to him must have sensed Ben's anxiety as she looked at him with concerned eyes. He offered a wry smile in return. "Sorry. Not a fan of flying."

"Never mind dear, we're almost there. We'll be on the ground soon enough."

He caught a whiff of her perfume, something old fashioned like Granny used to wear back when Pop was alive. Now they were both gone, and he wondered what she would have thought of his desperate efforts to win his girl back.

More than likely offer the sensible voice of reason like the straight shooter she'd been.

"No use in going back over old ground, Benny boy," would have been her likely advice. "Just deal with the fallout and learn from your mistakes." He missed Granny.

His lips curled as he remembered the day he'd hit the school bully, Will Cagley, in the nose for stealing his lunch box. They'd both been around nine years old and the shock at seeing blood dripping from Will's nose, along with the throbbing in his own knuckles, had Ben running off to Gran's house for moral support and a band-aid.

What he also received was the sage advice that had been her mantra - *"Can't change what happened, even if you're sorry. What's done is done."* She'd rubbed ointment into his reddened hands, covering them with gauze. "We'll see whether this kid learned his lesson, hmm," she'd added with a grin.

Her wink and smile gave Ben the encouragement to believe he'd been justified in his punishment of Will and he was soon proven right. From that day onwards, the boy changed his ways and become one of Ben's best friends through primary school.

Fond memories aside, Ben wasn't enough of an idiot to believe that his current predicament with Evie could be fixed with balm and band-aids. In fact, he didn't know if it was fixable at all. But he had to at least have one more go in trying to win her back. God knows, his last efforts had been feeble and half-hearted.

He'd been certain that asking Pauline for Evie's address would be met with a not-so-polite dismissal, so he hadn't even bothered going down that route.

Instead, he'd used his detecting skills to discover she'd accepted a job with the fire service in Queensland as a communications operator.

The risk of discovery had been worth it.

He'd deal with any fallout when he got back to Melbourne.

As the plane's wheels hit the tarmac and the force of the engine's speed slowed down, Ben's heart started pumping even faster.

He'd have his answer soon enough and one way or another, he could get his life back on track again.

Hopefully with Evie at his side.

Chapter 19

The roar of the plane's engines as it passed overhead did little to distract the divers below as they revelled in the wonder of the Barrier Reef.

"Wow, did you see that amazing stingray down there? It came within inches of your face, you know." Evie's delight and wonder at the teeming world beneath the sparkling water couldn't be denied as she surfaced next to Nathan.

He removed his mouthpiece, spitting out the salty water, before replying. "I saw it too. Even felt the swish of his tail as he came close. Awesome, eh? I promised you'd love it out here, didn't I? And who was the one who didn't want to try diving, hmmm?"

"Yeah, well, I've done nothing like this and yes, I admit I'm a wimp when it comes to adventure. But I'm glad I did now. It's gorgeous."

They'd surfaced about ten metres from the catamaran 'Ocean Lady' that had departed early that morning from the Cairns Marina. Along with several qualified dive instructors, there were about twenty others on board for a day of exploration and fun. On the trip out, the staff had provided the requisite introductory lesson for first timers on how to use the scuba gear and shortly after, the group completed their first dive.

Since then, they'd visited another two dive locations and now made ready to climb back on board to enjoy a break and some afternoon tea.

When Nathan had called and said they were going somewhere special, she'd been unsure of what to expect. After the balloon ride, she'd hoped they weren't upgrading to a bungy jump or leaping from a plane. Both activities were popular here, she knew, yet she wasn't too keen on trying them out just yet.

When he'd instructed her to bring swimming gear, Evie thought she'd be relatively safe and so felt less anxious.

Ben and I would never do this. On the rare occasion when he'd taken time off, most of their outings had either been attending football games, barbeques with his mates or snow skiing, the latter being something she was dismal at, much preferring to spend her day huddled over an open fire.

Diving the reef with Nathan seemed a world away from her previous life and she loved every minute of it.

Evie had never seen water so clear-the blue and green swell mesmerizing as it twinkled with rays of sunlight on its surface. The temperature remained mild yet she'd worked up a sweat wearing the scuba suit and oxygen tank, as it added considerable weight to her frame.

Coral coloured in pinks and oranges lay beneath the surface yet Evie had also spotted shades of blue and yellow as she swam, careful not to touch any due to its sensitivity to breakage and decay.

She'd spotted multi-coloured fish of various sizes, some small sharks and a large turtle nicknamed Arnie, a regular at ease with the swimmers that entered his domain, according to the instructors. He'd even sidled up beside her at one point, his soft flippers moving gently as he checked her out.

After several more dives in the afternoon, the crew conducted a head count before returning to the mainland. Evie sat next to Nathan on the upper deck, watching the pontoon disappear as they rode over the almost-calm water. Most of the others were inside the main cabin, grabbing a last snack or comparing photos before returning.

"Thanks for today, it's been amazing. Hopefully we can come back another time," Evie said, placing her hand on his knee.

"I'm glad you had a good time. I told you that diving wasn't too scary. You were a natural out there." He grasped her hand in his, taking it to his lips. His feather-light kiss to the inside of her wrist had her letting out a slight gasp.

This guy was overtaking her senses at a faster rate of knots than the boat.

Were things moving too fast?

Possibly, but right here, right now, she didn't care.

He cupped her face, whispering in her ear.

"Can I kiss you Evie?"

Her voice deserted her as she nodded her consent and closed her eyes.

He moved forward and Evie smelt the faint salty tang from the ocean and the heat emanating from his skin.

"Hey Mister…," his arm was yanked back, and the moment lost as Nathan turned towards a German speaking woman aged around seventy. Evie was momentarily stunned at the intrusion, sliding back in her seat as she ran sweaty palms down her shorts.

"Can you take a picture of Heinz and me?" Oblivious to the intimacy of the moment, the woman gestured towards a white-haired male standing less than a foot away.

Evie had noticed the couple briefly upon boarding, but had seen little of them during the day. The hapless Heinz appeared almost wizard-like, with his pointy white beard and floppy hat, stooped over whilst leaning on a cane for support. Undoubtedly incapable of diving the Reef, it appeared he'd been dragged along by his overbearing wife who now stood before the pair, demanding a happy snap.

"We like to capture each day with a picture, yes?"

Nathan's incredulous look of shock had Evie giggling to herself, even though she was just as pissed as he no doubt was at the couple's ill-timed photo shoot.

He almost grabbed the camera from the woman's hand and motioned for them to move closer together and smile.

"One more, yes?" she insisted, clicking her fingers. Nathan dutifully obeyed before handing the camera back to her.

"Thank you, thank you. Such lovely people," she shuffled off arm in arm with her docile husband, content now that they had a reminder of the day.

"Sorry 'bout that," Nathan turned back to Evie with a shrug. "Not so perfect timing."

"It's okay. It wasn't your fault. But the look on your face was kinda priceless," she couldn't help but giggle a little and he soon joined in with a hearty laugh.

Any prospect for privacy was further denied them as several crew members walked around, collecting scuba gear while other day trippers came on deck for a last look at the receding ocean.

Nathan, having given up any hope for intimacy now, sat down next to Evie, content to cosy up.

"Let's enjoy the last of the view before we get back," he said as she settled into his arms, feeling at home in his embrace.

* * * * *

Evie slept in the next morning, not bothering to set her alarm, as this was her last day off. It hadn't taken long to realise that the best perk of working at Firecom was the two day/two night roster, followed by four days leave, giving her time to kick back and enjoy the days as she pleased.

As much as she'd enjoyed her sleep-ins back in Melbourne, where the sun rose later, she was unable to resist the temptation of starting the day as the morning sun filled her bedroom. A quick look out the window confirmed another perfect blue-sky day ahead. Evie threw off the bedcover and stood to stretch. So far this wet season, there'd been no sign of any impending cyclones. Evie was more than happy for that to remain the case. She had no particular desire to experience that particular phenomenon of nature!

Spying several joggers along the Esplanade track made her keen to join them and thinking of Nathan, she grabbed her phone.

He picked up on the second ring.

"Hey Nathan. Hi, it's Evie."

"Evie, hi." He sounded distracted, and Evie thought she heard a muffled voice in the background. "What's up?"

"I'm just calling to see if you'd be up for a run this morning. The day looks perfect for some exercise. Maybe we can go back to the Red Arrow if you're keen?"

There was a moment's silence before he spoke.

"I'm sorry Evie, I can't right now. Something's come up and I…"

"Natey, stop talking and come back over here". A throaty female voice spoke in the background, and Evie's bright mood turned a little darker.

"Nathan, is someone there with you?" She hated the way her tone changed from cheerful to whiny but couldn't seem to stop the fear enveloping her.

"No. Well yes, it's no-one important". He murmured. "A friend's just turned up out of the blue under the weather so I'm just trying to help them out. Can I call you later?"

"Yeah, sure. Call me when you're keen." Evie made light of his rejection, certain she was being irrational in her mistrust. "I might ring Nicola and see if she's up for it."

It wasn't like we're an item or anything. He's free to see who he wants and isn't answerable to me.

"Great. I'll call you back. Promise." He disconnected before she had a chance to speak and she was left with the call-ended tone in her ear.

As she checked her contact list for Nicola's number, Evie couldn't help but wonder exactly what Nathan was doing at that moment.

And who he was with.

Chapter 20

Twenty minutes earlier and Nathan had been in *la la* land, enjoying the first dream he'd had in a long time. And a pleasant one at that.

He'd been swimming in the ocean, with Evie off to his left, pointing at something in the coral. He'd been about to swim over when the sound of someone pounding on his door interrupted the illusion and he woke with a start.

Cooper also raised his head at the noise and let out a few barks, rising on all fours in alert mode. "Easy fella," Nathan patted his head in reassurance.

He pulled on some shorts and walked to the door, Cooper's nails tapping on the floorboards as he followed his master, keen to see who the visitor was.

"Alright, alright, I'm coming," he grunted, as the knocking continued. *This had better be good*, he thought. *Otherwise, I won't be impressed.*

He yanked on the door and his stomach lurched when he saw Olivia, one hand in mid-air, ready to knock once again.

"'bout time, darling. I've been here for ages," she didn't wait for an acknowledgement before stepping inside, Nathan having little choice but to step back and let her pass.

"I knew you were home 'cos your car's out front," she offered, turning to pat Cooper's head.

The dog whined a little and crept backwards, not keen on the gesture.

"He never did like me much," she said, taking her hand back.

"It's not your fault. Cooper's wary around females, you know that. He's a boy dog, likes to mix with the guys." Nathan's lie was an attempt to disprove her theory, but he knew Olivia was correct-Cooper had never taken to her.

She gave a slight laugh that didn't touch her eyes, which he noticed looked glazed and unfocused.

She also appeared to have lost weight and her hair was wild, the light curls mussed around her face as if they hadn't been brushed in days.

Nathan waited for her to speak but she stood in silence, one arm across her chest, grabbing the other as she swayed, apparently having trouble with her balance.

"Did you drive over here drunk, Liv? he said.

"What? No. I've come off shift and haven't slept, that's all."

"Then you'd better sit down before you fall down," he said, taking her arm as he led her to the sofa.

"Such concern. I'm touched Natey," she said but followed anyway, sitting with a slight thud. "And here I was thinking you didn't care at all."

Nathan refused to bite at her sarcasm, returning to the kitchen to make coffee. He needed something to deal with this drama and caffeine was as good a fix as any.

"Do you want a drink?" he asked, receiving no response.

Typical, he thought. Liv had to be one of the most frustrating, obstinate, rude women he'd ever met but he'd grown to accept that was how she was. She did things on her own terms.

That had been a lot of the problem. She'd refused to let him into her inner world and he'd conceded defeat in her ever being able to be truly honest with him.

He prepared her usual strong black anyway, and walked back to the lounge, handing it over. She accepted with both hands without uttering a word.

He sat opposite as they sipped their drinks for a moment until he broke the silence.

"So, what are you doing here, Liv? What's going on with you?"

Nathan hated that he sounded uncaring yet frustrated she'd shoved her way back into his world.

A moment's silence before she placed the cup down with trembling fingers. "I'm being investigated at work, Natey. I don't know what to do. There's no one else I can go to."

She ran both hands through her already messed hair and leaned forward. "I think Matthew may have filed a report against me. No-one's said anything official though. I'm freakin' out about it."

Hearing his nickname on her lips grated, and he asked gruffly, "Who is this Matthew? Is he another ambo?"

"He's my new shift partner, yes. I've worked with him for a few weeks but he's really nerdy and by the book. I think he has it in for female paramedics, stupid weasel."

"So not really your type, eh?" He couldn't help but get the jibe in, the pain of her cheating on him still raw after all this time.

Olivia knew exactly what he meant as she hit her leg in frustration.

"God. Can't you forget about that. About me sleeping with Mike. It was a one-off. I told you that…," she looked down at the carpet, averting his gaze.

"Yeah, you told me all about it. It doesn't make it any better."

"Look, I… I'm sorry. What more can I say? I'm scared about what's happening. If I lose this job… well, I… I have nothing else." Her voice choked up and she wiped at the wetness on her face. He was surprised as he'd hardly ever seen her show much emotion before.

"Why come to me, though? Surely there's someone else you can talk to. A girlfriend, someone at work?" He saw the flicker of panic in her eyes and realised she possessed a real fear of losing the one thing he knew she cherished. He knew that Olivia's commitment to the job was the only thing important in her life.

On the other hand, he couldn't help but think she'd landed herself in this position.

"What made him put in a report about you, hmmm? Did you turn up half-stoned to work or give someone the wrong needle, maybe?

Her face paled at his last remark and he shoved his hands through his hair.

"Shit, Liv. Did you administer the wrong drug? You can't put people's lives at risk-even if you have a bad day. You of all people should know that."

She shrugged her shoulders. "It wasn't life threatening, just a sedative. I was strung out, I don't remember how it happened but it…"

Nathan's phone started ringing, and he moved to answer it. Evie's name was highlighted and his heart lightened.

"I have to get this. Give me a minute," he said to Olivia as he turned to walk back into the kitchen. "Evie, hi," he said.

"Don't be too long. I need you," Olivia's response came from behind and Nathan hoped Evie hadn't heard her plea. No sense in complicating things yet.

He felt like an even greater prick when he had to decline her offer to go running but knew he couldn't just dump Olivia when she was in this state. No matter what she'd done, he wasn't that much of a heartless bastard. At least, he didn't think so.

He hadn't realised she'd come into the kitchen until her voice came from close behind.

"Natey, stop talking and come back over here," Olivia whined, standing close enough for Evie to hear.

Damn you Olivia. Can't you keep your mouth shut?

It seemed her tears had miraculously subsided, probably because she'd figured it was a woman he was talking to.

He gestured with his hand for her silence and she turned away with a sulk. He said a quick goodbye to Evie, knowing he'd have some explaining to do, and turned back to face his ex…

Chapter 21

The next morning and Evie couldn't stop thinking about the woman she'd heard during Nathan's call.

Who was she?

It was driving her crazy, but she refused to hassle him with texts or calls. That wasn't her style. He'd said he would call and he would.

Best forget about it for now.

At least she had work to focus on for the time being, as A shift were at the start of a new tour.

She turned to speak to her workmate. "How did you pull up after the quiz night?" Evie asked Rylee, not having seen the younger girl for several days.

"Yeah, not too bad. I went clubbing with Jason and Julie from Regional. We met up with some friends at the Salthouse," she replied. Evie had heard that the hot spot was one of the more popular bars near the Marina. "You should come out with us sometime."

"Maybe. I'll see." Evie replied, not knowing where she stood with Nathan.

I thought I could trust him!

"Oh, but I forgot. You're off the market now that you're seeing Nathan, you lucky duck." Rylee must have noticed Evie's concerned look, as she lent forward. "Is everything alright with you two? You don't seem that happy today. Has something…"

"Firecom Far North, this is 9-11 Zulu. Radio check, over."

Evie shrugged as she responded to the transmission, glad for the interruption to Rylee's question. She hadn't realised her feelings were so obvious yet there was no way she could fight her uneasiness, it seemed.

Having to face another betrayal from someone she was starting to care for wasn't something she wanted to go through again. Especially, not when she was feeling something special for the first time in an age.

The women got busy then with several jobs that presented within minutes of each other-a gas leak and alarm activation, run-of-the-mill stuff. That was the nature of the work sometimes-each day brought something different, which made it interesting, in Evie's opinion. At times, she still struggled to get her brain around juggling several incidents at once but was slowly finding her groove.

They'd soon learn their day was about to get busier as the connecting door to Ambulance Comms opened and an operator poked her head inside.

"Guys, we're getting word of a traffic crash somewhere on Mulgrave Road. Still taking details but think there's three vehicles involved. We've notified the police already." She closed the door as Rylee picked up the phone.

"I'll contact Main Roads and see if they have any vision of it," she said as the job details appealed on their monitors.

"Seems like it might be serious. It mentions there are entrapments." Evie's heart raced a little faster as she began to turn out the appliances.

Regardless, she was happy for the distraction and placed her focus on the job rather than stressing over the drama that was her topsy-turvy love life.

* * * * *

"Mate, are you able to set up some road markers and keep the traffic away from here?" Nathan pointed to several onlookers driving past. "These idiot rubber-neckers are gonna cause another crash soon."

It was only human nature for people to have a good old sticky beak at most accidents, no matter what the emergency, or who was hurt, yet it was still an impediment he could do without. Some even had their phones hanging out their car window, hoping to snap a photo of whoever lay inside, for God's sake!

"Yep, sure thing. We'll close the lanes so they'll be diverted." Owen Forrester sounded calm but was more than pissed at having to attend this kind of job. Until recently, he'd held the rank of Detective Constable but had been demoted, and demoralised, back into Uniform for another week. Not for the first time, he cursed Sergeant Graham Holden, the moron who'd written him up on those crap insubordination charges.

Fighting back his resentment, Owen acknowledged Nathan's request, and jogged to the van to retrieve the red and white marker cones. He hadn't done this shit for so long he'd almost forgotten the process and as he was the only officer available, it was left to him to manage the chaos until back-up arrived.

He remembered seeing Nathan over recent years, trusting him as a good operator who knew how to run an incident. In situations like these, it was important that each service worked alongside the other, knowing their capabilities in order to achieve the best outcomes.

This time, with a woman and kid trapped in the Mazda's front seats, it was better to let the experts do what they did best, to operate their fancy equipment and cut them out.

The whirring of an ambulance siren interrupted his task, and he looked up to see the vehicle skid, hitting the median strip before stopping. A blonde jumped out of the driver's seat, slamming the door while her male counterpart exited from the other side. From the look on his face, he didn't seem too impressed by her driving skills and as they both moved to the rear to grab their equipment, she staggered for a moment.

Wonder what that's about?

The pair made their way towards the smashed vehicle, the male bending down at the crumpled driver's door where Nathan stood. The driver of the second vehicle was sitting down in the gutter holding a towel to his bleeding head.

Owen had already spoken to him, taking his details. Thankfully, he didn't appear to be suffering from any serious injuries but he'd still need checking out.

The other two, though, he wasn't so sure about.

The group spent several minutes in discussion before the male paramedic came towards him. The firies began using their cutting equipment and the sound of metal tearing from the vehicle's frame screeched in his ears, sensitive to the sound.

"Is that guy over there the only one from the other car?" the paramedic asked matter-of-factly, pointing to the male with the towel.

Mr Personality.

"Yeah, he seems not too bad. He's got a bit of a cut on his head but says he feels okay."

"Yeah, well, I'll be the judge of how bad he is," he said and walked off, leaving Owen to shrug his shoulders.

"Whatever you think best, mate," he muttered under his breath.

The cutting stopped and two firemen started pulling metal back, giving access to the female paramedic who knelt next to the driver.

They'd been talking intermittedly during the rescue process as the paramedic attempted to assess how badly the woman and girl were injured while in the wreck.

The firies moved to the top of the car then, cutting at the windscreen for further access as the passenger side remained wedged against a power pole.

Don't miss this part of the job at all, Owen thought, grabbing for his portable to update his Comms Centre.

By the look of this, he could be stuck here for quite a while!

* * * *

Nathan kept one eye on his crew as they worked at peeling back twisted metal, and the other on the female paramedic kneeling at the driver's door, assessing the woman inside. Olivia seemed relatively switched on now, although he'd seen her almost trip on arrival. He hoped, for her sake, she wasn't strung out on something. She required focus to deal with this job and couldn't afford to be off her game.

So far, she'd avoided any eye contact with him, even though he knew full well she sensed his presence.

Fine with me, he thought. *Maybe she's finally getting the message we're done.*

After trying to calm her down the other evening with common sense and a strong dose of caffeine, she'd all but stormed out after he refused her request to let her stay the night.

"For old time's sake," she'd said with a grin, quickly replaced with a look of... *What? Regret? Loneliness?*

He'd been dumbstruck at first, amazed she'd even think he'd agree to her crazy idea.

He'd shaken his head, trying to downplay the moment. "I don't think you mean that, Liv. We've both moved on from what we had. It's over."

The time he'd spent alone since their breakup had been freeing for him–given him time to work out exactly who he was and what he wanted in the future. He realised they'd probably never been compatible-wanting different things in life from the get-go.

He felt more in control now than he had in years, getting his life back on track.

Then she'd turned up again to turn things on their head. *Shit.*

He hadn't called Evie yet, either.

He knew he'd have some explaining to do about the phone call the other morning, no doubt hearing Olivia's deliberate jibe.

God knows what she's thinking. Probably thinks I'm the biggest asshole…

"Boss, we're just about through here. We can lift the roof off now," Oscar said, waking Nathan from his reverie. He returned his focus to the job, directing the team to follow through with the extrication.

Thirty minutes later, the ambulance drove off at a high speed, both mother and daughter on board. Olivia had shot daggers at him once, but he'd ignored her, refusing to play that little game in front of everyone.

No doubt, this wasn't the last he'd hear of her–of that, he was certain.

He returned to the crew, giving directions for the clean-up as he pulled his phone from his pocket, thoughts of Evie filling his mind.

"Dinner tonight? I can pick you up about 7 if you like," his text read, hoping she'd be in a forgiving frame of mind.

If he'd lost his chance with Evie because of Olivia, he'd be pissed as hell.

Chapter 22

Ben experienced a pang of guilt, sat as he was parked across from Firecom Headquarters in Anderson Street. He felt like the worst kind of stalker who was sizing up an opportunity to pounce upon his unsuspecting prey.

He'd been in town two days yet spent most of that time walking along the waterfront or brooding within the confines of his air-conditioned room, aimlessly flicking through tour brochures or scanning take-away menus.

None of them appealed in the slightest. He hadn't come for a weekend getaway.

From his vantage point across the road, he had a line of sight with the staff entrance yet he hadn't seen Evie leave even though two others had arrived a good ten minutes earlier.

He tapped the steering wheel again in frustration as sweat dripped from his forehead. *This heat is insane*, he thought, having lost the flow of cool air once he turned off the ignition. He'd been sitting here for over an hour, his shirt sticking to his skin and he once again contemplated whether this was the stupidest thing he'd ever done.

Maybe I should leave, before…

He spotted her then, long hair tied back, as she waved a cheery goodbye to a colleague. She looked cute in the navy blue uniform-it suited her slender frame to a tee. She looked just as beautiful as he remembered.

He thought briefly about exiting the car then and approaching, but she'd already jumped into hers and started it up so he remained where he was. *Probably for the best.* Not a great idea to waylay her in a public place, laying his heart at her feet. He needed to pick the right time.

I'll just see where she goes, he thought, turning the key as cool air once again fanned his face. He sighed in relief and wondered how Evie was coping with the intensity of this heat. Perhaps she'd be more than happy to return home, to what was familiar. Back to what they'd had before he'd gone and ruined everything.

His gut churned as he followed several lengths behind, like one of the surveillance operations he'd trained for. Yet, this wasn't any old job-this was someone he cared about.

He hoped he'd be able to make her understand exactly how much.

* * * * *

Seated at an intimate table for two at Verdes, Evie felt as giddy as a fifteen-year-old schoolgirl on her first date.

Idiotic but true.

The timing of Nathan's text had been perfect, and he'd remained uppermost in her mind throughout the day as she'd listened to his voice transmit over the radio during jobs. Rylee threw in some teasing comments to which Evie refused to bite, trying to play down any hint of a relationship between them.

Now, sitting opposite Nathan as she finished the seafood basket with relish, Evie was glad she'd accepted his offer.

More than glad.

They'd chatted about work for a while, laughing at Rylee's unfortunate lapse on the radio which had everyone in stitches. She'd been caught out swearing several choice profanities while leaving her foot on the operator pedal. "She was petrified an inspector would call about it," Evie said as Nathan nodded in agreement.

"Yeah, it was funny. Kenny thought it was hilarious." His eyes sparkled in amusement as he regaled Evie with some of his own embarrassing stories which had her chuckling in response.

So far, he'd made no mention of his phone call with the mysterious woman, and although it still weighed on her mind, Evie didn't feel comfortable digging for information, preferring he offered it up voluntarily.

They finished their meal, Nathan offering his usual compliments to the chef as they departed.

Upon arriving at her car, Evie made a clumsy effort at retrieving her keys from her handbag, more than aware of his gaze.

"Do you need help?" he said with a grin.

"Uh, no, they'll be… here somewhere." She continued to rummage around while trying to appear under control when in fact she felt like the biggest idiot. *Finally!* Success, as she touched cool metal tucked away right at the bottom. "Oh, here they are," she exclaimed, dangling the keys in front of him.

She hit the Unlock button and the driver's door gave an audible click as she half turned to pull it open. On impulse, she turned back to him, making an invitation she prayed he couldn't refuse.

"Do you want to come back to my place? For a coffee or… whatever you like. I have some wine I think although I can't promise." She looked up to gauge his response, once again sounding like the giddy girl out of her depth.

"Sounds like a great idea. I'm all yours." His reassuring tone had her confidence return and for a time, her doubts disappeared.

*　*　*　*　*

"This is nice," Nathan scanned the interior of Evie's apartment, the short passageway highlighted by a pair of colourful prints of the Barrier Reef.

Moving inside, the living area was dominated by several large floor to ceiling windows, presenting a panoramic night-time view of the city. A black three-seater settee filled the space alongside a wooden buffet lined with various bottles of blue and green glass.

"Take a seat and I'll make us coffee. You'll have to bear with me though. I have a new machine and I'm still experimenting," Evie said, walking through the open doorway into the tidy kitchen. "Choose whatever you like and I'll give it a go."

"Thanks. A cappuccino would be fine, if that one's not too hard," Nathan offered, sinking into the cool leather.

Evie poked her head back from the kitchen. "I reckon I can manage that. Won't be a minute so make yourself cosy." She flicked the switch on her iPod dock and soon after, he heard Bon Jovi lamenting about loving his girl *Always*.

Was the Universe playing games with him?

That had been one of Olivia's favourite songs and she'd flogged the popular band's CD so many times over the years, he knew each song by heart.

He realised that apart from a similar taste in music, Evie and Olivia were as different as chalk and cheese, in personality, looks and... just about everything.

Where Olivia had been highly strung and anxious, Evie seemed relaxed and laid back. She possessed little of the dominant ego or confidence of his former partner, yet this somehow made her more attractive, more real, unaware of how appealing and intelligent she really was.

Looking around the lounge, he noted the simplicity of the furnishings and the distinct lack of mess and jumble that had been part of Olivia's world. He'd often spent hours cleaning up her mess and casual regard towards house-keeping, which used to drive him crazy. Evie's place was neat and ordered, giving a calm relaxed vibe to the place.

"So. How do you like the view? Not too bad, eh," Evie said, returning with two steaming mugs of coffee.

"It's great. I'm impressed." He replied, taking the mug from her fingers as they brushed his. He noticed she sat slightly away from him, like a skittish cat not comfortable around strangers. "You get an amazing feel for the city, with the marina and ocean. Almost makes me jealous about not living in a high-rise."

"Somehow I don't think that's your style," she said. "The view from the home you're building will be just as spectacular, I'm sure."

He sipped the coffee which was good, strong but not too sweet. Just how he liked it.

"Mmm, this is good. I must order these more often," he said, placing the mug down.

"Careful. I may have to charge a fee," she replied with a smile. They spent several minutes in silence as they drank their night cap, each lost in thought until Nathan broke the silence.

"How's the complex manager going? Alan, wasn't it? Has he recovered from the alarm debacle the other week?" Nathan had felt sorry for the guy who'd had no clue on how to run an evacuation or deal with alarms. "I hope he'll be better prepared if it happens again."

"I reckon he's been avoiding me since that day," Evie said. "Probably scared him away with my sexy fireman outfit." They both laughed.

She had froth on her lip, and he brought his hand up to touch her mouth, running a finger across the sensitive skin ever so lightly.

When their eyes met, and he moved closer, Evie made no protest as he cupped her face with his hand.

"You're so gorgeous, Evie. I want to kiss you. And with no interruptions this time." Nathan paused, giving her time to back away, yet she didn't seem so inclined.

"Okay," was all she said as he lowered his head to hers.

His lips caressed hers for a moment before he deepened the pressure. Evie shifted to improve the angle, throwing a cushion across the carpeted rug. Nathan couldn't help but chuckle to himself as she did so.

Maybe not a neat freak all the time, he thought.

Minutes passed, and their coffees had cooled by the time Nathan lifted his head briefly, before lowering it once more.

* * * * *

The touch of his lips on hers was intoxicating as he caressed and licked his way around. He moaned, and she opened her mouth wider, inviting his tongue inside. His hands moved up and down her body in time with his lips as he discovered her curves and soft skin.

He pulled back, and Evie realised that the kiss had lasted what seemed like an eternity but was probably only seconds. Sparks of electricity had triggered in her limbs and she wondered at how she'd never experienced such an intensity with Ben. Sure, their lovemaking had been pleasant and satisfying but Nathan somehow took it to a whole new level. And they were both still fully clothed!

"That felt pretty good…," she offered, with a greater confidence than she'd felt earlier, "… but I'm not positive. Should we try again to see how good?"

"I think I can accommodate the lady's request," Nathan complied and lowered his mouth once more to hers.

Several minutes passed and it was Evie who pulled out of the embrace yet remained cuddled up close at his side. She rested her head on his shoulder and placed a hand on his knee, her breathing not yet back to normal.

The hardness of his thigh and his soft breath on her cheek had Evie sighing in contentment at how amazing it felt to be in his arms.

This all feels so good she thought, *yet I can't believe it's true.*

Doesn't he realise what he's getting into?

Shouldn't I just end it now before I get hurt again?

And the woman from the other night–what about her?

"Nathan, I was wondering about…"

Evie's words were cut short by a sharp rap at her front door which had her turning her head in surprise.

"Are you expecting anyone?" Nathan said, glancing at the wall clock which showed the time as past eleven.

"Uh, no, I'm not sure who it could be," she said, walking to the door as the rapping came again. "I don't know many people in the building. Maybe it's another alarm or something," Evie tried to lighten the mood yet had a sinking feeling in her gut that their moment of intimacy was over.

Her intuition was proven correct as she pulled open the door, only to see her ex-fiancé standing there, a bunch of wilted red roses held in front of him. Evie could only stare with confused eyes as her voice deserted her.

"Hi Evie." Ben said, moving forward to touch her arm but dropped it when she stepped back out of reach. "Guess I should have called to tell you I was coming, but I didn't, I'm sorry. I know it's late but...,"

"Evie, is everything all right?" Nathan moved to stand behind her. She turned with a blank look, lost for words as she tried to process the situation.

Evie realised she now had two very anxious males on either side of her–the alpha male she'd locked lips with only moments before to her left, and on the other, the desperate looking ex who looked like he'd been through hell and back.

What the hell was she supposed to do now?

Chapter 23

Evie wasn't sure how long she clung to the handle of the front door, watching as Nathan walked to his car.

What just happened?

One minute, they were getting hot and sweaty on the lounge and the next, he was disappearing from her sight in a less-than-perfect end to the evening. His sincere, "Call me if you need me," wasn't the way she'd imagined the night ending.

She finally closed the door, knowing she'd need to face her ex sooner rather than later yet trying to avoid the inevitable.

What in God's name was Ben thinking, anyway?

Running sweaty palms through her hair, Evie returned to the lounge where Ben paced up and down, a trait of his that had always driven her crazy.

She was more than annoyed with him right now.

She stood with arms crossed waiting for him to talk, doubting it would be anything she'd be interested in hearing.

He broke the silence as he cleared his throat. His, "Sorry for interrupting your date night," didn't exactly endear him back into her good books.

Gee, thanks Ben!

"Have you been dating other guys all these months?"

She didn't even acknowledge his sarcastic tone as her indignation grew.

"What are you doing here, Ben? Did Mum give you my address?" Evie's agitated tone saw him flinch.

"No. Pauline wouldn't give it to me." His face reddened. "I checked one of the government databases across the country." He shrugged his shoulders at her upraised eyebrows. "Not the first time I've done a little digging."

Damn his arrogance.

"I should have you reported for checking up on me."

"I know, I wouldn't blame you. But, well… Evie, the truth is, I was desperate to find you. To see you again in person and tell you what a total prick I've been. I haven't been able to stop thinking about what I did, what a…" Ben moved to sit down on the edge of the couch while she remained standing.

Now it was her turn to pace up and down.

"Ben, just stop. Stop whining about how sorry you are and how you made a big mistake. The chance for making up is gone. I've moved on. Why can't you?" Her voice faltered, struck by the memory of how much pain he'd inflicted.

She took a breath and continued. "You broke something in us, in me, and it can't…"

"Evie, don't say that. You don't know for sure. After all the time we had together, don't I at least get a second chance?

Don't *we* deserve a second chance? Or have you forgotten me already, with Lover Boy?"

"Don't you dare even start, Ben. Nathan's got nothing to do with this. I haven't known him that long."

"Yeah well, things looked pretty cosy when I arrived. What the hell am I supposed to think?"

"Think what you like, it's none of your business anymore." Evie snapped, the events of the day taking their toll.

She sat next to him on the couch, placing her hand on his knee. "Look, let's just take a breather." He knelt forward, placing elbows on knees, running both hands through his hair. "I'll make us some coffee and we'll talk about this when we've both calmed down a bit."She surprised herself at her suggestion yet realised she had little energy to argue.

"Okay, I guess." He sounded like a petulant child.

Her fingers remained on his leg for a moment longer, feeling his familiar heat, and he moved one hand onto hers, before she jumped up and pulled away.

"I'll be back soon," she said, escaping the overheated room to the comparative safety of the kitchen.

* * * * *

Nathan sat unmoving in his vehicle parked outside Evie's place, reluctant to leave her alone with Ben, even though he knew the guy probably didn't mean her any harm.

He didn't present as Nathan expected, showing a more confident attitude than the wimp he'd envisaged. About six-foot tall with broad shoulders and a toned build, it wasn't surprising Evie had been taken in with his suave smile and swagger.

He's still a dick, Nathan mused yet couldn't help but feel envious of their previous relationship and the connection they'd once shared.

He had no right to be. I mean, it wasn't as if things were serious between them. Not yet, anyway.

What were they doing right now?

At least half an hour and no sign of him leaving. Nathan's mind started racing.

Are they in bed having make-up sex?

Is he sweet talking his way back into her life?

He punched the steering wheel and bent to insert the key in the ignition yet couldn't bring himself to turn the damn thing.

His concern for Evie's safety if things turned sour kept him stuck in the driver's seat with nowhere to go. *I'd kill for a cigarette right now*, ran though his mind, even though he'd given them up years before.

Just when things had been going so well, why did the ex-lover have to turn up and ruin it?

What the hell was going on up there?

Chapter 24

Evie glanced up the wall clock, noting with surprise it was almost one in the morning. She groaned when remembering her early-bird session with Nicola before work. No doubt, she'd look, and feel, like hell.

They'd been talking for almost two hours or rather, Ben had done most of it. Evie almost felt like a counsellor meeting a long-suffering client yet didn't have the heart to kick him out.

Halfway through his telling about the grief he'd gotten from McDermott and how her "celebrity status" could potentially impact his march up the career ladder, she realised she no longer felt anything for Ben. Not love, not hate, just… indifference.

His capitulation under the pressure of the scandal had been what hurt her the most. They'd been planning their lives together, including children and a mortgage, for God's sake. But that had all come crashing down because of his capitulation.

Or at least, that's what Evie saw it as.

At the time when she'd needed him, he'd put her second to his career. There was no way around the truth. Yet, Ben was really just another victim of her father's thirst for greed.

Not only had she suffered the worst kind of betrayal from him, he'd stuffed up everyone else's dreams as well.

That was something she'd never be able to forgive. Or forget.

Ben turned to face her, his tired bloodshot eyes reflecting back some of the pain and regret for what they'd once had. "I can't just leave things the way they are, Evie. Not when there may be the slightest chance… you know, if you wanted to try again, I wouldn't say no. I think you know that."

Evie cupped her face in both hands before bringing them together in a moment's contemplation. "That's what you say now but I think we both know what your first love is. The fact you sacrificed me over your career proves it. And…"

"I don't think…"

"… the stigma of my father won't go away anytime soon." She continued. "There's not much we can do to change things," she said, facing him. "I've accepted that and you should too."

"Move on, Ben. That's really what you're saying."

Nathan's face popped into Evie's mind and she grimaced, believing she may have messed things up for good this time. She couldn't blame him, not after this fiasco tonight.

What must he be thinking?

She'd have to face that another time.

Right now, she had Ben to deal with and Evie's one hope was that she could convince him to put the past to rest, like she'd done.

"Ben, that's exactly what I'm saying…"

* * * * *

Nathan woke the next morning with a throbbing headache and a sick feeling in his gut when hit with memories of the evening before.

He'd finally made it home, reluctantly leaving Evie alone with dipshit but resigned to the fact that, because of the lateness of the hour, the guy was probably staying.

Whatever that meant.

He held out some hope that, from what he'd learned of Evie so far, he didn't think they'd spent the night in the same bed, but who knew?

She wouldn't be the first woman sweet-talked back into the arms of a desperate ex-lover. Could she resist his pleas or promises of "I want you back," pulling at her heartstrings?

The guy had looked anxious, standing at her doorway last night. All Nathan had wanted to do was punch his lights out.

But for Evie's sake, he'd played the gentleman and left, albeit with his tail between his legs.

And his reward?

For all he knew, right now they were sitting naked across from each other on the kitchen stools, sipping latte's while stroking…

Jesus, give it a rest, idiot. He cursed, throwing back the covers and standing for a moment, rubbing his aching eyes.

Cooper stirred from his mat outside the bedroom door and Nathan pulled it open, kneeling to give his faithful hound a quick pat.

"Hey fella, waiting to get outside?" Nathan said. Cooper gave a short bark in response and raced towards the rear door, as was his routine every morning.

Nathan felt decidedly out of his comfort zone, not used to being in competition for a woman's attentions, not for years. Not since Grade Four, when he and Shane Cummins had fought for the attention of the small blonde with the cute curls. *What was her name?* his mind searching, trying to conjure up her face.

Rebecca something, Nathan recalled, a small smile crossing his face as he thought back to the infamous punch-on in the courtyard earning both boys a week's detention. It had been worth it. Nathan had won both the fight *and* the girl–until the following week when she'd turned her attention onto some other boy.

He recalled tearfully telling his father about the loss of his first true love, something the old man assured him was one of life's lessons meant to toughen him up.

"Never trust the promises of a woman, son". He recalled his father's words as if spoken only yesterday. They'd been sitting on the old fence palings at the back gate, a place where they'd often chatted over the years. "God knows, if anyone can tell you about that, it's me."

Jack had always possessed a calming and insightful way about him, helping his son through the tough times as he grew from the boy into the man.

Pushing the memories aside, Nathan stripped off his jocks and stepped into the shower, turning the tap on straight cold as he contemplated the day ahead.

He stood for several minutes under its spray before turning off the taps with force, finally giving in to his need to know if Evie was okay.

Naked and dripping wet, he reached for his phone and punched in a message, "Evie, hope you're OK." *Weak*, he conceded, yet didn't want to seem like he was hassling her for details. Within minutes he had a response.

"I'm fine. Just sorting some stuff out. Speak soon."

At least she's replied, he thought, yet unsure what 'sorting stuff out' meant in terms of where he stood.

No doubt, he'd find out in time.

Chapter 25

Functioning on a little over three hours sleep, Evie checked her watch for about the tenth time, realising she wouldn't make it for the start of shift. She rummaged on the dresser for her name badge, plonking it on her shirt.

Grabbing her keys, phone and handbag, she slammed the front door closed and raced to the lift. No time for breakfast this morning, she'd grab something later. Pulling her mobile from her bag, she selected the work number as she pushed the lift button, telling Jason she may be late.

"That's cool. Don't worry about it," her workmate said, offering Evie some peace of mind as she scurried towards her car.

She hadn't enjoyed a restful night, only managing a few hours before the alarm sounded this morning.

When she'd finally convinced Ben it was best he returned to Melbourne, he'd had tears in his eyes, yet Evie had refused to succumb to the emotion. *Best to end it once and for all*, she'd decided. To break down in front of him wouldn't help either of them much.

He was probably in the airport lounge thinking her the biggest bitch on the planet but she'd cop that. She'd explained to him as best she could the feelings she'd once had were no longer there. Privately, she was sorry for their loss. The fact that he'd never once said the words, "I love you" during the whole visit also confirmed the fact she'd made the right decision.

The only thing she could picture in her mind at that moment was Nathan's smiling face as he'd bent to kiss her.

Shit.

Nathan.

That little conundrum re-surfaced as she placed the key in the car's ignition.

What the hell am I going to do to fix this?

She almost hit another vehicle as she pulled into the morning traffic, receiving the bird from an irate driver in response.

She didn't care.

Not taking the bait, she kept her eyes straight ahead, her focus on more important things than the angry motorist with the bad attitude.

* * * * *

"Olivia. Come on in and take a seat." Inspector William Charlton of the Queensland Ambulance Service prompted his employee to sit opposite his desk before closing the office door at Regional Headquarters.

Personally, he detested this part of the job, having to deal with issues of insubordination or malpractice by his staff. From all accounts, this problem had been brewing for some time.

Worse yet, women were a particular bugbear of his. *From the time they'd been let into the service, they'd done nothing but cause problems. Not a day passes when there isn't some drama going on with one of them.*

Sure, they had their good points but not many.

More trouble than they're worth.

Here he was again today, having to deal with yet another one.

Charlton kept his frustrations to himself.

Briefly checking the file he'd been provided by personnel, he noticed Ms Von Ryder had given over eight years of exemplary service as a paramedic but in recent months, her performance had deteriorated to the point of being less than satisfactory. It was past time to address whatever was going on.

The allegation by her shift partner that Olivia had administered incorrect medications to a patient could have catastrophic outcomes for both the victim involved and the organisation, not to mention him as Regional Inspector. If his workers didn't toe the line, *his* would be the first head to roll.

He'd be damned if he'd lose his career over the crazy antics of a hormonal, unstable female!

"Do you know why we're here today, Olivia?" Charlton began, glanced up to notice unruly hair and dark eyes. He knew for a fact she hadn't been on shift last night, so it was concerning she seemed so uncaring of her appearance in front of a superior.

"Ah, no, Sir, but I'm sure you're about to tell me," she replied curtly.

"Hmmm, well, I should say that there have been some concerns raised about your recent work performance and there may have to be some follow up." He shuffled several papers around his desk whilst talking, noting her eyes seemed fixed on the view outside his window.

"Olivia, are you alright?" the Inspector asked, his concern growing as she exhibited an air of insubordination and distinct lack of care about her situation.

"What? Oh yes, what were you saying? Something about my job." She squirmed in the chair, almost slipping out of it before grabbing the arm rest. "Has that Matthew been making up lies about me? He's so full of crap." It was clear Olivia's dislike for her partner was a contributing factor to her agitation. "He's not so perfect either, you know."

"Well, I can't say too much about who said what, but it seems there was an issue last week about some mismatched medications on one of your call-outs and the person involved may take legal action over it. Do you recall the job I'm referring to?"

Olivia rubbed her eyes which appeared red and glazed. "I think so."

"Well, I'll say no more on the matter right now until…" He held up a hand for silence as Olivia interjected.

"That's bullshit. I'm…"

He continued on, "We'll discuss it with our legal team but in the meantime, Olivia, I regret to inform you that you're to be suspended from duty until further notice …." When she sat in silence, he continued. "There will be an appointment made for you to see the staff psychologist to discuss any issues that may be affecting your work. All in confidence, of course. And at no cost to you. We'll have someone call you from their office soon." Charlton looked up to gauge her reaction, hoping he wasn't about to end up with a hysterical female on his hands.

He hated ugly confrontations. Not good for his blood pressure, or so his doctor keep telling him.

Luckily for Charlton, Olivia fell silent, tapping her fingers on the armrest for several seconds before standing, almost causing her to fall forward.

"Is that it? Can I go now?" she turned, not waiting for his response that the meeting was over.

The inspector moved round his desk, walking to open the door, but she already had it slamming back against the wall, marching into the hallway. "Olivia, we'll get this matter sorted and have you back at work in no time, I'm sure," he offered, not wanting to draw any attention to the office staff sitting wide-eyed in their cubicles. "We'll be in touch."

He was fairly certain from the behaviour he'd just witnessed, it would be some time, if ever, before this particular paramedic was operational again.

* * * * *

Olivia fumed as she pressed the button on the elevator, waiting for it to get her the hell out of here.

Having to sit and listen to the drivel pouring from the inspector's mouth had been a struggle. She'd had to fight back the urge not to slap his smug face. *Stupid man looked like her old school principal, Mr Hoskins, but with less hair.* She respected this guy even less, with his snooty air of superiority and formal tone.

Damn you to hell, Matthew. What will I do without my work?

I know-I'll call Nathan. He'll know what to do.

The *ding* of the lift sounded, and Olivia pushed past a woman exiting in her haste to get inside.

"Excuse me," the worker said with mild sarcasm, rubbing her arm where she'd been nudged by Olivia.

"Go to hell, stupid cow," Olivia returned as the doors closed and she descended to the foyer.

Walking to her car, reflecting on the meeting, Olivia's eyes welled up with the sudden realisation she may have just stuffed up her entire career.

Something which didn't bear thinking about.

* * * * *

Evie's focus was immediately occupied with work once she arrived, receiving a brief handover from the night crew who'd decided to wait for her.

Rylee offered her a wink. "Nice of you to make it," she said.

Little does she know!

Evie didn't feel inclined to chat, shrugging in response as she sat at her desk.

The morning flew by and as Evie manned the constant barrage of calls, there wasn't much chance to communicate with Nathan in any way until she switched over to the role of radio operator.

As an alarm popped up in his patch, her heart skipped a beat as she began the turnout procedure, activating the fire bells at Cairns North Station.

"8-11 Bravo, alarm activation at McLeod Street, Cairns. Key access is forty-two. Acknowledge," she prompted. A moment later, the sound of his sexy voice over the airwaves provided Evie a secret thrill, as she struggled to keep a professional manner, determined not to embarrass herself.

"Firecom, this is 8-11 Bravo, proceeding to alarm activation," Nathan said, keeping things businesslike.

She knew from experience, working alongside a partner in the same field required boundaries and rules.

Evie had always played her part, never crossing the line of mixing business with pleasure and she imagined that Nathan had the same views. After all, he'd dated a paramedic which no doubt had presented similar challenges.

Maybe that's it, she thought. T*hings are still raw after his break up with Olivia.*

Perhaps he's decided it's better to ditch the woman with too much baggage. To end things now before it's too late.

A million thoughts ran through her mind as she continued to manage the job, which turned out to be yet another false alarm.

"Firecom, from 8-11 Bravo, confirmed a Code Twelve and returning to station," Nathan said, before signing off.

"Roger that, 8-11 Bravo. Twelve-fourteen," she responded, with a heavy heart.

"Gees, they didn't even offer to get us coffee." Rylee said. "You need to speak to that man of yours about Firecom protocols."

"Rylee, we're not even…"

Her mobile pinged, and Evie moved to grab it from her bag, thankful for the distraction from Rylee's teasing. She wasn't in the mood today, struggling to make sense of what was happening in her personal life.

Shit, even I don't have a clue.

Her mood lightened considerably on reading the text. *"Can I come over tonite? Unless yr busy. N."*

Thank goodness.

A sign, at least, he hadn't given up on her yet. Or maybe he was planning to tell her it was over?

God, this not knowing is hell.

"Yes, free after work. See u then," she tapped in response, not wanting to leave anything to chance.

"Was that about our coffee order?" Rylee said.

"Oh, will you give it a rest," Evie blushed as she turned back to her console.

Chapter 26

Evie opened the door, only to be greeted with a large bunch of multi-coloured native flowers. Nathan's accompanying smile served to sweeten his gesture.

"They're lovely. Thanks so much," she said, accepting the blooms as she bent to inhale the woody scent as she led Nathan inside.

"I passed a roadside florist on the way. I thought the old ones may need replacing," he blurted, realising his mistake in reminding her of *that* night so soon.

The night lover boy returned.

Evie didn't seem to register his reference as she rummaged around several kitchen cupboards for another vase. "I've another one somewhere." She left the kitchen, searching the wooden cabinet in the lounge. "Oh, here's one. Just perfect."

Minutes later, the flowers holding pride of place in a glass vase, Evie invited Nathan to sit. "Can I get you a drink? I've got beer, 4-X if you like, or maybe another of my coffees?" she said.

"A beer's fine. Thanks." He sat back and ran a hand through his brown hair, still damp from the day's humidity. It had been a long shift, with nothing major apart from a ton of admin to plow through. It felt good to just sit back and relax. "I didn't know you liked beer," he called out.

"I don't. But I guessed that's the brand you prefer, so I bought a six pack, just in case."

"That's nice. Thanks". *A woman after his own heart.*

She walked in, balancing a plate of cheese and crackers in one hand, and his drink in the other. She returned inside to grab her soda water, sipping it now as she sat beside him.

"Hasn't this heat been horrendous?" she said with a grimace. "I can't imagine having to do jobs outside in this kind of humidity. It's so draining."

Nathan nodded in agreement. "Some never get used to it but I guess that's just part of living in the tropics." He raised his bottle, taking a long sip. "This makes it all better, though,"

"I'll bet it does." She fell silent.

He felt as awkward as she looked, eyes staring ahead as his mind raced.

What the hell do I say?

More small talk or jump right in?

Evie fanned herself with her hands before standing, moving to fiddle with the air conditioning thermostat.

"This thing plays up sometimes and I keep needing to adjust the temperature. I think I'll mention it to Al," Evie said.

As he opened his mouth to speak, it seemed Evie was also struggling with the smalltalk.

"Nathan, about Friday night with…"

"I just wanted to let you know…"

They laughed at the collision of words, Nathan patting the seat next to him.

"Sit down and let's start again, shall we?" he offered. "Why don't you go first."

"Oh. Okay." She took another sip and turned to face him.

"Nathan, you don't have to worry about Ben. Not anymore. I mean… you never did but…"

"It's fine, Evie. I know as far as you were concerned, things were over but he had other ideas, I'm guessing?" he prompted as she nodded.

"Yes, exactly. When he turned up with you here… Well, I could have killed him. I had no idea he was planning to do that."

"I guess you can't blame the guy for wanting to give it another go. I mean, if you'd been my fiancé, I sure as hell wouldn't give you up easily. But it was his choice so…his loss, I reckon."

She smiled. "Thanks for that. Ben did what he did to save his career and in a way, I don't blame him. To be engaged to the daughter of a convicted criminal isn't going to be thought of too highly by his superiors."

Nathan shook his head. "Na, that's crap, and he knows it. That's why he came up here, to make excuses." Nathan took her hand, caressing her fingers. "If he was man enough, he would stand up to the doubters and tell them all to piss off. There's no way I would ever do that to someone I cared about, especially my partner, whether or not it impacted my career. You have to work through things as best you can."

"Really?" Evie said. "I mean, it's only human nature to protect your own interests. If you were put in the same position and it meant you could lose your job or be demoted, I bet you'd think twice about it."

"I doubt it. It would need to be something pretty devastating to have that kind of impact." He drank some more, tugging at his shirt which was sticking uncomfortably to his skin.

"Right." He attempted to lighten the mood. "Now that's sorted and we both know the guy's gone for good…," he grinned and moved to stand up, "… would you mind if I change out of these work clothes. I've got some gear in the car and hoped I might take you out to dinner. How's that sound?"

"Sounds great. Go grab your clothes. You can have a shower before we leave."

Nathan picked up his car keys. "I'll be right back."

Feeling confident they seemed to have things back on track, Nathan only had one more pressing issue to clear up before he felt confident they could really move ahead.

* * * * *

Evie sat back, wiping a napkin to her mouth as Nathan provided an update on the house build—another hidden talent she'd come to know. A fireman *and* a carpenter—every girl's dream!

She hoped she'd get to see it one day soon.

Evie laughed as he described Cooper's recent encounter with a nasty cane toad he'd dug up at the site.

"Weren't you worried he'd bite it and get poisoned or something?" Evie said, having heard the toxic poison from the local pests could sometimes have fatal repercussions for unsuspecting pets.

"No, Coop's was fine. He's come across them before and learnt his lesson a long time ago," he reassured her. "It was still amusing seeing them both dance around each other 'til old mate got bored and hopped away."

"Well, I'm glad he's alright." Evie looked down at her plate, realising she'd hardly touched her grilled salmon. She'd been preoccupied listening to Nathan's stories, trying desperately to stop staring at the strong biceps defined by the black and white body shirt he wore.

Her mind flew back to her apartment earlier that evening and the fact she'd almost fallen over in a faint when he'd exited her bathroom wearing only a towel. "Just need to grab my deodorant," he'd apologised as he'd walked past.

"No problem," she'd squeaked, impressed by the strong and rippling muscles on display. She'd conjured up images of him lying in her bed-minus the towel-and had fought to keep a sense of normal when he returned, fully dressed.

Evie's focus returned. "Thanks for dinner tonight. Saved me from a night in the kitchen, slaving over the hot stove."

"My pleasure. I could tell you were getting a little flustered by the heat."

Oh God! He noticed.

She offered a slight smile before refocusing her attention on the plate before her. They continued chatting for a time before Nathan signalled for their bill. "I'd better get you home, seeing we're both on shift tomorrow."

Evie checked her watch, surprised to realise it was after ten. Her mind raced as they made their way to his car.

Dare I go the next step and make a move to take things to the next level?

Or am I just setting myself up for another heartache once he comes to his senses?

They strolled hand in hand for several minutes. The tide was out and the acrid smell of the mud flats on the Esplanade's edge had them speed up their pace.

"Shame the ocean doesn't make it all the way here," Evie said, poking her head over the wooden railing, noting the muddy surface several metres below. "I bet a lot of the tourists freak when they realise they can't swim down there."

"Yeah, it's a drawback but can be an attraction too. You often get the young ones on a dare or just drunk who walk out into it and get stuck. It's pretty funny watching them get rescued. I've seen it a few times."

Evie laughed, imagining how uncomfortable and messy the scenario would be. "I don't think it's something I'd do, that's for sure."

As they continued, Nathan's phone pinged and he shrugged before checking his messages.

"Anything important?" Evie asked.

"Not really. It can wait." He appeared to change his mind, stopping mid-stride, taking both her hands in his own. "Well, actually… No, I should tell you. My ex-girlfriend Olivia has been texting. And calling. She's going through a bit of a bad patch and needs some emotional support. Apparently, I'm the go-to guy in her mind that can fix all her problems."

Finally. He'd brought up the topic that had been nagging her for days as Evie felt relief at his honesty. "Was that the woman I heard on the phone the other day?"

He nodded. "Yes. That was her. She knew you'd hear-likes nothing more than to stir up trouble, she does. But don't worry. That chapter is well and truly closed. There's another girl high on my priority list now."

He smiled before lowering his head to hers. His lips caught her by surprise, yet she was ecstatic they appeared to be getting things back on track after the Ben fiasco.

Both were breathless as they came up for air and Nathan's eyes were bright and alert.

"Thanks for telling me. I'll admit, it had been on my mind." She straightened before continuing. "You know,…" Evie made a rash decision, "… you don't have to leave when you drop me home. You can stay the night. If you want to, I mean."

There. She'd done it.

Couldn't help herself. He was too much of an enticement and smelt way too sexy to resist.

"Are you sure?" Nathan replied after several seconds. He held her in his arms and tilted her chin up to meet his gaze. "I don't want to put the pressure on."

She breathed out.

"Yes. I'm sure. I'm not asking for anything else. Just… to feel like… It's what I want. If it's what you want, too."

He hugged her to him as they started walking again. At a faster pace this time.

"It is."

Chapter 27

Bright sunlight filtered through her bedroom window even though it wasn't yet six. Evie considered lowering the blinds before dropping her head back upon the pillow. She didn't want to lose the half-asleep, half-awake sensation which had her almost purring with satisfaction, her body as floppy as a rag doll. *A very satisfied rag doll.*

She raised her arms above her head to stretch, touching his warmth as she did so. She smiled as she turned on her side to gaze at his still sleeping face. He looked at peace, breathing lightly with a slight *puff* on the exhale.

That's cute, she thought.

She moved her fingers to touch his cheek but decided against it, not wanting to break the spell of having the chance to study him. She noticed the light stubble evident on his cheeks and chin, blushing when she remembered the feel of it on her skin last night.

Well into the early hours they'd explored and discovered each other. Evie had learned a whole new side to lovemaking, with Nathan as the considerate and patient teacher.

Ben had been her only other lover and although they'd enjoyed a healthy sex life, he'd often looked to his satisfaction first with Evie usually as an afterthought.

Nathan was different. He'd focused on her needs first and what made her feel good. More than good, actually.

Freakin' amazing.

His eyes fluttered then opened, and she was caught staring. He didn't seem to mind as a smile formed.

"Good morning," he said, a huskiness to his tone she hadn't heard before.

Not that she'd woken up beside him before.

"Good morning back," she said. "Did you sleep okay?"

He gave a slight chuckle. "Ah yeah, when I finally got to sleep, I did. Like a baby. I was kept up till all hours by some chick that kept wanting my body and I couldn't disappoint her."

"Oh, you liar," she gave him a punch to his shoulder, and he winced in mock pain. "You're the one who kept *me* up all night."

"I guess we're both guilty of staying up late so now we have to pay." He squeezed her nose before reaching for his phone to check the time. "Shit. It's after six. We'd better get moving. I've gotta ring Ernie and ask if he can feed Coops." He threw back the sheets, striding towards the bathroom before turning back. "Sorry. Did you want to go first? I'd forgotten I wasn't at my place."

Evie shook her head. "It's okay. I have another bathroom so I can use that one. You go ahead."

"Thanks. Oh, and Evie…," he poked his head back around the doorway.

"Yes?"

"… just for the record, it was an amazing night. I'd gladly lose sleep over you. Anytime." He gave her no chance to reply as he disappeared into the en-suite.

Evie smiled, relief replacing the dread she'd been experiencing that perhaps, he'd somehow found her less than exciting. Now, with his reassurance, she was more at ease. Yet, still the lingering doubts remained that somehow, sometime, the bubble would burst and the past would catch up with her all over again.

They both had little time to reflect any further as they prepared for the work day, Evie settling for coffee as she brewed Nathan a latte whilst he got dressed.

"Are you sure it's okay turning up in your civvies?" she said, referring to Nathan's casual clothes. Evie didn't want him drawing any unnecessary attention from his crew if he wasn't in uniform.

"It's okay. I often go for a run or to the gym before work. That's why I keep a spare set there. No-one will suspect a thing. It'll be our secret."

"I wonder how long that'll last," she said buttoning up her shirt, placing her name badge on the Velcro strip. "With gossips like Rylee, it won't take long to put two and two together."

He walked over, pulling her into his embrace. "Hey, it's okay. If you prefer to keep things quiet for a while, I'm up for that." He looked into her eyes. "I just hope that someday you'll let the entire world know and damn them all to hell."

"I realise I'm being paranoid, but I... just want to keep it special between us. While it's still new." Her eyes glazed over with uncertainty. "We don't know what will happen in the future."

Nathan stood for a minute, a look of confusion on his face.

Not choosing to push the issue, Evie grabbed her car keys from the bench, walking for the door. "Anyway, we should leave."

She hated causing him pain yet couldn't shake the uneasy stirring in her stomach that it was all too good to be true.

They descended the elevator in silence. As the doors opened and Evie made to exit, Nathan grabbed her arm and bent his head, stealing a kiss and she revelled in the familiar pressure.

"Bye, lovely. Have a great day." He left her dazed, offering a quick wave and toot of the horn as he sped away.

She couldn't help but grin as she forced her feet to move, following his lead.

Let's see what the day brings, she thought, before starting up and pulling into the morning's traffic.

* * * * *

"Someone's in a better mood this morning," Rylee said as Evie hung up the phone. "Looks like we've got the old Evie back today."

There were only the two of them on shift as Caroline was on holiday. Working solo with Rylee meant that Evie would have to be on her guard. She knew the young girl would love nothing more than to dig for details on her and Nathan.

"Guess I had a good night's sleep, that's all," she replied, hoping to distract her attention. "Did you read that email from the Inspector?"

"Which one? There's so many these days, it's hard to keep track." Rylee leaned back, continuing to stare at Evie for a moment before speaking once more. "Do you ever speak to your Dad or visit him?" she blurted out, catching Evie unawares.

Oh, God. Here we go again.

Evie sighed. She was still unused to her workmate's outspokenness yet couldn't blame her for being curious.

"No." Evie's reply was just as forthright, yet Rylee didn't seem to mind. "The last time I saw him was in court, being led away by the police. My mother and brother visit him, but I choose not to. I… don't really care if I ever see him again." She stood, entering Eileen's office to check the key cabinet, hoping to divert Rylee from asking any more questions she wasn't prepared to answer. "Do you have any idea where key thirty-one is?" she said.

Rylee persisted anyhow. "But why not? Contact him, that is? He might be really sorry about…"

"Look Rylee, can you drop it, please? It's not something I want to talk about, or even think about. I've put it behind me and he can just rot…," Evie sat back down, trying to fight the tears which now filled her eyes. She breathed out, feeling like a bitch for biting back, but Rylee's prying seemed to bring out the worst in her.

Why the hell do people expect me to forgive all the time?
Don't they know what he cost me? Cost all of us?

The radio crackled to life and Evie was thankful for the diversion.

"Firecom, this is 8-21 Delta. We're out on brigade business," one of the local crews advised.

"Copy that, brigade business, 8.21," Evie replied in a businesslike tone. She looked up to find Rylee raising her eyebrows.

"Yeah, brigade business, my foot. Bet they're heading out for coffee, dirty liars. They should get us one," she said. Both girls laughed as the tension disappeared.

Evie realised Rylee wasn't the type to hold a grudge. Thankfully, it seemed her questioning was over for now. Yet, it cast a stark reminder in Evie's mind of memories she couldn't erase as easily as she'd like.

* * * * *

Several days later and both Evie and Nathan had the weekend off to enjoy.

The trip up the Gillies Range had just the effect Nathan had been hoping for-an escape from work and the intense heat of the city. The cooler air and wide-open expanses seemed to be working its magic at lightening Evie's mood from earlier that morning.

When he'd arrived, he couldn't help but notice a slight tension in the air. Although the past few days had been awesome, it was obvious there was still something playing on her mind. *Maybe the texts from Olivia?* He'd promised that his relationship with her was over, but who knew women?

Or perhaps she was still processing the visit from Ben?

Still, he didn't push. Best to let Evie work it out in her own time.

God knows, break-ups were never easy. He and Olivia were proof of that.

"I bet you've had a few rescues on this road. It looks dangerous," her soft words were a welcome interruption to his thoughts.

From her vantage point as a passenger, the unfenced hillside presented a steep drop off the road into dense trees and scrub, descending into the Goldsborough Valley below.

Not a drive for the fainthearted, demanding his full concentration the entire time.

"We've had a few over my time. A lot of bikers get caught too, racing up and down the winding road for thrills. Sometimes, though, they end up kissing the bitumen," he said. "*Temporary Australians*, Dad used to call them."

She turned towards him. "Can't think that'd be much fun. I don't know how you guys do it sometimes, with some of the accidents you go to. I don't think I'd cope too well."

She looked cute today.

He glanced at her before returning his eyes back to the road. "It's not for the squeamish, I'll admit. I've had my share of call outs that haven't been too pleasant, but it's just part of the job. The ambos and cops see some gruesome stuff too. We just have to harden up and deal with it otherwise it can get to you."

"Hmmm, I can imagine. I never realised until I started working in Comms how stressful a lot of the jobs can be. It's a world most people don't understand."

Nathan smiled. "Guess that's why we get paid the big bucks," he said, and Evie laughed.

"I'm sure the money isn't the only reason you do it. I bet deep inside, there's a caring, sharing part of you that wants to help people and save the world. Isn't that what all firies are motivated by?" Evie asked.

"Na, I just do it for the time off. Don't care about that saving the world crap." Nathan kept a straight face but couldn't hold it for long before smiling.

They continued the drive, finally exiting the rainforest to emerge into the large open fields of the Tablelands, before proceeding towards the Atherton township.

When Nathan arrived at the house block, Cooper bounced up, pawing at the window, eager to escape the confines of the car. "Okay, boy, give me a sec," Nathan walked around to let the hound free and he made a quick beeline for the nearest tree, cocking his leg.

"Priorities first," Evie laughed as she exited. "Wow, this looks amazing. I know you've told me about it, but I hadn't imagined you'd managed to get so much of the house built," she said, pointing to the wooden framework.

"I don't muck around when I set my mind to it. My buddy Mason helps when he can. It'll be great when I can leave the Edge Hill rental and move in." He held her hand as he led her towards what was to be the front entrance. "Here, let me show you the latest."

He walked her around the build as the sun cast its mid-morning glow through the open gaps in the roof. There were three floor to ceiling windows at the front which had Evie offer a nod of appreciation.

"You'll get lots of light in here, which will be great in winter, I imagine," she said as they moved further inside. Stepping over piles of timber as they went, they bent their heads to avoid several large beams.

Nathan led her forward as she hopped over a large toolbox. "Come through here and you'll see the view from the kitchen. I reckon washing up won't seem a drag looking outside," he said.

Evie poked her head through the imaginary window, taking in the panoramic view before her. Several peaks rose in the distance, framed with large trees and rolling hills of green. A herd of black and white cows lazed on the ground, their bellies no doubt full of grass. The vision presented as the perfect mix of serenity and home-style comforts. "Wow, I see what you mean. It's amazing."

"You're building a lovely home here, Nathan. I'm jealous," she said.

He didn't answer for a moment, standing next to her as he lent both arms on the wooden frame.

He spied Cooper, nose down bum up, sniffing something of interest at the base of the large ghost gum and Nathan smiled to himself. They'd had a similar tree in the backyard at Elizabeth Street. Their old hound, Angus, had been Nathan's constant companion in his younger years, his only friend and confidante, apart from his father. For over twelve years, the kelpie had been the young boy's shadow as they'd spent countless hours exploring the local rivers and creeks.

The days of his youth spent learning stuff with his father were the memories he held most dear. Nathan only hoped he could be a similar positive influence on his own son or daughter one day.

Evie shuffled behind him and he realised he'd been lost in the past. *What was it she'd said?*

"Sorry, I was miles away," he turned, touching her gently on the shoulder. "Just reminiscing about the old times when Dad was alive. I wish he was still here to help me out with the build."

Nathan moved away, leading Evie towards the rear of the frame.

"It must have been hard for you when your mother left," Evie said. "Didn't you say you were only about six years old? That's awful."

He shrugged. "It wasn't the easiest of times, that's for sure. Still, we made the best of it. I think the old man suffered the most. Spent the rest of his days pretty much alone except for his poker buddies." He took her hand. "But enough about the past. Let's have a look at where the media room will be…"

They spent the next hour chatting as Nathan guided her around, spruiking his plans about what he planned to achieve with the block.

As the afternoon sun disappeared behind the hilltops, Nathan dared to dream that the appeal of his home and a country lifestyle would be enough of an inducement for Evie to stick around.

Chapter 28

Several days later, Nathan sat back at his desk, realising he couldn't put off the inevitable any longer. Olivia had been texting him all morning, begging almost, that he come to her house. It seemed she wouldn't leave him alone until he answered.

He yanked out his phone with a frustrated grunt. He wasn't sure why, but he still felt responsible for her somehow. Although she'd messed up and had screwed him over, he still worried that she was okay.

The mobile almost rang out before she answered in her usual abrupt tone. "Nathan? Where have you been? I've been waiting for ages."

"Its gotta be quick, Olivia. I'm at work so it's not a good time right now." Her words sounding slurred and breathless, and his worry increased. "What's happening? You shouldn't be calling me anymore." He realised he sounded more than heartless, yet it was usually the only way to get through to her.

"Nathan, I… shit," the phone gave a loud clang as it fell to the floor and for several seconds, he heard nothing but scratching and cursing.

"Olivia, are you alright? What happened? Have you been drinking?" he reclined further in his chair, wanting to end this fiasco as soon as possible.

"I'm back. I… dropped the… goddam phone. I… I really need… can you please come, Natey? It's all gone to shit and I miss you and…"

"I can't come now, Liv, I'm on shift. Whatever's going on, can't you ring one of your mates to come round?"

The volume of her voice increased, almost raising to a scream, and he held the device away from his ear to lessen its impact. "There's no one else. Only you. Only you." She started crying then, and he felt like the biggest heel for sounding like the heartless bastard that he was.

Hey, but she was the one who'd broken what they had, he reminded himself.

"Look, I'll try and come over later. But no promises. That's the best I can do." He received no response, only what sounded like her hyperventilating and sobbing in the background.

"Did you hear me, Liv? I'll try. I've gotta go now, alright." He pressed *End Call* before she could respond and tossed the phone on his desk.

Why did this shit have to happen now?

He'd just spent some one of the best days, and nights, of his life with an amazing woman, yet now had to deal with his ex-partner who may or may not be having some kind of psychotic breakdown.

Nathan hadn't really got around to discussing his previous relationship with Evie. For whatever reason, he'd only glossed over it, in the vain hope that Olivia was out of the picture for good.

Now, with this latest drama, he realised he'd have to come clean and open up old wounds he'd thought were well and truly closed.

Tonight, after dinner, he thought. *I'll tell her tonight.*

* * * * *

The intoxicating aroma of garlic, onions, herbs and spices filled the air as both Evie and Nathan attempted to replicate one of Jamie Oliver's dishes they'd chosen from his latest Italian cookbook.

Nathan had spied it on the bench the other night and felt inspired enough to offer to cook with her.

A moment of insanity, he'd thought more than once, as he looked down at his t-shirt, currently covered in sauce stains.

Evie had seemed impressed he'd made the offer, and he remained hopeful their efforts would at least be edible. Despite his doubts, the aroma of beef cheeks filled the kitchen, offering them both a mouth-watering tease.

"I'll put this pasta on. Shouldn't take long," Evie said, gently placing the tagliatelle into a boiling pot of water. "If this works, I'll get you to help me cook more often," she said as Nathan checked the meat for the tenth time.

"Believe it or not…," he looked up from where he lent over the oven, "… I can be a bit of a whiz in the kitchen." *Yeah, baked beans on toast, and lasagne, of course!* Can't forget that. I don't mind testing my culinary skills on willing victims," he said as more meat sauce dribbled down his chin. He placed the tasting spoon down. "This is awesome, I reckon. Can't wait to dig in."

"I agree. Me too. Seems you're a man of many talents." Evie moved to the cupboard, taking out two plates. "You save lives, build houses, know how to cook. Is there anything you can't do?"

"Well, let's see." He rubbed his chin, brows drawn together in mock contemplation. "I can't sing to save myself. And I'm not too keen on cleaning toilets. Apart from that, I'm up for anything."

"Well, I'll keep that in mind," she chuckled and moved to drain the pasta. "Let's get this served up. I'm starving."

* * * * *

"Wow, I'm pleasantly stuffed," Nathan rubbed his belly as he plonked himself down on the lounge following dinner.

"Yeah, me too," Evie followed him in. "Do you want to watch something or listen to music? I'm happy either way," she asked, placing a hand on his leg as she leaned back.

"Mmm, some chill out music would be nice. Don't think I'm up for any reality tv or whatever crap is on," he said, passing her the remote.

"Okay". She switched the screen on and hit the button for Smooth Music. Within seconds, the dulcet tones of Michael Buble's *Everything* filled the room.

"Nice," he commented, happy with her choice.

"I aim to please," she smiled back before kissing him on his lips, taking him by surprise.

"Well, I'm certainly that," he said, as she settled back into his arms and he gently stroked her smooth hair. "No complaints from where I'm sitting."

"Well, that's good to know."

They sat for a moment before Nathan broke the silence. It was now or never. "Evie. I think it's about time I explained about Olivia and our time together. Especially since you shared everything about Ben and what happened between you."

She turned to face him. "Nathan, I don't need all the details and I'm not pushing, if it's too painful. But…, I won't deny it has been playing on my mind a little."

"That's alright, I understand." He rubbed her arms up and down. "I should have told you earlier, but there never seemed to be a right time." His gaze was drawn to his phone which had pinged once again with another text notification. This was as good a time as any to set the record straight.

Evie waited for him to continue.

"Olivia is…, unique in her own way, I guess. She's always been a bit highly strung. Didn't have the best childhood either, which didn't help things," Nathan eyes glazed over as his mind was taken back to the first time he'd met Liv, not through the job but in the local supermarket, of all places.

Talk about a cliché.

He told Evie about that first meeting-how he'd been shopping after work, wandering the aisles when a woman's voice had startled him from behind.

"Have you got any idea what *galangal* is?" He remembered her pickup line like it was yesterday and had often teased her for its originality afterwards.

He'd been amused at her boldness, yet glad for the interruption to his otherwise ho-hum day. He wasn't normally in the habit of trying to pick up women at the local food store himself which is why she'd caught him off guard.

Nathan's track record with women until that time hadn't been great, unwilling to make a full commitment to a relationship while in his twenties. Still, like any normal guy, he was partial to female company *and* a warm body in his bed occasionally.

As he'd reached his third decade, he'd realised he needed to change his ways if his dreams of a having a family to become a reality. When he'd met Olivia, he'd thought she may have been the woman he'd been looking for.

"Don't I know you from somewhere?" she'd said, as he stood mutely in the herb and spices aisle. "I'm sure I've seen you before. Do you work at the hospital?"

Nathan was sure she hadn't crossed his path. He would have remembered someone like her. "No, I'm a firefighter. Don't get to the hospital much." "Is that where you work?"

"Yes, and no. I'm a paramedic. We come and go from there all the time. We've probably been to jobs together but never formally met. I'm Olivia Von Ryder," she said, holding out her hand, and he took it in his.

"Hi, I'm Nathan. Nice to meet you, Olivia."

We never did find the galangal, he thought. Things had moved quickly after that meeting, which he soon discovered, was all part of Livvy's personality. She was like a whirlwind, breezing in and sweeping everyone, and everything, up in her path.

They'd moved in together not long after, yet Nathan had often felt he was on a rollercoaster he couldn't get off. Things were good for a time and he'd imagined they might last the distance until he'd discovered Olivia's little indiscretions, both with her shift partner and the pills. Later on, she'd started to hit the bottle as well.

Evie didn't interrupt his story, listening with intent as he continued. Nathan talked further, describing Olivia's deterioration into a dark place he wasn't able to get her out of. No matter what he'd tried or offered to help, she'd refused to let go of what he called her relentless path of self-destruction.

"Now, with these latest texts and the issue with her job…," he explained further, "… it seems like she still can't forget the past. Or me, it seems." He sighed and hit his hand to his knee. "I can't help but feel I'm responsible somehow."

Evie shook her head. "I'm sure that's not true. You shouldn't blame yourself, Nathan. She chose to do the things she did, to cheat on you, which seems something only a crazy person would do."

He breathed out a long sigh. "Yeah, I hear what you're saying but I still can't help it." He stood up to stretch and picked up his phone but not before kissing Evie's mouth lightly. "You're amazing, you know, to take this on board and be so understanding. It can't be easy after what you've already gone through." He noted her smile.

"I hope you understand Evie, but I need to see her one last time. To make sure she's alright," he said. "This has nothing to do with you and me. Once I see her, we're done for good. I will make that clear to her, so you don't have to worry."

"It's fine, Nathan. You do what you need to do. I'm okay with that," Evie said, as he began to tap the keys on his phone.

Chapter 29

As she stumbled from the kitchen, glass in hand, Olivia tripped over an empty bottle lying on the tiles and cursed. *Stupid freakin' shit.* She had no recollection of how it got there-she'd probably thrown it at some point, useless to her once empty.

Rubbing her eyes, she sat down and reached for her phone to check again for messages. Noting the most recent to be from the bastards at work, hassling her again, she felt like throwing it across the room. Instead, she ignored it.

Still nothing from Nathan.

When is he coming? He promised he'd be here.

The Nathan she knew always went out of his way to support people, couldn't help himself. That was one reason she'd been drawn to him in the first place.

She'd been that way once too-caring about others. The bright-eyed recruit, wanting to save the world, to help the sick and injured in their time of need. In the beginning, those first whirlwind years of learning the job, gaining the confidence and skills to perform at her best, had her feeling invincible and valued.

But recently, it'd all gone to shit.

She was tired all the time, expected to perform hour after hour, day after day, job after job. They were abused, threatened, even assaulted occasionally but expected to take it and keep going, as if nothing could hurt or penetrate their shields.

Yet it did.

The dreams had been the starting point though. They'd returned not long after she and Nathan got together. Almost every time she'd closed her eyes, *he'd* be there, haunting her thoughts, day and night.

"You're no good, daughter." His evil smile would penetrate her mind, relentless in his abuse. "Who'd want someone like you?"

She took a deep breath and recognised the unpleasant odour of sweat on her skin. She raised her armpit and turned her head, confirming it came from her.

Couldn't remember the last time she'd showered. Didn't really care.

Had no energy for that. Or anything else.

Not since they'd taken her job away. "Suspended pending investigation" the letter had read.

She raised an unsteady hand and took a sip, grimacing as she realised it was water. *Ahhh, God, I need to get more stuff.*

Maybe later.

She almost dropped the glass when she heard the ping of a new text.

About time.

Her heart sped up with anticipation as she read his words.

Liv, tied up but will come over to see you soon.

Finally. He'd answered and was coming over. Not right away, but she'd wait. She could be patient when she needed to be, yet not for much longer.

What the hell was he doing, anyway?

Is he seeing someone else?

She stood on uneasy legs and let out a groan. She didn't care if he was—no one else would be good enough for him, he'd find out soon enough. *They* were perfect for each other, even if Nathan didn't realise it. All that bullshit about wanting a family…

Tonight, she'd convince him otherwise. She had to.

He was the only one who could make everything right again.

* * * * *

Next morning, at the monthly station officers' meeting at Regional Headquarters, Nathan rubbed his temple in frustration as Inspector Wilde recited the latest budgetary figures.

As riveting as the information regarding corporate card expenditure and missing firefighting equipment no doubt was, Nathan had other things on his mind.

He was desperate to contact Evie, to explain about what happened after he'd left her place last night. Yet, he'd been strapped for time so far, forgetting to set his alarm meant he'd only just made the meeting with a minute to spare.

For the time being, at least, he was stuck until it finished.

As Station Officer Mark McCann stood to provide an update on his station's performance, Nathan's mind wandered back to last evening.

In hindsight, leaving Evie alone hadn't been ideal, but she'd seemed to understand his need to sort things with Olivia once and for all.

When he'd arrived at her house, he couldn't help but notice the mess that greeted him. Unwashed dishes, empty bottles tossed around, and the stale smell of perspiration overwhelming as he entered.

"I have something to show you," she'd said upon seeing him, grabbing his hand. Her almost childlike demeanour had him concerned as he'd worried about her state of mind. "Come and have a look."

He'd said nothing, following her into the lounge where she pointed at the coffee table. A large 12" x 8" photograph framed in gold took pride of place in the centre, surrounded by six small multi-coloured candles, burning bright in a luminous glow. Nathan moved forward with a slow sense of dread, remembering it as one they'd taken on a holiday somewhere, *Bali or Fiji perhaps*?

"Do you like it?" she'd asked breathlessly, almost as if she'd been running a marathon. "I think it's one of our best." She continued to grip his hand as if afraid to let go.

"Liv." He didn't want to upset her, but needed to put a stop to her delusional fantasy about him. "I'm not sure what this is about but…"

She put a hand to her lips. "Shh. Don't say anything. I set it up for you, put another one in the bedroom on your side of…"

"Liv, stop, will you? Please. Just for a second." He grabbed her in both hands, leading her to the couch. "We should talk about this. About us."

She looked at him with confused eyes, and he'd felt like the biggest heel, but there was no getting around it. The fantasy had to end.

They sat for a moment and she rubbed her arms up and down, shivering as if cold, even though the humidity was high.

"I'm seeing someone else, Olivia. Have been for a while now. You need to forget about me and move on with your life." *There.* He'd said it. *Best not to hide the truth anymore.*

Silence had filled the room for several minutes as she attempted to process Nathan's words. He knew when realisation hit, as she shook her head in denial and rose to her feet. He sensed the tempest beginning to build.

"What the hell do you mean–'*You're seeing some else?*'" her tone mocking in its delivery. "Why would you…" Her eyes widened as she spat at him in a venomous tone. "Was that her? The one at the accident a few weeks ago? In the pretty fireman's outfit? Do you bring all your girlfriends to work now, Nathan, you bastard?"

He put his hand to his temple, feeling the need to escape as quickly as he could. "Don't talk about her like that. You know nothing about Evie."

"Well, I know she's trying to steal my boyfriend. She's nothing but a…"

"I'm not your boyfriend, Liv. Not anymore. Remember? We're done with–have been for a long time now." He stood and stepped to the window, attempting to put some distance between her and the intensity of her anger.

It only served to rile her up more.

"But we're not, Nathan. Don't you see. You said you'd be there for me–to help me. I…," her voice grew softer as she paced, "I need you. I… love you." She stopped in front of him then, trying to take his face in her hands, yet he moved back.

"No Liv. You don't love me. It's just you wanting someone to support you deal with what's happening in your life. You and me–we're not getting back together." He thought of the pain he was inflicting yet it had to be done–to make a clean break. "You should get some help, I think. Someone to help you sort out your issues. Including the ones about your father…"

Her eyes grew wide in fury and she moved forward to punch him, but he stepped back. "Don't you dare bring him into this. Don't you dare. It's not about him. He's dead and gone, and I'm glad…" Her voice raised, almost to a screaming pitch, and Nathan took it as his cue to leave. There was no reasoning with her in this state. His presence only seemed to be igniting her irrational behaviour. He moved to the front door.

"Liv, I've gotta go. I'm sorry." He opened it, even though reluctant to leave her alone. "I'll get Natalie to drop by and check on you tomorrow, to see how you're doing." He referred to Olivia's supervisor who was the only person he could think of who may be able to help.

"Go then, just get the hell out," she screamed, ignoring his offer. "Run back to your little bitch, if that's what you want."

Nathan realised he wasn't going to make her see reason—not tonight anyway—closing the door behind him. He could hear her yelling as he descended the steps to the front gate.

"You'll never be happy without me, Nathan. You hear me?

Never be happy again. You'll see."

Still lost in the memories, Nathan fought to focus as he heard his name being called.

"Nathan. Are you ready to give us your figures?" Inspector Wilde said, all eyes upon him.

Nathan scrambled for his notes. "Yeah, I have them here, Sir."

All thoughts of the night's events were put aside as Nathan fumbled his way through the next ten minutes, his monotone delivery reflecting his current level of interest.

As he sat down upon its conclusion, his thoughts returned to the upheaval that was his personal life as he wondered how in the hell he'd figure out a solution that would keep everyone happy.

Chapter 30

The next evening and Evie switched on the bedroom lamp as they prepared for bed.

"What's happening with Cooper? Have you got someone to watch him when you're here?" she asked as she pulled back the bed covers, sitting to set her alarm. He'd said little about his visit to Olivia last night, his only comment was that *"hopefully, it's sorted."* She hoped so too, yet decided against pushing for details. He'd tell her in his own time.

Nathan popped his head out from the en-suite, toothbrush in hand as he spoke. "He's fine," he said, naked except for his black jocks, offering Evie an enticing view of his impressive six pack, and more. Any anxiety she felt disappeared out the window.

Gees, he so sexy. Can't believe this guy is sleeping in my bed!

She tried to keep the smile from forming as she scooted past, patting his butt as he bent to rinse.

"Cheeky girl," he muttered through water. He stood and wiped his mouth with his towel before giving her room to brush. "My neighbour Ernie feeds Coops when I'm away. Takes him for walks too. He's an old retired navy guy with a lot of free time on his hands. I've helped him with building stuff too, over the years."

"That's nice. It's hard to find good neighbours these days".

An understatement, if ever there was one.

They'd had that too, once upon a time.

Evie's mind wandered to Rebecca, her best friend through primary school, and daughter of Margaret and Robin Wilde who'd lived next door to the family.

The girls were inseparable in their younger years, spending countless hours in each other's backyards, particularly after Evie's parents installed their pool. Summers had been the best of times with Beckie, the sister Evie never had.

Her father, Robin, was a lawyer who got on well with Eric, whilst both women took turns ferrying the kids to school and helping each other out, as neighbours and good friends do.

As the years passed, the girls slowly grew apart as they followed different paths yet remained friends until Beckie accepted a job in publishing and moved to London. Pauline and Margaret continued socializing, playing tennis together and often catching up for coffee and a chat.

Everything had changed when Eric's indiscretion became public and the relationship with their neighbours turned sour.

As the media set up camp, it was the underlying tension around the drama that eventually ended their friendship.

One evening, during the trial, Margaret had come storming over, ranting that she couldn't have anything more to do with Pauline or the family, accusing them of being "a deceitful lying bunch of scumbags" or something similar. She continued on with her rant about the reputation of the neighbourhood being destroyed and how she'd been accosted by a reporter hassling her for an interview.

Her mother, dumbstruck by her friend's hurtful words, was left speechless, so it was left to Evie to demand Margaret leave the house.

"And don't come back," she'd yelled as the front door had slammed in the woman's wake.

A few weeks later, the Wilde house was put on the market and they'd moved away. Pauline had been devastated to lose her longstanding friend and hadn't spoken much of the episode since.

"This is gonna be nice," Nathan interrupted her thoughts as he lay down in her bed, pulling up the cotton sheet. She smiled as she switched off the lamp, settling herself in.

"I know. Best place in…"

She was interrupted by the ringing of her phone, making her jump.

"I hope this isn't Firecom wanting me to work tomorrow," she said, picking up. "I'm not cancelling our day off together." Evie's heart raced a little faster when she noticed her mother's name on the Caller ID. *Not like her to ring this late*.

"Hey Mum, is everything okay?" she asked as Nathan rolled over, touching her arm in a reassuring gesture.

Her mother's tone was soft. "Evie, sorry to call you so late. You're not at work are you?"

"No, I'm at home. Just got into bed." Evie put a finger to her lips, signalling Nathan to keep quiet. He nodded and stayed silent.

Evie hadn't offered up many details to Pauline about the sexy fireman currently lying naked in her bed, only that she'd met someone from work and "he was nice". She'd decided to wait until she knew what was going on before getting her mother's hopes up.

"I could have called in the morning I suppose, but Cameron thought you should know straight away. It's just that… well Evie, your father…"

Evie held the phone close to her ear as she moved to the door, wanting to keep Nathan out of earshot of her family's issues. She turned to see him propped up on his elbows and left the room with a shrug, closing the door behind her.

"Mum, I don't want to hear what's happening to him, I've told you. I don't care anymore. I…"

"… he has cancer, Evie. They think it's… bad, but treatable." Her mother's voice waivered and Evie hardened her resolve not to resort to tears. Not for him. He didn't deserve them.

Evie ran a hand through her still damp hair as her heart pumped faster. *Cancer.* Him, of all people. She couldn't even remember him having a cold. Or the flu.

Where the hell did cancer come from?

Guess this is Karma, Dad. This is what you get for messing up people's lives.

There was a moment's silence before Pauline spoke again. Evie guessed what was coming.

"I hoped… well, you could come home. If only for a few days. I have Cameron, but I'd like to have you here as well."

Evie decided to stick by her resolve and not give in to her mother's tears or pleas.

"Mum, I can't right now. Work's too busy and I don't think I can get away," As soon as the words left her mouth, Evie felt like the biggest bitch, hearing a soft sob over the line. She took a breath and waited.

Silence.

"Are you still there, Mum?"

"Yes, yes, I'm here. I just wish you'd think about…"

"I have thought about it Mum, trust me. Over all these months." Evie wiped her eyes as tears welled but she refused to let fall. "I'm sorry but I have to go now. I'll call you back soon. Bye."

She disconnected before any reply came, and stood for a minute shaking, her hands hanging at her side before turning back towards the bedroom. She was more than startled to find Nathan standing barefoot in the doorway with a worried expression.

"Everything okay?" he asked.

* * * * *

Evie took a moment before answering.

"Yeah, everything's fine. Just Mum getting upset over stuff, as usual. Asking if I can visit, but I said I can't right now. She still has Cameron so…" Evie moved to walk past him back to the bedroom, but he stopped her with a light touch on her shoulder.

"Are you sure? You look pretty upset." He tilted her chin towards him. "It must have been something important for your mother to call this late." He glanced at the wall clock. "Is it something I can help with?"

Evie sighed, taking a moment to respond.

"Not really. She called to tell me that my… father has cancer. I'm not sure what type, but it sounds serious." Evie moved into the bedroom and sat on the bed, avoiding his gaze as he followed her. "There's nothing I can do so I don't see a need to go down there. Not that I want to connect with him, anyway."

She turned her head towards the window, obviously trying to process the news.

"You don't mean that," Nathan said after a moment. He wanted to hold her but sensed she wouldn't appreciate it right now so he remained standing with his arms crossed.

"Yes, I bloody well do. Don't tell me how I should feel. You wouldn't understand." Her eyes appeared bright with anger and Nathan realised he was seeing a side to Evie he hadn't until now. Not that it made her any less attractive to him, but he'd obviously underestimated the deep hurt she'd suffered at the hands of her father.

But to ignore a dying man…

If he had the chance to spend five more minutes with his father, he'd give anything to have that time. One last conversation.

But that wouldn't happen. Not for him. But it could for Evie. Before it was too late.

"I know I can't tell you how to feel. No one can," he said, moving to sit next to her. He placed a hand on her knee and she tensed. "But I understand a bit about giving people a second chance." His brows drew together as he thought for a moment on what she'd told him about the incident. "Do you even know the other side of the story, Evie? I mean, why he stole the money."

She gasped and stood, forcing his hand to drop back down to his side. "Other side? Nathan, are you kidding? There was no other side. He did it for greed, pure and simple. Stuffed everything up just for lousy money." There was a slight break in her voice as she began pacing, moving in and out of the moon's glow.

"He… he left Mum and Cam and me to pick up the pieces and get on with things. While he's sitting back in jail getting stupid cancer." She sobbed the last words out, putting her hands to her face to wipe away tears.

Nathan moved towards her, but she turned away. "No, Nathan, don't. Please. Just don't." She held up a hand to stop his embrace, and he stepped back.

He waited a moment, weighing up his words, fearing what he said next could either make or break them. But he had to stay true to what he believed in.

"Evie, you realise that if you can't get past this and visit your father, you might not get that option again. He might die, and you'll never get that closure, to let him know you still care. I know deep inside you still do" he said, measuring her reaction to see if it had the impact he hoped. "Sometimes we have to forgive the people that hurt us the most if only so we can move on with our own lives."

She crossed her arms across her chest and turned to face him. "Like you did with Olivia? How you *forgave* her for cheating on you and sticking up for her, running over whenever she calls. She's using you, Nathan, and you can't even see it," Evie croaked, her voice sounding dry and scratchy, no doubt trying to keep the tears in check.

He sighed, realising she wasn't prepared to see sense, at least, not tonight. "Olivia's got nothing to do with this. She's out of my life for good but yes, I still care about what happens to her. We were together for a long time."

He patted the bed. "Look, it's late and we're both tired and stressed out. Let's go to bed and talk about this tomorrow. It's not doing either of us any good standing here arguing about it," he lay back down pulling the sheet up to his chest. "Please, babe, just come back in."

She studied his face, rubbing her arms before moving to the door. "I can't sleep right now. I'm going to make coffee. I'll be back soon." She opened the bedroom door and walked out, closing it with a slight click.

He watched her go and lay back, placing a hand behind his head, staring at the ceiling.

It was some time before his eyes closed as his mind filled with thoughts about what he should do next.

Chapter 31

Steaming coffee in hand, Evie pulled her legs underneath her as she settled into the cosy wicker chair, breathing out as she felt her body relax.

She glanced up to see the moon briefly before it was overshadowed by a mass of cloud making its leisurely journey through the night sky.

She'd had to escape the intensity of Nathan's grilling about her father, hating the fact she'd fought back with accusations about his own past-accusations she had no right to make. Still, he'd managed to push the buttons which forced her to think of a time she'd rather forget, yet couldn't.

The night her father admitted he was a thief.

The lights had been off when she'd called in, and as Evie walked down the hallway past the family portraits, she was met with what smelled like something rotting. As she continued, the wilting flowers in a crystal vase proved to be the culprit. "God, that's awful," lowering her nose closer for confirmation.

Not like Mum to leave these here.

Pauline always took pride in keeping a bright and cheery welcome, the weekly delivery of blooms part of her efforts.

"Mum, Dad, are you in here?" Evie placed the bridal magazines down she'd brought for her mother to peruse, opening the dining-room door. *Surely they haven't gone to bed?* It was just after eight.

It was only when she'd turned on the lamp she noticed her father sitting on the settee, making her jump in fright.

"Shit, Dad, you scared the hell out of me," she said, raising a hand to her chest. He sat leaning forward, head bent, as he swished the liquid around in his glass. He glanced at her before returning his gaze downward.

"Is everything okay?"

Are they tears on his face?

Her father's behaviour seemed out of character, and he didn't seem overly enthused at her intrusion. She understood his job could be stressful, but there was obviously something serious going on.

Evie placed a hand his shoulder, and he patted it in response. "I'm okay, darling. Just had a bad day, that's all." His voice sounded croaky and broken, not his usual confident tone at all.

"Well, we all have those, Dad. Don't let it get to you too much. It's not worth it." She sat down beside him, noting his paled expression.

He gave a short laugh which didn't reach his eyes and he stood, the liquid sploshing to the point it almost spilled. He placed the glass on the table with a thud and clasped his hands in front of him.

"Evie, I have to tell you some news and it's not good, I'm afraid." He turned back to face her, his nervous expression making her uncomfortable. She couldn't remember the last time she'd seen her father so rattled and uptight.

"Okay," she offered, willing him take his time. Whatever it was, she had the feeling she wasn't going to like it.

Does Mum know about this?

Is that why she isn't around?

"Evie, it's likely that in the next few days…" he avoided her gaze, "… certain facts will come out in the media, accusations about me and some others at work. Things that will be upsetting to our family and friends."

Evie's stomach began to tighten, and she found herself unable to speak for a moment.

What is he talking about?

Have they arrested some celebrity or well-known person which had the bosses in an uproar? Some big shot criminal? It wasn't the first time something similar had happened.

"What do you mean, Dad? What kinds of things?"

He looked at her with an intensity. "There's likely to be allegations made that some detectives have been stealing proceeds of crime, and that the CMC are investigating. I'm… I'm caught up in it so there could be some trouble ahead, I'm afraid."

Evie shook her head, trying to understand what he was trying to say.

"But that's so stupid. Why would they think you'd be involved? Don't they know who you are? Your reputation? It's ridiculous." *If the Crime and Misconduct Commission were involved, this must be serious.* It was crazy that anyone who had met her father could think any bad of him. He was one of the most honest and conscientious people she knew. He was the one she'd looked up to since she was a little girl for his…

"Because it's true, Evie." Eric knelt on his haunches as he touched her face. "It's true and God help me, I…". His voice stopped on a sob, and she'd found herself lost for words momentarily.

"Dad, I don't understand what's going on. Is Mum aware of this? Where is she?

He spoke with hesitation in his voice. "Your mother has gone out to see friends, I think. I said I wasn't… up to it tonight. And yes, Evie, she's aware of what's been happening. Has been for a while but I asked her not to say anything."

Evie let out a loud sigh and rubbed her neck, trying to release some of the tension that had settled there. Her mind flew to Ben and whether he was implicated as well. *If he knew something and hadn't told her…*

Her father must have read her mind. "Ben's not involved, if that's what you're thinking. Even though he's part of the team, I would never have got him mixed up in all this mess. Couldn't do that to him. Or you." He took her hand in his and rubbed his fingers over hers.

"I'm expecting some officers to come knocking any minute. I didn't want you here to see this, to have to …," he stood, running both hands through his hair. "Dammit! This isn't the way I wanted it to end up. I never expected…"

Evie shook her head again as the sense of dread refused to leave her. She felt compelled to ask. "Did you do it, Dad? Did you take the money, like they're saying?" Her heart thumped in her chest, willing him to deny what she was asking yet half expecting what his reply would be. "Why would you do that?"

He said nothing, an expression of emptiness in his eyes. "Dad?"

"I just lost my way somehow. I… don't know. It was just… easy and seemed excusable because the other guys were in on it. I wanted to give us a better life, all of us. To give you and your mother and Cameron, more of hate good things in life. The wedding you dreamed of…"

"Don't you dare blame this on us, Dad," she stood as a rising anger gave her courage to challenge him. "Me and Ben. We never asked for more from you. I'm sure as hell that Mum wouldn't either. I mean, look around you, for God's sake." She swept her hand around the room. "You make good money, anyway. You have a beautiful house that's paid off. A nice car. Everything you worked hard for." Her voice started to break as tears came to her eyes. "Why would you put that at risk? For stupid money. It's just dumb."

She started crying and put her hands to her face to try and stop the flow, but it was useless. Eric moved forward and took his daughter in his arms, stroking her hair in a soothing gesture. Like he used to when she'd been little, running to him with scraped knees or elbows from a fall off her scooter.

He'd always been there, her hero who could make her world right again. His "fairy princess," he'd always called her.

They didn't hear the knocking at first, distracted by the sound of muffled sobs and laboured breathing. It was only when the rapping became more insistent that her father raised his head, resting his chin on her crown, stealing one more moment together.

"Don't answer it, Dad. Let them wait," she grabbed at his arm, but he'd already released her and moved across the room.

"I can't Evie. I need to face it. What I've done." He stood at the doorway to the room, leaning on it for support. "In some ways, I'm glad it will be over." A look of resignation came across his face and he attempted a smile. "You'll have to be here for your mother, sweetheart. She's going to need you and Cam more than ever now."

"But Dad, just wait….," she made to join him, but he'd already gone, walking the short distance to the front door.

After that, Evie recalled, all hell had broken loose, with the house all at once full of uniformed and plain clothes officers, as well as several inspectors she recognised from family barbeques they'd held at their home. People they'd called friends now wore faces as cold as steel.

No happy banter now, though, mate talking to mate. Just formal cautions and stilted words as numerous cops walked through their home, taking everything from computers, laptops and phones to pulling out drawers, strewing items everywhere.

Her mother had returned home during it all, collapsing in hysterics as her husband of thirty-two years had been led away to a squad car, leaving Evie alone to console her as it disappeared out of sight.

* * * * *

Evie woke in what seemed only minutes later to find the moon long gone and sunlight creeping through the drawn blinds. A familiar smell stirred her senses, and she spied Nathan standing next to the bed, his hand outstretched with a steaming mug of coffee.

"Good morning, sleepy. Thought you might like this. But be warned…," he pulled it back towards him, raising one brow, "… it's my first try at using the machine, so I can't promise it's up to scratch."

She sat up and took the offering in both hands, bringing it closer to her face. "I'm sure it'll be fine," . She inhaled the familiar aroma before taking a tentative sip. "Mmm, it's perfect. You're an angel for this."

She meant it.

Nathan seemed unaffected by the tension of the night before, which she saw as a positive.

How do you do that? she wondered. *Not hold on to anger or grudges, even when those who say they love you are the ones who hurt you the most?*

He moved to leave, stopping in the doorway. "I'm about to make brekkie. How about bacon and eggs?" He'd made no mention of their disagreement of last night, and Evie was grateful for the chance to get her thoughts in order.

"Ah, that would be great. I'll finish this…" she said, holding up the mug, "… and go take a shower. Give me ten."

"Fine, take your time. We have the whole day," he closed the door.

Evie propped herself on a linen pillow, taking the time to enjoy the coffee. Without warning, the tearful words of her mother's plea replayed in her mind and she felt an overwhelming sense of guilt that she was only adding to her mother's pain.

Am I just being stubborn, to punish him even more?

Don't I have the right to stand by my beliefs? He deserves nothing from me, after what he's done.

It was all too hard.

Evie thumped the pillow in frustration before heading to the bathroom and shower.

Nathan was waiting.

And she had a decision to make.

Chapter 32

Driving through the wrought-iron gates of the cemetery entrance, Moira slowed the hatchback to a crawl to avoid the elderly couple shuffling their way along the dirt path.

She passed a white calico marquee where several rows of matching white chairs were placed, ready for the imminent arrival of mourners.

Wonder who the poor soul is they're coming to see, she mused as she continued towards Parkmore Avenue. A row of flame trees stood guard over the plaques of the permanent residents, its fallen blooms forming a carpet of red-tipped petals, almost regal in appearance.

After driving for hours from Cairns, Moira once again leaned forward over the steering wheel to stretch her back, attempting to relieve the tightness that had settled there. Despite the pain, she much preferred to make the journey by car, the silence of its interior providing ample opportunity for reflection.

She'd made several trips here over recent years, on the special dates of significance. He'd have said she was wasting her time.

She could still hear his voice as if he sat beside her.

"Can't dwell on the past," he'd say, when she'd suggested they visit the graves of his parents, but he'd refused. "Once they're gone, that's it. No point in going to stand over them, crying and all."

She'd disagreed, believing to visit the departed a way of keeping their memory alive. She'd stopped pestering him after a time, not wanting to see the pained expression upon his face–reigniting memories he'd long put to rest.

Even after all these years, she continued to hear his voice, sometimes when she least expected it. Seven years married wasn't long, yet Jack had been her first true love. He'd rescued her at the very time he'd needed a saviour. Unfortunately, it hadn't been enough for the younger, immature version of herself, and running away had seemed the more exciting option.

Something she regretted to this day.

She pulled up and reached across to the passenger seat for the bunch of bright red and yellow tulips which had not wilted, despite the heat of the day. Moira realised they weren't likely to last long in the midday sun, yet he'd been fond of the blooms, surprising her on more than one occasion with his thoughtful gesture of love.

Least she could do now was return the favour.

She owed him that.

Today would have been his 72nd birthday.

Knowing the location by heart, she walked down the grassy pathway of Aisle C, having dedicated it to memory from past visits. No evidence of her last offering remained, most likely removed by grounds staff who kept the facility well-tended.

More than once, she'd thought that perhaps this would be her final resting place as well. As morbid as that was, Moira knew she wasn't getting any younger and needed to face facts. There may be no one else to organise it for her and she hated the idea of burdening others with the hassle, anyway.

Tomorrow, she'd make enquiries about securing a plot, even though the one next to him was taken. When visiting that first time, Moira was surprised Jack had chosen cremation over burial, particularly when his parents had been strict Catholics. But then again, it wasn't unlike him to go for the simpler option. Easier to maintain. No chance of oversized headstones crumbling to the ground or the words of loved ones fading over time before disappearing forever.

Looking at the small plaque now, she felt a familiar tinge of pride mixed with sadness at his simple epitaph:

In Loving Memory of
Jack Alfred Barrett
30/3/1947 - 17/12/2016
Father to Nathan
Friend to all
Sadly, missed.

No mention of her. Why would there be? Even her own mother hadn't forgiven her desertion. "The joy disappeared from her eyes overnight," cousin May had written in one of her letters. Apparently, her mother had spent the rest of her days staring at old photos of her daughter who'd done the unthinkable and they'd never spoken again.

Moira knelt, placing the flowers in the plastic holder, half full with last night's rainwater. Most of the other receptacles held artificial blooms, brightly coloured and gaudy yet guaranteed to last more than the two days of her fresh bunch, yet she didn't care.

He'd loved his tulips, growing them in pots which had lined the doorway on the front porch.

She could picture the cottage now, complete with its white picket fence, bright red front door, chimney on the roof.

Every girl's dream—isn't that what they used to say?

Just not her dream.

Or so she'd thought.

Happy birthday, Jack, my darling.

She balanced on both knees and sat back on her haunches, his framed face smiling at her from the plaque.

A myriad of memories flashed through her mind as she recalled the happier times, the fun days before she'd ruined it all. The selfish whim of an immature girl.

Would she have done things differently if she had her time over again?

She'd asked herself many times over the years but still didn't have an answer.

Sorry, Jack. I hope you can forgive me. One day, when we see each other again.

She stood, wiping at the grass on her knees and skirt, bemoaning the fact she wasn't as nimble as she'd thought as her joints creaked in protest as she rose.

"Until next time," she said, blowing a kiss to her one true love. "I'll say hello to our boy for you," she wiped away a tear as she began the short walk back to her car.

Chapter 33

Evie popped a Bon Jovi CD into the player as she drove to work Sunday morning, opening the window to let the gentle breeze tease her face.

She sang along with her favourite eighties band, "Whoa, we're halfway there, whoa living on a prayer," albeit off key. She'd win no karaoke competitions with her voice, that was certain, but today, she didn't care. Today, she felt like singing.

To hell with anyone who complained!

In all truth, Evie's singing was her way of avoiding having to think about Paulina's phone call and request to come home.

To complicate matters, she had Nathan and the ongoing issue of Olivia to deal with, as well.

Sometimes, it felt like the past wasn't always ready to let go-regardless of how much you wished it would.

Evie clung to the hope the Universe was on her side this time.

She continued humming as she approached the security gate, swiping her pass to give her access. Driving through the gates, she selected a park close to the entrance, noting a woman sitting on the bonnet of one vehicle. Wearing dark glasses and casual clothes, Evie sensed she may have seen her somewhere before yet couldn't quite place where.

Grabbing her bag and lunch container, Evie locked her car, offering a smile to the woman as she walked past.

"Hey, I wanna talk to you," the woman said, startling her with the hostile tone." Her words sounded slurred, and as she moved to block Evie's path, it caused her to pull up sharply.

It appeared the bright start to her day was quickly diminishing into something less than perfect.

"Sorry, do I know you?" Evie stepped back. Obviously, the woman had her confused with someone else.

"Don't act all innocent." The female removed her glasses and it was then Evie recognised the ice-blue eyes as belonging to the paramedic from the road crash weeks ago. "I know who you are."

This must be Nathan's ex, Olivia.

A real charmer!

Not wanting to incite her obvious anger further, Evie attempted to diffuse the situation. "You must be Olivia". The woman put her hands on her hips, looking unimpressed at her attempt at friendliness. "I know I'm probably not your favourite person but that's not my fault. I…"

"I can't believe that Nathan would be interested in someone like you. You're not his type at all." She continued to stand in front of Evie, blocking her pathway into the office.

Taking in Olivia's dishevelled appearance and obvious agitation, Evie struggled to contain her own rising anger but refused to rise to the bait.

She wasn't about to defend herself to someone she hardly knew, let alone someone unprepared to listen to reason.

Still, the comments hit home. She'd obviously been a topic of conversation between Nathan and his ex-partner. He'd promised Evie he'd made it clear to Olivia they were over but obviously she was having a hard time accepting that truth.

She'd had her chance and thrown it away.

If she'd loved him that much, she wouldn't have cheated - end of story.

"Look Olivia, I'm late for work. I'm not going to stand here, arguing about Nathan with you," Evie moved to pass, hoping to cool the situation, but Olivia grabbed at her arm.

"He doesn't care about you, you know. He told me. He realised he missed me and wants to try again." She gave a short laugh and her eyes darted wildly.

Evie took a step back, momentarily speechless by the venom in Olivia's voice. Wanting to ignore her taunts, she couldn't help but be thrown by her words.

What has Nathan been saying about me?

Had he made his ex-girlfriend promises as she'd claimed, or were her dramatics part of some delusional game?

Evie drew her handbag tighter as she faced her accuser. "I'm not interested in what you have to say, Olivia." She moved towards the staffroom entrance. "Just stay away from us. Away from Nathan. You need to get on with your life and forget about it."

Evie's skin crawled as she took a breath and turned away, hoping her parting comments would put an end to the confrontation. Olivia remained silent, standing with her arms crossed as Evie swiped her key card at the door.

She refused to turn her head as Olivia screamed in parting, "I'll get him back, you'll see. He's mine and always …"

Her last words were drowned out by the banging of the door as Evie stepped inside the office where she was met by Rylee's inquisitive look.

"What was that all about," her workmate said.

Great, Evie thought. *Just what I need.*

* * * * *

Evie was still shaking from the confrontation as Rylee watched her with wide eyes. "Hey, are you alright? You look like you've seen a ghost." Rylee peered through the window, no doubt spying Olivia outside. "Wow, she looks kinda scary."

Evie walked towards her desk, placing her bag down before replying. "Don't worry about it, I'm fine," she said, not wanting to provide Rylee with more fuel to fan the fire of gossip. "She's just upset about work or something. It's nothing to do with me."

The younger girl turned from the window, sitting at her desk. "I've heard about her. She's been suspended for overdosing someone. God, can you imagine? Not the kind of help I'd like to get, that's for sure."

"Mmm," came Evie's non-committal response, as she tidied her work space. Rylee's shrug and sudden fascination with her mobile gave Evie hope that she'd managed to divert the incident from the young girls' mind.

If she could put it from her own thoughts as easily, she'd be in a much happier mood herself.

They spent several minutes catching up on the night's incidents before performing the daily checks required at the start of each shift.

"Hey, did you see the latest email from the Assistant Commissioner?" Rylee popped her head above the computer console facing Evie's desk. "It's got the latest job opportunities and promotions listed. There's a position come up for a supervisor at Townsville," she said, as a smile crossed her face.

Evie knew her young workmate had future aspirations of moving up the ladder sometime. "Would you apply for that one, the supervisor down south?" Evie said. "Am I driving you that crazy already that you want to leave?"

"I'm thinking about it though I'm not sure if I want to move down south. It's different, and I've made a lot of friends here," Rylee said. "Have you been there yet?"

"No, I haven't got around to it but I will some time. I've been told it's pretty dry."

"Yeah, that's why its nicknamed 'Brownsville'." Doesn't rain as much as here, just constant dry heat. But it's got its good points too. More shops for starters."

"Well, that's a bonus," Evie smiled in return. "You can never have too many shops."

"I know, right?" Rylee said in all seriousness. "Can't even buy decent heels in this place."

She continued in the next breath. "Hey, is it true Nathan is going for one of the inspector jobs? I can't believe he'd get off the trucks, but maybe he's had enough, hey?"

Evie stiffened in her seat, her eyes widening in surprise, yet Rylee seemed not to notice. "Ah no, he hasn't mentioned anything to me. What makes you think he's doing that?"

"When I was out with Oscar and some others last week, they mentioned he was talking about it." Rylee stood as she stretched her back. "Hasn't he said anything to you?" He might want to surprise you, or something."

"Maybe," was all Evie managed although her mind was racing. "I'm sure he'll let me know when he's ready."

Who the hell am I kidding?

If Nathan is thinking about taking a promotion, is he too scared to tell me about it?

Because of what happened with Ben?

"Evie, did you hear the radio message from 8-11 Bravo? They're calling again," Rylee said, interrupting her thoughts. She'd been so distracted, she hadn't heard the transmission in her headset.

Gees, get a grip, Evie, you idiot, she chastised herself.

"Ah, thanks, Rylee. I got it," as she focused her mind on the job for the next few minutes.

The rest of the day, however, proved more than challenging as Evie couldn't rid the nauseous feeling in the pit of her stomach at the morning's events.

The day that had begun so well had gone from bad to worse.

Not to mention that Nathan had more than his fair share of explaining to do.

Chapter 34

"I'm sorry Maam, but I can't honour this script. It doesn't look genuine. And…," the chemist sensed the customer was soon to depart the premises, "… I'm obliged to contact the police about this," she said, raising the slip of paper in her hand.

"Thanks for nothing, bitch," Olivia hissed, grabbing at the script before she could act on her threat. "I'll be reporting this. You don't have the right to not give it to me." Olivia turned away from the counter and stormed down the aisle, pushing past an elderly woman who momentarily tottered on her frame.

"Well, how rude," the lady muttered, but her tormenter was out of earshot, walking at a brisk rate out of the pharmacy.

"Are you alright, Mrs Barkley?" the junior clerk rushed to the side of the woman. "She had no right to do that to you."

"Yes dear, I'm fine. Obviously, she's not having a very good day of it." They both caught a brief glimpse of tattered blonde hair as Olivia exited the shop.

A loud clap of thunder sounded directly overhead the building, shaking its foundations. "Heavens, that gave me a fright," Mrs Barkley held a hand to her chest as the clerk directed her towards a seat, her run in with the agitated young woman fading from her memory.

Exiting as the rain began to fall steadily, Olivia raised a hand over her head briefly but realised the futility of that as large droplets pelted her skin and clothing. She directed her thoughts to a more immediate issue.

Six days now without her regular supply from work, and she was getting desperate. Clumsily forging an old prescription, she wasn't totally surprised when the chemist refused to honour it.

Olivia had specifically chosen this time of day to come, and knowing it was a busy time, hoped that the staff may overlook her deception. Unfortunately, her ploy hadn't worked, the astute chemist no doubt used to these types of tactics and on the lookout for culprits.

Damn.

What am I going to do now?

Olivia gave up any attempt to remain dry, and slowed her pace as she thought about what to do next. Dazed eyes darted around the carpark, and she swayed slightly on her feet, almost falling before steadying herself.

A guy pushing a shopping trolley walked past, glancing at her with concern, but she ignored him and turned her head, the sudden action causing her vision to blur.

She couldn't remember the last time she'd eaten anything.

Maybe two days ago?

Where was Nathan? Why hadn't he called?

"Nathan." She spoke the word aloud, which had the effect of jolting her back to reality. "That's where I'll go. To see Nathan. He'll be able to help."

Olivia moved forward with a greater sense of purpose, walking towards the rear carpark, finally locating her vehicle.

Her hands shook as she unlocked the door and slid inside, water dripping down her hair, face and clothing, saturating the sheepskin seat cover, yet she was oblivious to the discomfort.

She had a new focus now-and as she screeched out of the carpark, she smiled in anticipation of seeing him again.

* * * * *

Nathan stepped outside the office, notepad in hand, to find Kenny and Oscar chatting, supposedly checking the gear in the appliance. "Kenny, can you run a siren check with Firecom on the appliance? I want to get it done early so we can get some building inspections done."

"Sure thing, boss," the senior firefighter said as Nathan returned inside. "I'll do it now." "Bloody pain in the ass," he muttered, and Oscar laughed, giving him a consoling pat.

"Come on mate, you can do it," he teased, waving a hand in the air as he escaped towards the tearoom. "Glad it's you and not me". Oscar missed Kenny's finger gesture in response and the older man grunted, yelling to his younger counterpart, "Hey, what about helping with these other checks?" His voice fell on deaf ears, the outer door closing to leave him alone in the engine bay.

He spent the next few minutes complying with Nathan's request, testing the siren on the fire truck was operating as it should and confirming all equipment was still intact.

Kenny sat down on the truck step and brought out his phone to check if there were any messages from Moira.

The woman had him tied up in knots, the most anxious he'd been for years. Hadn't felt this way since, well… not since Mary, and that was a lifetime ago.

Keeping company with her these past few weeks had given him a new lease on life, and to his surprise, she seemed to be enjoying herself too.

Bowling, dancing the tango, walking through Flecker Gardens-all these things were new to him but with her enthusiasm and spirit, Kenny was determined to do all he could to impress her any way he could.

No messages yet. *That's fine, she's probably busy.*

It was slightly frustrating that she put up an invisible wall with him at times, not keen to discuss the past or anything much about her life other than what she was up to now. He knew virtually next to nothing about her dead husband or the son who was apparently in the fire service as well. On the times he'd tried to make conversation, she'd shut him down pretty quickly, so he let it lie. For now.

He didn't need to scare her off by being nosy. She'd let him in eventually, he just needed to…

"Christ, what's she doing here?" Kenny muttered, as he noticed the woman who'd entered the engine bay from the street.

On the few times he'd socialised with her, back when she was dating the boss, she'd been rude bordering on possessive. He remembered her as being almost paranoid about the guys talking to Nathan while she hung possessively onto his arm like a leech on a succulent thigh.

Olivia hadn't spotted him, concealed behind the truck, and he planned on keeping it that way.

He, for one, hadn't been surprised when news got out that they'd broken up. In fact, he'd often wondered why Nathan hadn't ditched her sooner, putting it down to the crazy things we do when we're in *love*. Or think we are.

"Hey, you over there," she shouted out, his hiding spot obviously not as well concealed as he'd hoped.

"Oh, hello, luv. Didn't see you there," Kenny lied through gritted teeth, attempting a fake smile. "Haven't seen you around for a while."

"Yeah, well, I've been dumped, so that's no surprise," she said, walking towards him yet not lowering her voice at all, which seemed raised to an unusually high pitch, almost a yell.

Hang on. Wasn't it you who did the dirty on him?

"Is Nathan here? I need to talk to him. Now."

Yep—pretty much true to form.

"Uh, yeah. He's in the office. I can get him…"

"Don't bother," she turned back towards the glass door leading to the departmental offices, dismissing Kenny without a second thought. "I know where it is."

"Righto then. Looks like you know where you're going."

Think I'll leave them to it, Kenny thought, as he crossed the engine bay, and escaped to the tearoom.

He didn't particularly want to be around when the sparks started flying, which they were obviously about to do.

Good luck boss!

He pulled on the door and stepped inside, joining Oscar and Will at the dining table. "Hey guys, you'll never guess who just turned up…

* * * * *

"So, how did the date go last night?" Nathan sat at his desk as his friend sauntered in, taking a seat opposite. "Any luck this time?" He'd asked this question many times over the years as Mason liked to play the field yet insisted he was looking for that *someone special*.

"Na, bombed out again." Mason shook his head, not appearing too upset at his misfortune. "I mean, Kirsty's nice enough and everything but we don't click right. She's cashed up though and would be a real catch."

"Maybe you're being too fussy. You know you'll never find *the* perfect match, they don't exist. If you really want to have something serious, you may need to reassess your criteria."

Nathan leaned back in the chair, lacing his hands behind his head.

He'd had this conversation many times with Mason, yet his friend didn't seem to understand what it took to form a lasting relationship. Heck, he couldn't remember the last time Mason had dated someone for more than a month or two. Nathan figured his friend wasn't ready to settle down yet. Perhaps he never would. Perhaps the love of his job would keep him happy over the coming years.

Unlike Mason, Nathan saw more to his life than work, although that was still important to him. Otherwise, he wouldn't be considering a move up the ladder, something Mason had prompted him to think seriously about.

One of the reasons Nathan was delaying his application for the inspector role was that it would mean giving up the day-to-day firefighting duties, putting him at a desk Monday to Friday, not to mention the increase in paperwork, which was something he wasn't' fond of. At least now, being able to ride the trucks brought variation and *some* excitement to his day, making the office tasks more bearable.

Yet Mason kept spruiking the perks of the senior role and Nathan couldn't deny the extra pay was a huge incentive.

His attention was diverted from their chat by loud voices coming from outside his office door.

Shit. His face reddened when he realised his ex-partner was about to come inside.

He stood as Mason turned around to check what the fuss was.

Jesus, she looks like hell. Worse than before.

"Well, I've found you at last," Olivia said in greeting. She slammed the glass door, rattling the thin pane, before standing in front of his desk with hands on hips. "Why didn't you answer my calls? I've been waiting and waiting". She lent forward, placing both hands on the desk to steady herself and he caught a brief whiff of an unpleasant stale odour that had him raising his brows.

Mason stood, gesturing towards his chair. "Nice to see you too, Olivia. Why don't you take my seat? I was just leaving anyway." He gave his friend a wink as he left, obviously not needing to interrupt the reunion. "I'll catch up later, bro," as he departed.

"Yeah, right Mason. Thanks," Nathan said, not blaming his friend for hot footing it out of there. He'd never liked Olivia much, and the two had only ever tolerated each other for Nathan's sake. Now, he studied her with a sense of dread. "Why don't you sit and calm down a bit, Liv, before you fall over," he said, rising to help her, but she put up a hand in defiance.

"I don't want to freakin' sit down. I need you to talk to me. To stop ignoring... I've been calling and calling but... I just..." Olivia had moved her feet to keep a distance between them, but they became entangled and as he'd predicted, she fell onto the carpet, landing unceremoniously on her butt.

"Oh, for God's sake," Nathan muttered, bending to help her up, and he half lifted, half walked her to the chair before turning to the water cooler and filling a glass. "Here, drink this and don't say a word," he raised his hand as she'd been about to protest but instead, took the water and drank.

Taking his seat, he contemplated the woman before him, finding it hard to believe this was the same vibrant, outspoken Olivia he'd once known. He'd never seen this broken-down version, and he experienced an uneasy sensation in his gut.

His mind traced back to the few times she'd spoken of her father Kurt and the demons he'd spent years fighting himself, albeit unsuccessfully, only to end it all with a rope when Olivia was only about eleven years old.

He hoped she wasn't headed down the same path of self destruction.

For the time being, she appeared to have calmed.

"Aren't you hot in those things?" he said, gesturing towards the woollen pants she wore, in an attempt to lighten the tension in the room. "It's boiling outside even with the rain. They look hotter than our turnout gear."

"What? These?" she tapped a hand on her thigh before looking around the room. "Nah, I'm feeling cold, actually. You've got the air con up too high."

"Mmm, maybe," he said, more concerned about her mental and physical states. *Should he call a doctor to come over?*

"Anyway, I've been thinking a lot about us... and how good... well, most times were good, and now that I'm not working... ummm, suspended, I'd have more time to spend with you, and..."

"Liv, you need to stop," he placed one hand over hers and she raised her eyes to look at him, making direct eye contact for the first time since she'd arrived. "It's just not going to work anymore. You and me. It can't."

"What do you mean, '*It can't*?'" she pushed the chair back on its wheels. "I thought you still loved me. You said you'd always feel that way. Said it lots of times." Bringing one hand up, she started pulling at her bottom lip, pinching it with a nail in a repeated notion.

"Well, that was before you… We've been through all this before, Liv. More than once. It's a little late for a change of heart now, don't you think?

"No, it's not, you selfish bastard," she yelled, standing suddenly which caused the chair to topple and fall with a thud. "It's because of her, isn't it," her voice raised in volume and Nathan sighed in exasperation, knowing how thin the walls of his office were. "That slut you've been seeing. She's no good, you know. Some mousy little Comms operator. A nobody."

"Olivia, calm down. This has nothing…"

"… a thief, that's what she is. A bloody thief that can't keep her hands to herself."

"Right, that's enough," Nathan's voice also raised a notch, moving around the desk to take her arm. "I want you to sit while I call you a taxi to get you home."

Olivia pulled back from his grasp, moving towards the door before flinging it back against the wall, this time shattering the rectangular pane of glass which fell like confetti onto the carpet. "I don't need a taxi, you pig. I can get back without you. Without any of you," Olivia said, noticing

Kenny and Will standing close to the office door, having left the tearoom to investigate what the commotion was.

"You alright, boss?" Kenny asked, mindful of keeping back from the *guest* who didn't seem keen on accepting any help.

"Fine, Kenny. Everything's fine. Just get back to the checks, like I asked," Nathan said in a clipped tone, instantly regretting his abrupt response yet unable to stop it.

"Yeah, that'd be right. Everything's okay with Nathan. He's such a hero," Olivia said at high volume. "Nathan Barrett is a real hero," she looked outside the engine bay, where several more people now stood wide eyed, having ventured to check out what was causing the disturbance.

Nathan remained standing by the door, not wanting to incite his ex-partner into any form of further abuse, not with his work colleagues around. They didn't deserve to have to listen to the ravings of his ex-girlfriend. Still-her demeanour and agitated state had him concerned. He still felt responsible in a way and couldn't just send her off without knowing she'd be okay.

He stepped towards her slowly. "Why don't I get someone to pick you up and take you home then," he offered, but Olivia had already turned to leave, aware of several pairs of eyes now fixed upon her. "Or organise a doctor's appointment for you to speak to…"

"Fuck you, Nathan. I don't need your help." Olivia walked backwards out into the street and ran towards her vehicle which she started up, spinning the tyres as she took off at speed down Brown Street. He prayed that she wouldn't kill anyone in her rage.

"Sorry about that everyone. Just a little misunderstanding," Nathan said, noting the confused gazes as he returned inside.

Shit of a day, he thought. *Could it get any worse?*

Recognising the crunch of glass under his boot, he cursed as he realised he would now spend the better part of the afternoon on hold to organise building maintenance.

Chapter 35

The next morning saw Nathan in a better frame of mind as he made his way downstairs to start breakfast. The ringing of his phone distracted him from yesterday's memories which he hadn't yet raised with Evie, not wanting to spoil their evening together. Yet, he knew he'd have to tell her sometime as the word would no doubt get out.

Noting Mason's number, he accepted the call. "Hey, what's up".

After having spent an amazing night with Evie, he'd had little sleep, yet still felt energised. He'd left her upstairs, snoring like a trooper, as he'd showered and dressed without her moving a muscle.

Talk about sleep like the dead!

It had stirred something in him-her being in his bed. She'd agreed to stay over at his place, and her presence gave the place an aura of feminine charm he hadn't realised he'd missed.

Sure, the single life was okay. He got to go where he wanted, when he wanted, buy takeaway, and spend hours goofing around with Coops at the dog park, all without having to answer to anyone.

Even so, there were times when he missed having a woman around-the feel of soft skin, being fussed over and cared for, even nagging about not washing up dinner dishes. *Well, they weren't quite at that point yet, but he hoped to be sometime.*

"Nathan, you there?" Mason's voice snapped him from his daydream, and he repositioned the phone to his ear.

"Sorry mate, I'm here," he said. Cooper trotted to sit in front of him, part of his daily ritual, reminding Nathan it was food time. "This is early, even for you. Don't you have any fire stations to run?" he said as his friend gave a sarcastic grunt in response.

"Yeah, right. I'll have you know us inspectors work our butts off behind the scenes..."

"Sure, sure you do".

"... but everyone is of the opinion we just sit around, drinking lattes and..."

"Mason, that's not true at all, man," Nathan said. "We appreciate you all work hard. I mean, think of *all* those emails you write–must be hundreds every day."

"Screw you," Mason replied. "I had *actually* called to help you out in your application for the very position you're bagging. But if you believe it's below you, well... I'm wasting my time. I tried to talk about it yesterday but as you know, other matters had us slightly distracted."

"Yeah, sorry about that," Nathan said. "It was kinda out of my hands, I'm afraid." He wanted nothing more than to put the episode from his mind yet knowing Olivia as he did, that may not be as easy as he'd like.

He remembered his friend's offer. "I'd appreciate your help. That's why I left you the message." Nathan gave Cooper a pat as he remained patiently positioned at his owner's feet. "Hey, hold on a minute. I'll put you on speaker while I feed Coops. He's hassling me.

"Alright, I'll wait, even though…"

Nathan missed half the reply as he placed the phone on the bench, pressing the "Speaker" button to reconnect with his friend.

"… my valuable time, you know."

"Keep talking while I do this. It won't take long," Nathan said, smiling as Cooper dropped his empty food bowl at Nathan's feet. "You're a clever boy," he said, giving the canine another pat.

Mason continued. "I've sent you a copy of my application when I went through the process, although you'd have to change it up. Old Smithy may still be on the interview panel, so he'll recognise if it's a straight copy of mine, the old prick."

"Thanks. It'll help me get an idea of what I need to put in," Nathan said. "I'll get onto the computer later and check it out. Thanks."

"You'll need three referees that can pile on the bullshit and tell them how fantastic you are."

Nathan grunted, used to his friend's sarcasm. Mason was constantly trying to get a rise out of him but usually failed.

"Yeah, got those sorted, too," his comeback was short. "Hang on a sec," he said, picking up the bowl and placing it in the laundry for Cooper to enjoy.

Mason remained silent for a moment before continuing. "In all seriousness Nathan, I'm hoping that your recent run-in with the ex doesn't make the rounds at the Station. It may not look too good for you to be seen associating with someone so volatile-if you catch my drift."

Nathan walked back to the kitchen, placing both hands on the counter and lent over. "Sorry, I missed your last. What was that?"

"I said, having a girlfriend with a reputation like hers isn't going to do your chances at promotion much good. It's probably all around the station by now and if any of the seniors get wind of it…"

"Oh, for God's sake. That's crap. For one thing, she's not my girlfriend, she's just someone I feel sorry for. And if they're that concerned about trivial…"

"I realise it's crazy, but that's the way it is sometimes. It's what this place is like. Any bad publicity that's connected to one of its employees and its goodbye career. Remember that guy from Cardwell, Callum something? He ended up having to quit and got a job at the mines after they found him out screwing one of the paramedics in the back of a van."

"Yeah, well there's not much chance of that happening with me." Nathan sighed. "I'm trying to keep seeing her under wraps so she can sort herself out."

Nathan's mood began to darken. He couldn't believe anyone could be so petty as to disregard his abilities because of a failed relationship.

That was just dumb.

He heard a slight click, figuring Cooper had finished his meal and wanted to be let outside. "Look, I've gotta go, mate. Thanks for the heads up. I'll think about it and get back to you." He picked up the phone, taking it off Speaker mode whilst walking to the lounge. He found Cooper sitting at the front door which was ajar.

What the hell was it doing open?

"Okay, no problem," Mason said. Then added, "Oh, and how's the new woman in your life? Making any progress there?"

Nathan felt his heart pump in his chest. "Yeah, she's amazing. I'll fill you in another time, but I gotta go. Bye." He broke off the call, opening the door and looked out into the street which was empty of people.

Strange, he mused.

Maybe Evie got up and went for a walk.

He returned inside, closing the door but left it unlocked, just in case.

"Good boy for not running out," he said to Cooper, as the dog looked at his master, tail wagging.

Once Cooper was free to roam in the rear yard, Nathan filled the kettle before going to check on Evie. He knew how much she enjoyed her early morning brew.

Grabbing the hot mugs, he made his way upstairs and on entering the bedroom, noticed the door wide open and the room empty.

Yep, he thought. *She must be out walking.*

Perhaps she'd heard him on the call to Mason and didn't want to disturb him as she left.

He set the cups down, sat on the bed and waited.

* * * * *

Evie had stirred slowly, the warmth of the early morning sun creeping through the blinds, touching her forearm with heat. Her eyelids fluttered and opened, and she took a moment to gather her senses to remember where she was.

Nathan's place.

The first time she'd spent the night, and it was, *well… pretty damn good actually,* she thought.

When he'd called her late yesterday afternoon, suggesting dinner at his place, she took it as an offer she couldn't refuse. After the day she'd had, chilling out together sounded more than heavenly.

When she'd arrived, any thought of telling him of her recent altercation with Olivia left her, as his tired appearance showed his day had fared little better. She'd decided to save it for another time.

Raising her arms above her head, she noticed the slight, almost enjoyable, ache in parts of her body that hadn't felt that way in a long time.

Nathan's lovemaking skills were impressive-his desire to please and look after her needs first making Evie realise how much of an unselfish lover he was. Experienced at drawing out her pleasure first and not concentrating on his own.

He'd made her laugh, teasing her when she'd bemoaned her breasts for being too small. "Yeah, you're right. You should get implants. Massive ones. So they come out here," he'd gestured with his hands out in front of him to emphasise his meaning. "They can never be too big, baby!".

"Ohhhhh, you…," she'd laughed at his description, enjoying the fact he made light of her faults.

Would he be that accepting of all her imperfections?

"No, Evie. They're perfect, just as they are," he'd said, tweaking her nose as she toppled on top of him. "Wouldn't change a thing at all," he'd said before showing her just how much her abundant features impressed him.

It had been quite some time later when they'd both gotten to sleep.

Now, she couldn't wait to see him again and sensing she must have got up with the birds, decided she'd better get moving too.

They'd talked about visiting the aquarium today and getting an early start would mean avoiding the tourists who usually flocked there later in the day.

She took her essentials to the bathroom, taking a brief shower as she hummed, *I'm walking on sunshine. Whoaaa. And don't it feel good!*

Returning refreshed, she rummaged through her bag, checking her phone for messages. "Oh, great," she realised, reading the text from her mother. "Please call me darling, when you can," leaving her feeling less than cheery.

She'd avoided calling Pauline again about her father's illness, but Evie knew she couldn't ignore the issue for much longer. Like it or not, she would have to face facts—either risk not seeing him again or taking a huge leap of faith and…

And what?

Give up everything I believe in?

Is that what I should do?

Dropping the phone in her overnight bag, she tidied the bedcovers before heading downstairs. She heard what sounded like male voices coming from the kitchen and wondered if he had a visitor.

Putting a hand to wet hair, Evie decided it best to keep out of sight, not wanting to embarrass him with a sudden *Surprise!* as she blundered her way in.

She tiptoed closer to the door, peeping round to check who Nathan was talking to. Spying his phone on the kitchen counter, she made to step inside, but a male voice had her halting in her tracks. It could be his friend Mason, but she wasn't sure.

"I said, that having a girlfriend with a reputation like hers isn't going to do your chances at promotion much good. It's probably all around the station by now and if any of the seniors get wind of it…"

"Oh, for God's sake. That's crap. She's not my girlfriend, she's just someone I feel sorry for. And if they're that concerned about trivial…"

"I know, it's crazy, but that's the way it is sometimes. You know what this place is like. Any bad publicity that's connected to one of its employees and it's 'goodbye career'.

Evie raised a fist to her mouth, attempting to stifle the sob that had risen in her throat, leaning backward on the wall for support.

She couldn't believe what she was hearing. Not from him, of all people.

"Someone I feel sorry for!"

Is that all she was?

A relationship built on pity because she'd been dumped before and was an easy screw?

Discussing her with one of his mates like they were discussing last night's footy scores cut to the core, and she turned away in disgust.

How could I have been so stupid?

I have to leave before…

Rubbing at the tears in her eyes, she turned on bare feet and made for the stairs. Taking them two at a time, she re-entered the bedroom, grabbed her things and put on her thongs, before tip toeing back down.

Noticing Cooper looking at her with pleading eyes, she gave him a quick pat. "Sorry, fella," she rubbed the soft fur before raising her hand. "I have to get out of here."

He made a small whine as she opened the front door and exited without a backward glance.

* * * * *

He'd been sitting on the bed for some time before it hit him that something wasn't right. He scanned the room, realising with a sense of alarm that all her stuff was gone. Her clothes, her phone, her overnight bag. Everything.

Nathan rose and entered the bathroom, noting the second towel hanging wet on the rack but none of her other items remained where she'd placed them.

Where the hell was she?

It wasn't like Evie to just up and leave—he knew that much at least.

He skipped downstairs two at a time, and picked up his phone, dialling her number. No answer. *Hate these damn things*. Punching on the keys, he left a message.

Hey babe, worried about you. Is everything ok? Pls call me.

Chapter 36

Easing into the soft leather of her brother's Landcruiser, Evie let out a sigh as she rubbed her aching eyes.

The last few hours-no few days-had been a whirlwind and the pent-up tension had her on edge. From the time she'd left Nathan's place to the phone call with Eileen arranging emergency leave, Evie had made the decision to leave town. Returning home, where her mother wanted her to be had presented as the best solution when she'd needed to escape.

Beyond that… who knew?

Unaware of his sister's anxiety, Cameron had been as excited as a child at Christmas when meeting her in the arrivals hall, tackling her in a bear hug which had several bystanders giving the pair questioning looks. Ignoring them, she'd kissed her brother, thankful to be back in the embrace of someone she trusted implicitly.

Just what her breaking heart needed…

She looked at him now as he focused on navigating the road from the airport, crazy busy as usual. Once on the freeway, he reached for his phone on the dash, passing it to her as she admired the screen shot of his smiling young daughter.

"Cam, she's so adorable," Evie said, looking at the recent picture of her niece, the light blond curls framing Bethany's angelic face. A pang of regret hit her as Evie realised the little girl was no longer a baby, but a vibrant toddler. She'd missed out on her reaching some of life's early milestones. "I can't believe how much she's grown."

"I know, right," her brother said as he manoeuvred through the busy traffic. "Unbelievable to think she's a toddler already. Chatters like a real trooper, too. Just like her mother." Cam couldn't keep the obvious pride from his face as he spoke.

Evie laughed and marvelled at the transformation in him, a far cry from the dark days after their father's disgrace. Cam and Lizzie appeared to have put the negativity behind them, although Evie knew it hadn't been easy. Certainly, the birth of their daughter had eased some of the pain during that time.

The architectural business Cam had worked hard to establish over the years had taken a heavy hit because of the publicity when several clients recognised his association to Eric, cancelling contracts and ending long-term associations. Still, he'd told her, things seemed to be picking up again, with more work booked in the months ahead.

"Mum will be over the moon to see you," he said, interrupting her thoughts. "I understand it's been hard for her since you left, even though she doesn't say so. With the wedding falling through and everything, I mean." He gave her knee a gentle squeeze. "She was distraught about you and Ben when it happened. Thought you were the perfect couple. We all did."

"Yeah, join the club," Evie couldn't keep her sarcasm from her voice as old memories played out again. Yet, she refused to be drawn into the same tired old conversations about what could have been. "I'm not here to rekindle things with Ben, Cam, if that's what you're thinking. Besides, he already tried that, and I sent him back home."

"Wow, really. I didn't know that." Cameron's look of surprise was genuine, and Evie realised her mother hadn't mentioned Ben's trip to him. *Good ol' Mum. Always good at keeping secrets.*

"I liked him. Wasn't such a bad guy."

"Yeah. It was a shitty time for everyone."

She turned her head to gaze out the window as they continued in silence for several minutes.

She took in the approaching skyline and realised just how big the city of Melbourne was compared to Cairns. *Like chalk and cheese.* She thought of the quieter life she'd grown accustomed to, realising she didn't feel as homesick for her birthplace as she'd imagined she would.

Was the smaller city weaving its magic upon her?

Or was it a certain someone whose personality and charm had deepened her connection to the quieter town?

She fought back tears as Nathan's face popped into her mind and she thought of the missed calls and texts he'd made in the past couple of days.

Let him wait. I'm not ready to hear any excuses right now.

Anyway, this trip wasn't about her—it was about helping her mother get through her husband's diagnosis.

"Have you decided whether you're going to visit Dad yet?" Cameron read her mind at that moment, raising the very issue she'd so far tried to ignore.

"I…, I'm not sure, Cam. I'm just not sure if I'm ready. If I'll ever be ready. Have you been?"

"Yeah. I went to see him last week." Cameron said, and turned left off the freeway, merging onto the road leading to the family home. "He seemed not too bad. I believe he's started the chemo treatments. He seems positive about it all, or at least, from what I can tell. Asks about you a lot. What you're doing and stuff."

"Mmm, I'll bet," she said, and sighed. There was no way she'd feel sorry for her father now, just because he was sick.

That doesn't excuse what you did, Dad. It just doesn't.

"Oh look, is that a new David Jones they're building there?" Evie pointed to a construction site as Cameron nodded.

"Yes, it should be finished by the end of the year. As a matter of fact, I've been leading the design on that one so I can't wait to see how it looks." He smiled, and Evie experienced a surge of pride in her brother in having made such a success of his life.

While she still struggled to sort her mess out.

"Almost there," her brother said as their home came into view. He gave a toot of the horn and within seconds, Pauline was at the gate waving excitedly at the car.

Evie waved back, feeling both anticipation and trepidation, uncertain at what the next few days would bring.

* * * * *

"Evie darling, so glad you're here. Was the flight bearable?" Pauline embraced the daughter she hadn't seen in months, barely able to curb her excitement at her return, even if it was only temporary.

Better that than nothing.

The house had felt empty over recent times, the only outlet was babysitting Bethany several days a week. If she didn't have that, Pauline would have been at her wit's end trying to fill in her days.

"Yes Mum. I flew Qantas, so it was fine," her daughter remarked, giving her mother a kiss on the cheek.

"I've gotta run, Mum," Cameron waved, standing at the car door. "I've promised to take the little one to the zoo this afternoon and Lizzie just texted that they're ready to go."

"Okay dear. I'll see you soon," his mother called out, her arm tucked around Evie's waist, still unable to contain the joy that her daughter had come home.

Not permanently, she knew, for Evie seemed determined to make a new start in Cairns. Far enough away from the dramas she'd left behind.

But at least for a while, she would enjoy the fact they'd be together.

Time enough to put things right.

It was the least she could do. For everyone.

Chapter 37

Over the next few days, mother and daughter spent time catching up, enjoying outings to their favourite cafes for coffee and lunch, all the while avoiding the real reason for Evie's return. An air of tension seemed to follow them both-a shadow cast upon them which neither were willing to face.

Eric's presence remained strong within the home. Old family photos, including their wedding portrait, hung over the fireplace, while the framed graduation photo from the police academy held pride of place in the main hallway.

Evie paused in front of it now, noting the familiar smile of her father as he'd stood in line to shake the hand of the Police Commissioner of the day.

"One of the best days of my life, that was," she remembered him saying. Like his father before him, Eric had worked hard over the years to establish a policing career to be proud of, yet had thrown it all away on a whim.

Lucky Pop hadn't been around to see the events that led to the ending of his son's eminent career.

He'd turn in his grave, Evie thought, shaking her head as she touched fingers lightly to his smiling face.

Evie didn't hear her mother's footsteps as she came to stand behind her. "He was so handsome then, wasn't he?" Evie dropped her hand by her side. "I always said he was my own version of Paul Newman. Those sparkling blue eyes had me from the first day we met." Pauline laughed and touched Evie's shoulder, facing her.

"It's time we talked about things, Evie." Pauline's eyes started to tear up." Let's go to the sitting room and I'll tell you about what's going on."

Evie realised there was no more avoiding the inevitable. She would break it to her mother about the decision she'd made-that she wasn't able to bring herself to see him.

Shit! Why did I have to be put in this position, anyway? It's not fair.

Why couldn't he have stayed the honest, hardworking man in the photo–the man I've looked up to all my life?

They walked along the short hallway into the cosiness of the quiet sitting room, once Evie's favourite but which now reminded her of that last fateful conversation with her father.

Her mother spoke first. "I can imagine what you're thinking. I saw it in your face looking at your father's photo." Her mother always had the uncanny ability to get inside her head. Drove Evie crazy sometimes. "But your father's not a bad man. He… he just did what he did because he cared about us. Wanted to give us more."

Evie squirmed on the settee, her temper beginning to raise as her mother attempted to make excuses for him. *Again.*

"Mum, I know you've found it hard, having to play the faithful wife and standing by your man and all that, but you can't be that blind to the truth." She turned to Pauline, noting her tired eyes. "He stole money. Dirty money. It's not something you do, especially someone in his position. He threw it all away. The career that he'd worked so hard for. Not to mention the embarrassment and shame it brought onto all of us. If he now expects me to feel sorry…"

"Evie, that's enough," her mother's raised voice had her momentarily silenced. "Please." She rubbed a hand behind her neck, obviously trying to relieve some tension and momentarily looked to the ceiling. "It's time I told you the truth. The actual reason your father's in prison. Suffering. Because of me."

A look of confusion crossed Evie's face.

What the hell is she talking about?

There's only ever been one truth, hasn't there? He stole. Pure and simple.

She waited in silence as Pauline seemed to struggle to find the words. When she eventually spoke, Evie jumped in surprise.

"It was for me, you see. The money was for me. This whole thing… the trial, your wedding, Cam's business… he made me promise not to tell you or your brother but now I…" Pauline placed her face in her hands and began sobbing.

"Oh Mum," Evie said, sliding over to place her arms around her parent, shocked at seeing her this vulnerable. She'd never seen her mother cry. Not like this. "I don't understand, *'it was for you'*. Why would it be your fault?"

Her mind spinning with questions, Evie remained silent for several minutes as her mother's soft weeping continued, until she wiped her eyes and faced her daughter.

"I… I've been gambling, Evie. At the pokies."

Evie's mouth widened in an "O," not quite comprehending what she was hearing.

"Your father found out and tried to get me to stop, but I couldn't. The Club made me happy and was something that got me out of the house. With you and Cam gone, well, it just seemed so empty. The pokies gave me something to look forward to."

Evie recovered her voice. "How much did you lose, Mum? Evie asked, guessing it wasn't only a couple of hundred dollars.

Pauline sighed and looked down. "The debt ended up over $250,000." Evie couldn't contain her gasp as her mother continued. "I managed to re-mortgage the house without your father knowing, but God help me, it disappeared. It went so quickly. He only found out when the bank called, asking about a discrepancy in the accounts."

Pauline eased herself from Evie's embrace and began pacing.

"So what happened?" Evie said, guessing what came next but needing to hear it for herself. She felt pity for her mother, not realising until now how hard it must have been to watch her children up and leave, with not much care for how she was coping. The occasional dinner and phone call obviously weren't enough to compensate for losing the ones she cherished the most.

Knowing her father and how protective of his family he was, it began to make sense that he'd try to put things right. Any way he could.

"I had to own up, of course. The whole story." She stood by the window, parting the curtains to peer outside briefly before drawing the blind. "You know what he's like. He always loves to take control, to make things right. *'Don't worry, darling'*, he said. *'I'll work it out, you'll see'*. He made it sound like we could find an easy way out of the mess I'd got us into."

She sat back down. "It wasn't long after that he began making payments back to the bank. It never occurred to me to ask where the money came from, but I guess...," Pauline began crying softly again, "... I guess I knew that he had to be doing something illegal to get the money. Whenever I tried to ask him about it, he'd tell me *'Don't worry, love, it's fine. It'll all be...'*. She broke down, sobbing in Evie's arms.

Evie felt sick to her stomach, yet ignored it, stroking her mother's hair as she attempted to console her.

Honestly, she wasn't sure what to believe.

So many emotions ran through her, trying to take it all in.

She felt anger, for one thing.

Anger at her mother for doing something so stupid, throwing money away for no good reason.

Everyone knows that gambling is a mug's game. No-one ever comes out on top.

But that soon gave way to compassion, recognising her mother's desperate attempt to fill the void in her life.

Anger at her father. For not telling her and Cam the facts up front. Letting them believe that he was the villain when he wasn't really to blame at all. It was so like the Dad she knew to protect his wife, although he must have known his chances of getting caught were high.

Then the shame kicked in. Shame at herself for not believing in him, not trusting him enough or looking for other answers but accepting the story her parents had concocted without digging further for details.

What a bloody mess!

A thought entered her mind which had Evie tense, yet she felt compelled to ask. "You're not still doing it, are you Mum? The gambling, I mean?" She worried that with her mother being alone with no-one to talk to or confide in, the likelihood of her returning to her addiction wasn't an impossibility.

"No, no, darling," Pauline touched a hand to Evie's face. "I've been getting help for that, seeing a doctor who I can talk to about things. Actually, that's been the best thing to come out of all this."

"I'm sorry I wasn't there for you Mum, through all this shit. I didn't realise." Evie's voice choked, rendering her silent as she fought to regain her composure.

"I didn't expect you to be, darling. It's not your fault. It's the way things turned out. But, your father… he's the one suffering the most. And it's all because of me. He's sitting in a rotten jail cell because of me."

Evie hated hearing the distress in her mother's voice. "Mum, you can't blame this all on yourself. Dad made the choice he did, and even though he meant to help, it wasn't the best decision. It was just plain crazy.

"Perhaps you're right." Her mother blew her nose into a hankie. "I'm tired. Let's go to bed now, shall we?" Pauline said, the weariness clear on her features. "It's been a lot for you to take in and I think we both need to get some sleep. We can talk more tomorrow."

Nodding in agreement, Evie rose and switched off the table lamp as they moved out of the room, making their way along the hall to the stairs.

Outside her mother's bedroom, Evie bent to kiss Pauline. "Goodnight, Mum. Try and get some rest, if you can."

"You too, darling. Goodnight," Pauline whispered, closing the door.

Moments later, laying back in the familiar comfort of her old queen size bed, Evie's mind was spinning. What she'd discovered tonight had left her exhausted and overwhelmed. What she'd believed to be the truth for months now had been proven to be a lie and it wasn't until the early hours of morning that Evie finally succumbed to a restless sleep.

Chapter 38

Debra and Jeff Cunningham turned left into Herbert Street, returning home after their regular Saturday lunch date which had given them the afternoon free from their three young children.

Not that they didn't adore their tribe, but to have an hour or two's reprieve had proved to be a saving grace for their marriage, and was definitely one of Jeff's better ideas!

Driving past their neighbour's place, Debra couldn't help but notice how its appearance had deteriorated in recent weeks. A growing pile of large palm fronds lay scattered across the front yard where the grass stood several inches higher than it should, in desperate need of a mow.

A pile of uncollected newspapers lay scattered near the letterbox, the protective plastic wet from the recent rain. Several mynah birds pecked at the shiny material, no doubt attracted by the prospect it may make good nest building material.

"Do you think she's sick or something?" Debra asked her husband. "I mean, she was always so good at keeping the garden and pool area, but it looks out of control. And I'm sure I heard glass breaking the other night. Wonder what that was about?"

"Who knows?" came her husband's usual deadpan response.

Debra knew that Jeff rarely took note of what other people did, preferring to focus on his own growing family. "*Best not get involved*" was his mantra, which conveniently excused him from any involvement or conflict. Debra was the more social of the pair, observant to what went on in their street. "Maybe she lost her job or something. Or she might be on holidays and couldn't be bothered to hire a gardener. Come to think of it, I haven't seen her go out much lately at all."

"I'm sure it's nothing to worry about."

Jeff parked, turning off the ignition as his wife reached for the door. "Yeah, maybe." She exited then faced her husband, lowering her voice lest anyone hear. "But if it gets too bad, I'll have to call the estate agent and get something done."

"Yes honey, if that's what you want," Jeff replied, a wry smile touching his lips as they sauntered towards their front door. "I'm staying out of it."

"Typical male," Debra said, as they walked inside and closed the door.

* * * * *

Upstairs at number twenty-six Herbert, Olivia sat in the dark, the only twinkle of light coming from the two candles framing Nathan's photo.

It was one of her favourite pictures, taken on their trip to Bali when he'd been surfing Balangan Beach. She'd preferred to sit and sunbake, snapping random pictures of him in different poses. This one had him standing up on the board, arms outstretched, his smile almost as wide as the ocean itself.

What a great holiday it was.

Seems like such a long time ago.

When had it been? Three-no four-years?

She felt beside her for the scotch bottle, tipping the last of it into the glass, taking a sip and grimaced at its bitterness.

Not her drink of choice but she'd run out of rum so *this*, she swirled the liquid in her glass, would have to do.

She was tired all the time, and her head ached with a constant battering behind her eyes, which started to tear up for what seemed like the hundredth time that day.

Am I such a bad person to deserve all this shit?

Was it because I cheated on him?

Jesus.

Plenty of people do worse.

She looked back at the photo, at Nathan's eyes, so alive and full of energy. Laughing eyes. Her mind continued its tortuous game.

Were they mocking her? Laughing at her now after her little performance at the station?

Bet the whole crew are sitting around, joking about how pathetic I am.

He was so damn smug. Showing off his new girlfriend to the entire world.

"Goddamn bastard," she screamed, throwing the glass at the gold frame, knocking both it and one candle, before hitting the floor with a thud.

She put her face in her hands as she started sobbing. For several minutes, the only sounds heard, apart from the squawk of the cicadas, were the frenetic gasps and moans of a woman in despair.

Locking both arms around her legs, she swayed back and forth until the sobs lessened and she swiped at her eyes with a forearm.

The pounding in her head had increased in tempo and she brought out a steadying hand, raising herself from where she sat. She staggered to the bathroom to search the drugs cabinet for something, anything, to get rid of the pain.

Finding a half-empty packet of some yellow pills, she dropped six into her hand and swallowed them down with water from the tap.

Collapsing into bed, she entered a troubled sleep where the waves of the beach lapped at her feet as Nathan rubbed sunscreen onto her naked back. His touch felt soothing and lulled her into an uneasy slumber.

Outside in the lounge, a flickering flame gently touched Nathan's face, illuminating both it and the room in a radiant glow.

* * * * *

"Been up long?" Evie asked as she entered the kitchen, the enticing aroma of bacon and eggs filling the air. Not starving but unwilling to reject her mother's efforts, she walked over, giving Pauline a gentle hug. "Smells yummy."

"I didn't sleep much, so I thought I'd do something useful," Pauline said. "Been up since five, but I don't feel tired. Quite the opposite, in fact." She turned back to the stove, flipping eggs as Evie took a seat on one of the red leather stools. "I'll need to call Cameron soon, make sure he can come over and see me." She rubbed her hands down the frilled white apron she wore over a cotton shirt and matching pants. "Now that I've told you the truth of things, I think Cameron and Lizzie should know the truth too. They deserve to."

Evie nodded and looked down, realising the admission can't have been easy for her parent. To expose the secret she'd hung onto could risk the strong bond she had with her children.

Evie didn't hate her-that would never happen. What she felt most was a sense of disappointment, betrayal even, by both her parents.

Dad should've told me straight up.

I can't believe I was so stupid I didn't see what was going on.

Evie knew her parents were devoted to each other, having experienced a lot over their long marriage. It can't have always been easy, dealing with her and Cameron as they grew from teens to adults. Added to that was the pressure of her father's job. His wife had stuck by him all this time, offering support and creating a loving home worth coming home to each night.

Maybe that's what it was–their commitment to stick by each other no matter what obstacles they faced?

How would I know? I can't even find the right guy to marry.

Whatever the reason was, after learning the truth last night, Evie had thought long and hard about the state of her relationship with her father.

She'd ached to talk to Nathan about it. Sharing what she felt might have helped ease the confusion in her mind and her heart. Yet, just thinking about him made her despair even worse.

Remembering his betrayal, she'd so far refused to answer any of his calls or messages.

Whatever bullshit excuse he gave couldn't justify his behaviour and what he'd said to Mason.

For the time being, Evie put him from her thoughts to concentrate on how to deal with the issues closer to home.

"Do you think we can visit Dad today, Mum? Is that possible?" Evie voiced her thoughts and Pauline faced her with a surprised look. "It's what I need to do, I think. Now that I know what really happened, I mean."

Her mother turned off the stove, and moved to the bench, clasping her daughter's hands. "You don't have to love, if it's not what you want. That's not why I told you." She gripped them tighter. "But if you do want to see your father then, yes, we can go today. I'll need to make a call and check we can be included on the visitor's list. Sometimes they have a limit on the numbers."

Tears came to Evie's eyes as she sensed her mother's need to be forgiven, which Evie felt powerless to deny. She laughed, attempting to make light of the tension. "Of course, I want to. Let's eat up and hit the road."

The beaming smile that touched Pauline's face confirmed to Evie that she'd made the right decision as she held out a plate for her mother to fill.

Chapter 39

The country town of Ararat lay approximately 200 kilometres west of Melbourne city, the journey taking the women over two-and-a-half hours.

Typical of regional centres of its time, the town was dotted with examples of both modern and historical architecture. It owed much to its former glory days of the gold boom, which had peaked midway through the nineteenth century. The small tourism industry focused on showcasing several of the old-style buildings which included the original hospital and mental asylum, itself a popular attraction with regular ghost tours.

Ararat also had the dubious honour of hosting one of Victoria's minimum-security prisons, the Hopkins Correctional Centre. In its planning phase, residents of the town had raised a ruckus, worried about the kind of people the establishment would bring to the region. But in the years since its opening, the fact the prison housed only low to medium security prisoners had seen the locals more accepting of the facility, some even boasting about the benefit of encouraging more visitors to the town.

Arriving at the prison entrance, Evie noticed the unusually designed frontage incorporating white concrete panels in differing geometric shapes. She thought it looked more suited to an art gallery than a home for criminals.

Being a weekend, the carpark was full and a long queue had formed at the front doorway, most visitors with heads bowed, avoiding any eye contact.

Evie noted the eerie silence as she and Pauline joined the line, almost like they were attending a church service, with small whispers and several coughs the only sounds heard. The sky shone blue overhead, almost teasing in its cheeriness and Evie looked up, shading her eyes.

She wondered if her father got to appreciate the sky much these days-its vastness and clarity representing a freedom he'd been denied for months. He'd always liked to sit outside on the backyard deck, enjoying the view of trees and city skyline, glass of whisky in hand. Said it helped him relax.

Bet he missed it a lot.

Bet he missed a lot of things.

How would I cope in a place like this?

Two burly prison officers stood to receive the visitors, one holding a metal detector, the other a clipboard as he marked off names and checked IDs as each person filed in. Evie crept forward with her mother, showed her drivers licence and was told to proceed. Approaching the second officer, he held up a hand for her to stop as he waved the detector around her body.

She looked back at Pauline, who offered a slight smile and a shrug, no doubt used to the process as she'd been coming here for months. Experiencing the check-in procedure herself, almost made to feel like a criminal, Evie became even more conscious of the stress her mother had suffered over recent times.

Not to mention the hell her father was going through.

She couldn't help but stifle a sob at the thought and the officer gave her a concerned look. "Are you alright, miss?" he said, moving to stand in front of her. *God. Maybe he thinks I've got something hidden or secreted somewhere, planning to break her father out, like in Prison Break or something.* She offered a weak smile and tried to slow her racing heart rate, squeaking out a "No, I'm fine, officer," before moving to the next checkpoint, head bowed.

Several minutes later, the group shuffled like sheep toward another door, this one marked "Prisoner & Visitor Meeting Room" in bold metallic lettering, and Pauline laid a hand on her arm.

Before she could speak, one officer raised a hand, and all eyes focused on him. "Folks, now that we have checked you in, just a few ground rules." He pointed towards the large metal door behind him and continued. "Through this door are a number of tables and chairs. Go in, take a seat and we'll let the prisoners in shortly after." His eyes darted around the group, mouth tightly pursed without a smile or any hint of emotion, delivering the monotone instructions he'd no doubt recited many times before.

"Keep physical contact to a minimum, brief touches only. No shouting or yelling please or you may have to be escorted from the room. You have thirty minutes." He stood aside and moved towards the back of the room to take up his position with his co-worker as they kept keen eyes on the group.

Her mother's voice whispered in her ear. "I won't go in today, dear, not now that you're here. This visit is for you. Eric knows that you're coming."

An overriding sense of guilt hit Evie's chest like a sledge hammer knowing her mother was sacrificing her visitation time for her. "But Mum, can't we both…"

"No Evie, it's alright. I think you need time to talk together, not with me hanging over your shoulder. After all…," she bowed her head and looked to the side, "… it's my fault he's here. You need to spend some time together. I'll come visit next weekend."

"Excuse me, love." An elderly man brushed Evie's arm as he stepped around her to grab the door handle and move inside. She realised several other people also filed past, keen to meet up with their loved ones.

Evie hesitated, unable to move. Her heart pounded in her chest, and she felt a mixture of fear, guilt and regret all at once.

She hadn't seen her father for months, had blamed him for everything. All the shit she'd gone through, from the time he'd been marched out of the house by the police.

The man she'd looked up to her whole life.

The man who'd betrayed her with his lies.

But now, she knew the truth.

Now, it was Evie who had to face up to her own guilt.

She took a deep breath, glancing around the room. Apart from Pauline, she was the last one left to enter. Giving her mother a quick wave, she grabbed the handle and opened the door.

* * * * *

Rylee and Caroline were well into their Saturday shift at Firecom which was proving to be busier than usual.

Could have used Evie's help today, Rylee thought more than once, wondering what the drama was that had seen her co-worker disappear back to Melbourne at short notice. She'd asked Eileen, but the Manager had refused to say anything, other than it was "something personal".

Rylee hated not knowing what was going on.

I always share everything that happens in my life but some of the others... Well, they just like to keep secrets.

Caroline snapped her fingers, drawing Rylee's attention back to the radio, where she'd missed the last transmission.

Better keep focused on the job.

They had three incidents running, and she needed to keep on top of things.

Already there'd been three alarm activations, a not too insignificant car crash, and a lengthy water rescue at Josephine Falls.

"Bloody hell," Caroline cursed as the Triple 000 line started buzzing again. "Queensland Fire, where is the location of your emergency?"

"I'm at number twenty-four Herbert Street and I'm ringing about some smoke coming from my neighbor's house at number twenty-six."

"Okay Maam, so there's smoke from next door at twenty-six. Is it inside or outside the house?" Caroline queried.

"It's coming from inside, upstairs actually. I could smell something a while ago but now I can see smoke and it seems to be getting bigger." Debra Cunningham grabbed one of her boys, intent on pulling the cat's tail. "Billy, stop that right now."

"Is there anyone at home that you're aware of?" Caroline asked as she prompted the woman for more details while mapping the address.

Rylee's ears pricked at the conversation, waiting for more information to be transferred as Caroline continued talking.

"Well, I know who lives there but I'm not sure if she's home." Debra poked her head out the window of her bedroom, spying a red sedan parked in her neighbour's driveway. "Oh, but her car is there so I reckon she must be home. Should I go and… Shit, did you hear that," Debra's voice raised a level as there was a loud bang. "Oh my God, there's flames now. I think you guys need to hurry."

"Yes, Maam, don't worry. My partner is dispatching crews right now as we're talking. So just confirming, you don't know if anyone is inside and there are flames, right?"

"Yes, yes. Oh, I'm really scared. Should I leave my house too? I have my three boys with me." Debra's panic was reflected in her voice as the orange of the flames grew brighter and larger, stretching out beyond the window frame of the upper level to lick hungrily at the leaves of overhanging branches.

Caroline looked to Rylee who was already radioing crews and nodded, signalling the girl that this wasn't a hoax.

"7-11 Alpha, turnout to reported structure fire, Herbert Street, Mooroobool. Further details en route. All other agencies have been notified," the younger girl declared.

I hope they get there in time, Rylee thought, as Caroline advised Debra to get herself and her kids to safety before ending the call.

All they could do now was sit, and wait.

Chapter 40

Sweat began to bead in Evie's palms as she sat, tapping the cool white plastic of the table. Feeling as if she'd been waiting for ages when in fact it was only minutes, her eyes constantly darted to the door where the prisoners would enter.

What the hell is taking so long?

Glancing around, she noticed how calm and unaffected the other visitors appeared. A young woman in her twenties bounced a baby on her lap, the soft *cooing* and *ahhhing* keeping the young tot happy as they waited. The elderly man who'd pushed past Evie moments ago had a racing guide or something similar laid out in front of him and studied it with fixed intensity, flicking from page to page while he too whiled away the time.

Evie had nothing to keep her occupied and so gazed at the monochrome wall clock, its *tick tick* sounding louder with each passing second.

Just when she thought she couldn't stand it any longer, the black door opened with a creak and an officer stood back as a parade of men entered the room. Dressed identically in dark navy trousers and matching shirt, some had smiles on their faces, some looked anxious and others kept their gaze down as they entered, single file.

Evie spied her father immediately with his silver hair that was now a stark white, the once thick locks considerably thinner than she remembered. It was evident that recent events had definitely taken their toll.

Eric scanned the room, his eyes lighting up once he spied his daughter, and he almost skipped over to the table. She rose from her chair, still for a moment, before sobbing and putting her arms around him briefly, remembering the warning from the guard about minimal contact. Her father did likewise, his bear grip reminding her of years gone by when he'd thrown her high above his head as she squealed with delight.

He didn't look as though he could handle that now.

He's lost weight. Probably over twenty kilos by her estimation.

Her mother had said he'd been undergoing chemotherapy treatment for his cancer for several weeks already, the impact more than obvious.

"How's my girl?" He held her at arm's length, gripping tight as if afraid to let go. "I can't believe you're actually here. So happy you came. So happy." He smiled from ear to ear as he released her, motioning for her to sit. He glanced towards the guard eyeing them from the doorway. "Don't want to get scolded by grumps over there for getting all touchy, feely, heaven forbid!"

Evie laughed. *Trust Dad to make light of the situation. Just like the old days.*

"Yeah, they look scary, don't they? Her brows drew together, as she lowered her voice. "Seriously, though, I hope they're treating you alright Dad," she said, settling back in the chair.

"Yes darling, don't worry. They're looking after me pretty well, what with this damn illness and all." He pointed to his left arm, bandaged at the elbow where several bruises were clear. "The treatment they provide is the best you can get. It's not something I saw coming, that's all."

She breathed out, not knowing how to respond without sounding trite or clichéd. She decided truth was the best option. "I don't know what to say, Dad. It's just…"

"Don't worry about it, Evie".

They fell silent for a moment before both speaking at once.

"Darling, I understand you must…"

"Dad, I'm so sorry. I can't…"

They laughed and Eric pointed to her. "You first then. Seems we're both keen to talk. So much to catch up on."

"Yes," she said. "You could say that." She rubbed at her temple, not knowing where to start. She looked around the room, noting the two officers involved in conversation while most other prisoners chatted with their visitors. Even the old guy had ditched his racing guide to focus on a young inmate who looked to be little more than twenty years old.

Evie leaned in a little closer to her father. "Mum told me the truth, Dad. What really happened, I mean." His eyes widened and his skin paled while he straightened in his chair. "I can't imagine that you'd do something like that. Risking yourself for her, I mean. Especially your job."

Eric placed a hand on hers. "Evie. I…". He sighed and leaned forward on his elbows as they rested on the table. "How much did Pauline tell you?"

"Everything Dad. She told me about the gambling, the mortgage and debts she'd racked up. I can't believe it. Anyone else but Mum. But to cover up for her…

"Shh now," he whispered, looking around. "What's done is done. There's no changing it. I did what I did, which in hindsight, was bloody stupid. But the cash was there, sitting useless in plastic evidence bags, and I thought if I just… well, it was dumb, and I got caught out. Should never have even considered it. Not someone in my position. But there you go." He rubbed his hands up and down his legs several times. "We all do crazy things for love, sometimes. And I'd do anything for that mother of yours. We all would."

"Oh Dad." Evie started crying then, pulling a tissue from her pocket. Luckily, she'd remembered to stash some before the guards had taken her handbag at the entrance. Otherwise, she'd be sitting her now, a snivelling mess. She glanced up and noticed that her father's eyes were also wet with tears.

Evie fought to pull herself together and took his hand in hers. She'd forgotten how comforting his touch was, the strong hands that had soothed her as she grew up. She missed the hugs and the teasing pats on the head he'd been fond of giving her.

"You should have told us, you know. Me and Cam. We're both adults. If Mum was in trouble, don't you think we deserved to know about it?" Evie couldn't help but keep the frustration from her voice, even though she'd promised herself not to go too hard on him.

He's a sick man, Evie, give him a break!

"I considered it more than once, trust me." Eric rubbed his forehead and took a breath, his skin paling a little more as he answered.

"Are you okay, Dad? Do you need some water? I can get..."

"No, I'm fine darling. Just the after effects of the chemo hits me sometimes. I'll be bloody glad when it's over, which should be soon, I'm told." He smiled. "It was my decision not to tell you both. I know your mother was ashamed of her addiction and didn't want to bring embarrassment to the family. Pauline was petrified of running into people she knew so went to clubs out-of-town where she wouldn't be recognised. She's getting better though. Been seeing a counsellor and that's helping, from what she tells me. It kills me I can't be there for her."

"God, what a mess," Evie said. She looked around, noting everyone in deep conversation. One young couple now seemed to be arguing, trying hard to contain the tension as the male gripped the sides of his chair, his knuckles turning red.

Everyone has their own shit going on, just like our family, dealing with it anyway they can.

Yet, she'd chosen to run away.

From her father, her mother, Cameron, her friends and workmates.

Now she'd done the same thing with Nathan.

Run away before giving him the chance to explain.

Nathan.

I miss him.

As soon as I get back to Mum's, I'm going to…

"So, tell me all about life up north." Her father broke her daydreams. Evie experienced a sense of guilt for not focusing on him and pushed thoughts of Nathan aside. For the next while, she filled him on the details of her new life and Eric listened intently. Before long, their allocated visitation time was at an end.

"Five minutes people, then time's up," one of the officers interrupted her thoughts and a loud groan echoed around the room. Evie refocused on her father as he spoke.

"I'm so glad you came, darling. It's been a thrill for me to look at you again." The grip on her hands was intense, yet she understood his need for the contact. Being ripped apart from your loved ones was one of the hardest things anyone could go through.

But if anyone could make it, it was her father.

Evie was confident of that.

Beat the bloody cancer too.

"So, how's life in the Far North? Your mother says you're getting on well there. Also, something about a new fella, hmmm?" He chuckled. "I hoped you'd be able to find some happiness again. After Ben."

"Mum talks too much." Evie felt her cheeks redden, not surprised her mother had kept him up to date with her news. "I'm getting used to it but it's a lot different to home. Less traffic, though. And people. Which is a good thing."

"And the new man? How's that going?"

"Well, I… I'm not sure. We'll have to see. I think I may have…"

"Time's up, folks. Need to say your goodbyes. Remember to keep contact to a minimum." Officer bossy boots was taking charge again and moved to the black door, preparing to escort the prisoners back inside.

They both stood, as Evie fought off the tears she didn't want him to see.

The time had by gone so quickly.

"Goodbye darling, for now. I can't tell you… how wonderful it was to see you again. I hope you can come back soon." He took her into his arms, glancing at one guard who nodded as Eric embraced her, holding tight as she sobbed into his shoulder. "Don't get upset now. I'll be fine." He kissed her head. "You get things sorted with that fella of yours. I hear he's a good catch."

Evie smiled, rubbing at her wet eyes. "I will Dad. I'll try. And you look after yourself in here. I'll call you soon."

"That'd be great. Would make my day." He gave her another quick squeeze and moved away towards the exit, joining the queue of males as they walked single file out the door into the centre. Evie waved a goodbye as he smiled and disappeared from sight.

* * * * *

Pauline and Evie spent the drive back to Caulfield, each lost in their own thoughts. For Evie, the last few days had been a rollercoaster of emotion as she struggled to make sense of what was going on-with Nathan, her mother and father. Her world had been flung into chaos, and it was exhausting.

"Are you alright, Evie?" her mother shot her a concerned glance before returning her focus to the road. "I hope seeing your father wasn't too upsetting. It can be a shock, going into a place like that for the first time. I know I was petrified."

"I'm okay, Mum." She said. "It's not easy, that's for sure. It's just… I can't remember Dad ever looking like that, not even when he was working day and night on big cases. He was always the strong one." She returned her gaze to stare out the window. "But I guess even strong people find it hard when your freedom is taken away. I know I wouldn't cope."

"That's why your father's such an amazing man. That's why I… why I love him so much."

Hearing the break in her mother's voice, Evie touched her arm in support. "He loves you too, Mum. And you'll both get through this. They'll be better times ahead. You'll see."

"You're right darling. There's better days ahead," Pauline said, resuming the silence as they continued the trip home.

Later, as they turned into their street, Evie breathed a sigh of relief. It had been a long day. She'd be glad to sit back, relax and process everything that had happened in the peace and quiet of her bedroom. Yet, it seemed her mother had other ideas. "Let's go out for dinner, darling. To Angelo's perhaps? I don't feel like cooking tonight. What do you think?" her mother asked, as she parked in the driveway.

All I want to do is curl up in a ball in my baggy track pants with a wine, Evie mused, but didn't want to disappoint her mother, who seemed keen on getting out of the house.

"Sure Mum, that's fine. Let's shout ourselves a night out. I think we deserve it." Grabbing her handbag, she closed the door and headed to the entrance when her phone began to ring.

Her heart started pumping as she rummaged around in her bag-hoping, and dreading at the same time, it was Nathan calling.

What am I going to say?

She needed to get her thoughts straight before she spoke to him again.

Needed to fix the mess she'd created by running away.

Looking at the screen, her heart sank a little when she saw Rylee's ID instead.

What would she possibly be ringing for?

Chapter 41

"Rylee, for God's sake, calm down," Evie shook her head as Pauline cast an inquisitive glance her way. Evie shrugged in response. "I don't understand what you're saying. What crew at what fire?" She stepped into the kitchen, placing her handbag on the bench as her mother wandered off to freshen up for dinner.

"I said, there was a house fire today… it was a rough one, really impressive, double storey structure." *Rylee and her usual dramatics–nothing new there.* "Anyway, I just thought… well, that you'd prefer to know." The girl stopped and started talking to someone on the background, her voice raised. "Yes, Caroline, she deserves to be told. It's her boyfriend, isn't it?"

Evie's breath left her chest, and she began to feel sick. *House fire. Bad one. Did that mean Nathan was involved? Was he alright?*

"Rylee, are you there? Tell me what happened? Is… is Nathan, I mean, is everyone alright?

"Well, no, not really. The whole thing collapsed. The guys who went said it happened fast. That he shouldn't have tried to save that stupid cow. But it was his ex, and…"

"Olivia? Was it Olivia's house that was burning?" *This was crazy. What the hell had happened?*

I should never have left him. Or run out like that, no matter what he'd said.

But then I wouldn't have seen Dad and…

"I think you should come back, Evie. Back to Cairns. Nathan and Kenny are both in hospital and I'm not sure how bad they are. No one's saying anything. But I really think you should," Rylee said, her voice unusually sombre.

If Rylee sounded that serious, things must be bad.

Nathan must be injured. But how badly?

"Okay, Rylee. I'll come back, tonight, if I can. Just… keep me updated if you hear anything else, alright? I want to know what's happening," Evie started walking towards the door and headed upstairs, her mind racing.

"Yep, will do," Rylee said before disconnecting, Evie hearing the *beep beep* in her ear before she could reply. She stood at the top of the stairs for a moment, a million scenarios running through her mind. Of flames, Nathan's face, her father's smile, Olivia threatening her in the carpark.

Yet she just as quickly dismissed them, determined to focus on what she needed to do—get back home as quickly as possible.

"Mum, where are you?" Evie called out, almost running along the carpeted hallway. "I need to pack and go—as soon as I can".

* * * * *

The main entrance to Cairns Base Hospital was teaming with people, not unusual for mid-afternoon which often saw the Emergency Department full to overflowing. The external facade of red brick was adorned with over-sized red, yellow and green panels in a half-hearted attempt to brighten up the entrance, most likely more for the benefit of children than anybody else.

Evie took little notice of either the building's architecture or its facilities, her mind pre-occupied on seeing Nathan and discovering his condition.

She hurried to the Main Entry, halted in her tracks by the squealing siren of an ambulance as it sped towards Emergency. She took a moment to regain her composure, her head spinning after her frantic dash from Melbourne in the early hours of Monday morning. That had been the earliest direct flight with vacancies following Rylee's call.

Deciding that "Enquiries" was likely her best option, she scooted over to join the line of two ahead of her.

The sole occupier of the desk was an elderly, grey-haired woman, who wore thick-rimmed glasses and a mother-of-pearl brooch on her hospital apron.

"What name did you say, luvvie?" Evie overheard her ask the young woman at the head of the line. She fought down a silent urge to scream.

I don't have time for this, she thought, yet immediately felt remorseful as she noted the volunteer's smiling face as the woman moved away from the counter.

Chill out, Evie. She's doing the best she can. Your turn will come. Another minute and you'll be out of here.

Sure enough, thirty seconds passed and the male in front of Evie went on his way. Finally it was her turn.

"How can I help you today, luvvie?" the lady asked, her name badge identifying her as "Betty–Volunteer," which was worn with obvious pride.

"I'm here to see Nathan Barrett. He's a fireman and was hurt a few days ago."

Betty turned to the computer, tapping at the keys. Evie was impressed with her dexterity and speed, surprisingly agile fingers which belied her senior years. "Barrett." Her eyes scanned the monitor. "Yes, I may have seen that name. Just a moment." Evie had to forcibly restrain herself from tapping the counter in frustration.

Nearly there, her mind screamed.

"Yes," Betty offered seconds later. "Here he is. Are you a relative dear? He's in ICU and they don't just let anyone up there."

Evie's heart sank, yet she had a response ready. "Ah, yes. I'm his... his girlfriend. I've been away, you see. Interstate. Only just found out yesterday." Evie hoped she didn't sound as unsure as she felt as she announced their relationship status.

Was she Nathan's girlfriend? His lover? They'd never talked about it. Were they even a couple? Did she even have the right to be visiting?

Doubt consumed her but was pushed aside by a sudden determination and conviction she hadn't experienced before.

I'm entitled to be here, she reasoned. *I care about him. A lot. He's all I think about. I might even…*

"Oh, that's terrible dear," Betty said, jolting Evie's awareness to the present. "I heard something about a bad house fire in town. Someone died there too, I believe. Poor soul." She gave Evie's hand a light pat and pointed. "It should be fine. Take the lifts over there to the First Floor, and follow the signs to Intensive Care. There should be someone there who can help you find your man."

"Thanks so much," Evie offered, touched by the Betty's caring gesture, before scooting away from the desk towards the lift lobby. Her heart began a steady drumbeat once more as she found herself one step closer to her goal.

Chapter 42

Mason stood again from the uncomfortable waiting room chair, raising his arms overhead in a stretch. Spending hours on end with his six-foot five-inch frame squeezed a little too snugly into the vinyl wasn't his idea of fun but, hell, what was a little discomfort when his best friend lay out to it in a hospital bed.

He checked his watch again, having lost track of time within the sterile confines of ICU. He'd been in and out visiting over the last forty-eight hours, with little word on Nathan's condition other than the initial "He's come through surgery, which is a good sign," from Dr Singh, whom Mason hadn't sighted since.

What the hell is taking so long?

Why doesn't he wake up and start giving attitude to the nursing staff or something? Amusing them with his smart-ass jokes about fishing or fireman's hoses or…

Mason began pacing once again. Truth was—he was as scared as hell. Scared he'd lose his best mate.

Christ, we've known each other for a long time. We know things about each other, shared stuff that… it couldn't all be gone, could it? Not like this.

When you wake up, hero, he thought, *I'm gonna kick your ass from here to Rockie.*

The ping of a lift door sounded, and the *clang clunk* of a metal trolley broke the silence as an orderly turned the corner, walking past Mason with a slight nod. Not far behind him, a brunette followed, and he realised she was coming his way.

He was glad for any diversion he could get right now, whoever she was.

She arrived by his side, and addressed him. "I'm here to see Nathan Barrett. Do you know him? I noticed you're wearing the service uniform." She checked his name badge briefly. "I'm Evie."

He recognised his friend's latest squeeze from a photo Nathan had shown him and took her into his arms in a quick hug. "Hey, Evie. Glad you're here." He stood back before the embrace got too awkward and she offered a smile.

"I came as soon as I could arrange a flight. I was in Melbourne when Rylee called me." Her words came out quickly, and she was obviously on edge. "It's… a lot to take in, I guess. For everyone."

"Yeah, it hasn't been much fun these last few days, that's for sure."

"Have you heard anything? I mean, how badly is he hurt? And Kenny too. Rylee said they'd both been brought in. I…"

Mason took her arm as he led her back to the chairs of doom. "Let's take a seat and I'll fill you in." He eased his large frame down beside her. "What did Rylee tell you?" No doubt the young drama queen would have embellished the facts, knowing from previous experience Rylee's liking for gossip and exaggeration. She'd tried to hit on him once, but he'd put her in her place, for her own sake. Immature millennials weren't what he was looking for in a relationship.

Evie put her hands to her face, in an obvious attempt to stem the threatening tears. "Only that they were injured when the house collapsed. But that's it. It's just so…".

He didn't know Evie well at all, but from what he'd been told by Nathan, she appeared to be the real deal. Nathan had filled him in on her story, telling how her ex-fiance had dumped her over bad publicity and the fact her father was currently doing time for fraud.

Mason had to admit he was impressed by her obvious commitment to his friend. Most would find it hard to move on from a past like hers, yet here she was. Worrying about his mate, obviously head over heels, trying to keep her emotions under control. Proud yet stubborn. Dedicated and caring.

Qualities he admired in a woman. Seems he'd missed the boat, yet again.

You're a lucky bugger, Nathan.

Mason decided to be straight up with her and not pussy foot around. He didn't think she'd want that. He relayed the most recent news he'd been given from the duty nurse less than an hour before.

"Well, that is true, to a point," he said. "Unfortunately, Nathan copped the worst of it. For some stupid reason…"– he knew why his friend had broken protocol but kept that to himself– "… hero boy went back into the fire to look for Oliv… ah, the victim." Mason looked at Evie. "You do know whose house it was, don't you?" he asked.

Evie nodded. "Rylee said it was Olivia's. I can… I understand why he'd do that. Take the risk, I mean. Even though they weren't together, they kept in contact and I know she'd been hassling him with texting and calls. She'd gotten into trouble at work and wasn't coping very well. Nathan offered to help her." Her brows drew together, and she looked at Mason before asking. "I knew she had some issues, but… Did she set the fire deliberately? Is that what you think?"

Mason shook his head. "The investigators who checked the building formed the opinion that a candle upstairs started it. From what I remember of Olivia, and the other evidence they found including broken bottles and… well, it's more than likely she was knocked out on booze and pills. The toxicology report from the coroner will probably confirm it."

His voice cracked with anger as he went on. "I warned him to keep his distance. Especially with a possible promotion coming up." Mason didn't notice Evie's widening eyes and her quiet gasp, as he continued. "The crazy bitch was messed up, regardless of what happened with her job. I don't know how Nathan put up with her. She was no good for him. Told him lots of times. But there you go."

Evie looked like she'd seen a ghost and Mason offered a steadying hand to make sure she wasn't about to faint.

"Can I get you something? Water maybe?" Her voice had dropped to a whisper, as he looked at her with concern.

* * * * *

Mason's comments had jolted Evie's memory back to the fateful conversation she'd overhead at Nathan's house, the day she'd run off. *"I said, a girlfriend with a reputation like hers isn't going to do your chances at promotion much good. It's probably all around the station by now."* And Nathans' reply, *"That's crap. For one thing, she's not my girlfriend, she's just someone I feel sorry for."*

Had Mason been talking about Olivia and not her when he'd called Nathan that day?

Had she made a terrible mistake?

"Mason, can I ask you something? Did you call Nathan recently? About Olivia, I mean. I think I may have…"

A young nurse walked by and nodded at Mason in quick acknowledgment but continued on past, entering a patient's room as she pulled the sliding door closed behind her.

Mason turned to Evie. "I've seen her before, but that's not Nathan's room. I don't think she's looking after him." Mason pointed in the opposite direction down the passageway. "He's in Room 201. Can't get in, though. Only for immediate family, they say. Not that he has anyone left." He took her hand in his and shook it. "We're all he has now. They should let you in."

Evie breathed in, the smell of disinfectant filling her nose, amplifying her distaste for hospitals and waiting rooms.

She couldn't put it off any longer.

She had to ask him.

If Nathan didn't make it, she didn't know what she'd do next. Who she'd turn to?

"Just how bad is he, Mason?"

"The surgeon who operated said it was touch and go," Mason said. "The wooden beam falling onto his thick skull didn't help much and created a clot that settled somewhere in his brain." She couldn't contain a gasp as he continued. "They put him in an induced coma to relieve the pressure and I understand that's been working."

Evie shook her head as she wiped at her face. "And Kenny? What about him?"

Mason let out a throaty chuckle. "That old codger. Didn't he turn out to be the hero? Followed his senior inside the house, dodged falling beams and dragged Nathan out. I've been told he's ricked a few back muscles and received some burns on his hands when he took his gloves off, but apart from that, he's not too bad." Mason smiled. "Been milking it, though. Still in a ward downstairs, lapping up the attention from the nurses and that lady friend of his. I reckon he's just here for the free food."

Evie laughed, appreciating his attempt to lighten the mood. "That sounds about right, from what I've seen of Kenny. I know he and the other guys think a lot of Nathan, so

I'm not surprised at what happened. Behind Kenny's gruff exterior, he's all marshmallow, I bet."

"And a ladies' man too, apparently. That woman who visits the station-Moira, I think it is. She's been here night and day, visiting Kenny and taking him treats. She comes up here a lot too, asking how Nathan is and hassling the staff for updates. Seems like a real mother hen, that's for sure!"

"She's probably just worried, like we all are."

Evie stood, stretching her back to ease the tension caused by the stiff chair. Uncertainty and frustration starting to jangle her nerves, the edge of a tension headache beginning to creep into her front temple. *Damn, that's all I need right now*. She looked up and down the corridor, yet it remained empty of staff.

Now seemed like the perfect chance.

"What room did you say he was in?" she asked. Even though she hadn't been given clearance to see him, the fact there was no one around to ask negated that requirement. In her mind, at least.

"Room 201," Mason said, pointing left of where they stood. "Second from the end. I won't tell, don't worry," he offered a wink, and she took off before she lost her nerve.

Chapter 43

Evie's heart pounded as she neared the room, half terrified of being discovered by security who'd have no problem in escorting her from the building.

Stop being ridiculous, she thought. *I've done nothing wrong. I'm within my rights to be doing this.*

She checked the cardboard name identifiers pinned to each door as she passed-Taylor, Anthony in Room 199, Haddad, Eli in Room 200, Barrett, Nathan in Room 201. *Finally*. Evie tried to peer inside, yet the white vertical blinds kept prying eyes out and she saw nothing.

Once inside, she wouldn't know what to expect.

Evie peered down the corridor to where she'd left Mason and waved, which he returned, giving her a small amount of confidence.

She pushed the door open, it's weight surprising her and she used both hands to gain access. The room was larger than she'd imagined, designed to accommodate two beds, one of which was empty.

The maroon-coloured curtains that hung from metal frames around each bed contrasted starkly with the walls painted a shade of off-white. An array of equipment filled most of the remaining space which included an assortment of monitors, IV poles and cords.

The steady *beep beep* of a heart monitor was the only sound Evie registered as she approached Nathan who lay still, unaware of her presence.

An oxygen mask covered his nose and mouth, and a plastic tube connected his left hand to a bag containing IV fluid. A thick crepe bandage circled the top of his head.

The image was as shocking to Evie as it was frightening.

Seeing Nathan so vulnerable like this, lifeless almost, sent her heart into overdrive. She wondered that he couldn't hear its drumming a steady beat as she fought to keep her panic under control.

Evie scanned the room for a chair, noting one in a corner, and lifted it gently off the floor to not make a sound. Ridiculous really, when all she wanted was for him to wake up. But any loud noises may also attract the unwanted attention she desperately wanted to avoid. She didn't want to be kicked out. Not now.

Evie took a limp hand in hers as she leaned in close. "Nathan. It's Evie. I'm here," His skin was warm to the touch, and she rubbed at the dark hairs, before placing her lips there for a light kiss.

"I'm sorry I couldn't get here sooner, but I've been in Melbourne. I even visited Dad." She couldn't fight the tears any longer, and they fell as she talked. "I'm so ashamed I ran away without explaining but I… I heard your call with Mason and I… I just assumed you were… Oh shit." She let go of his hand and stood beside him.

"It's because of you I went, you know. All your talk about forgiveness and not regretting the past–it's all because of you, Nathan. You've made my life so happy. I know you wouldn't do anything to hurt me or talk about me behind my back." She thought back to the dreaded call before she'd left, realising what a terrible mistake she'd made in not talking to him about it, not trusting him enough. "I… please just… come back, please. Nathan. You're everything to me."

She sat back down, burying her head on his arm and wept. He remained motionless as she continued to sob. Just how long she gave in to her grief, she wasn't sure.

It was only when she sensed the door opening Evie attempted to wipe her face and turn around.

A middle-aged nurse stood before her, hands on hips with a disapproving scowl upon her face.

"And just what are you doin' in here Missy, might I ask?"

* * * * *

Moira exited the lift onto the First Floor, having just come from visiting Kenny. He was such a kind man, sweet and funny, the complete opposite to most of the men she'd known in the past. *He doesn't take life too seriously*, she thought, as she headed towards Nathan's room. *Something I should do more myself.*

Perhaps we wouldn't make such a bad match after all.

She was surprised, if not slightly alarmed, as she noted a group of people standing outside Nathan's room and wondered if there'd been any news. She spotted his friend Mason standing next to Nurse McCafferty who seemed to be chastising a young woman Moira didn't recognise at first glance.

As she drew closer, she realised it was Nathan's girlfriend Evie who stood red-faced as the nurse continued her rant. They'd met on the night of the trivia quiz and had seemed most pleasant. "I understand you say you're his partner, Miss, but you can't just waltz into an ICU room without permission," Moira heard McCafferty say in her strong Irish lilt.

"Is everything alright here?" Moira said, trying to ease the tension surrounding the group. It was obvious the young woman had been crying.

Moira embraced Evie in her arms, hoping to lessen some of the nurse's aggravation. "Evie, I'm glad you made it, dear. Exactly what Nathan would need, I'd say." She'd become used to the brusque yet efficient manner of the head ICU nurse, knowing McCafferty's bark was worse than her bite.

"So, you know this lassie too, Moira?," McCafferty said, a wry smile on her lips. "You'd best not be pulling the wool over my eyes."

"No, not at all, Mavis. I wouldn't dare. But I can say that Evie is most definitely Nathan's partner. She deserves to be here as much as… no, more than, anyone." Moira's voice dropped, and she led Evie back a few steps. "Why don't we go to the Cafeteria and grab a coffee, dear? I'll fill you in on everything."

Evie nodded and the two women left Mason and McCafferty standing for a moment before the nurse wandered off, no doubt content Evie's identity had been sorted out.

Chapter 44

Tuesday evening and for those keeping vigil at the hospital, the wait for any news on Nathan continued.

Content that Kenny was sleeping now, Moira tiptoed out of the room into the bustling corridor filled with nurses, empty trolleys and a cleaning lady wielding her mop along the tiles.

Checking her watch, she noted it was already after nine, surprised she'd been sitting and talking for well over three hours. Kenny's injuries from the fire were serious but not severe, *thank goodness*. Regardless of the fact he claimed he'd need "at least six months" off work to recover, he'd come out of it better than Nathan.

Nathan.

Moira was more than worried about him.

The last update she'd received had been that he was still in the induced coma with no visible signs of awareness. *Yet.* McCafferty had made a point of emphasising the last word to give Moira hope that everything would be alright-that he'd wake up soon.

Moira prayed that he did. More than once.

Jack would have laughed at the sight–her kneeling down in front of the flickering candles of the chapel, praying to a God she had no right talking to.

She'd spent her life avoiding churches like the plague, having grown up with devout Catholics as parents who'd often berated her choice of friends and any opportunity she could to have fun. Well, her kind of fun anyway.

In her early years, she'd been subjected to more than enough religion, philosophy and rules to last her a lifetime, not to mention the occasional beatings from her *holier than thou* father. When she'd met Jack, he'd seemed like the answer to her prayers.

"Footloose and fancy free," that's me, she'd told him on their first date, with an inflated sense of bravado. He'd been quick to see through her facade, though. He'd always been sensitive to the troubles of others and willing to help those in need. Before long, he'd won her over with his attentive manner and adoration.

Too bad she'd failed to appreciate it.

Moira sighed and started towards the lift before thinking better of it. Evie and Mason had been regular visitors to Nathan's room over recent days, and she didn't want to overstep her mark.

Fighting the urge to return to the ICU, Moira decided to have a coffee instead. Perhaps she'd pop in before going home. She took a seat in the downstairs café, ordering a latte from the waitress before leaning back and closing her eyes as her mind wandered back to a past she'd not thought of in an age.

* * * * *

"Bill, I told you before, I can't leave Jack now. It's... well, it's not the right time, can't you understand? I can't take his boy away from him. Not yet."

Bill grunted, repositioning his arms from where they'd cradled Moira's naked body and raised them, placing both behind his head. She could tell from his sudden withdrawal that he wasn't taking her plea well. But she had no choice. She couldn't leave Jack and take their son away. Not now. Maybe never. It would kill him, she knew it would. He idolised the boy, that much was obvious. Probably more than he did her.

But she didn't mind. Not really.

It wasn't like she'd been faithful to him, all these years.

Yet, she couldn't imagine having to give Bill up either.

There was something compelling about the rugged ambulance driver she couldn't resist.

Built like a young Kirk Douglas, complete with sexy dimple in the chin, he made her feel more like a woman than any other man ever had. *What that man could do with his hands–well, he was certainly talented in that department!* The spark that had ignited years earlier still burned, despite his rough edges, the chronic smoking habit and sometimes fiery temper.

He'd never hit her though. That was something she wouldn't tolerate, no way. Not from him. Not from any man.

She'd seen enough of her mother's beatings over the years from her *oh-so-righteous* father to have made that vow to herself. If it hadn't been for Jack having the guts to stand up to the old man, who knows how she would have ended up? Probably dying before her time–like her mother before her. She'd only been fifty-two years old.

Moira owed Jack for getting her out of there.

Bill interrupted her memories. "I think you should do it. Just leave. You can bring the kid, if that's what you want. I know I said I don't like them, but I'd put up with it for you. I think we should move away, ya know. Somewhere away from this crap town." He moved to roll over, grabbing for the half-empty packet of Benson & Hedges on the dresser, shaking it as one fell into his fingers. "We should do it, babe."

Moira had felt fear grip her chest as she watched him strike the match and put it to the cigarette before shaking the flame away.

Where had this come from?

He'd never talked about leaving, or children, or not being happy in the town they'd grown up in.

Why now?

She sat up, resting on both elbows, and turned towards him. "Has something happened, Bill? Is that what all this is about?" She waited as he sucked on the smoke, the air filling with the fumes she detested but put up with, anyway. She didn't want to sound like a nagging wife.

"Na. Not really. I'm just getting tired of all this sneakin' around shit. I want to take you out, show you off in public, not have to hide all the time like bloody criminals or something. And I may have plans too. To get…"

"I've told you–it's not that easy. I can't just--".

"Yeah, yeah, I've heard the spiel. You can't walk out on *poor old Jackey boy* 'cos that would hurt his feelings, and…"

"Shut up, Bill. Just… shut your big fat mouth for once," Moira jerked upright, placing her legs on the carpeted floor. She missed his look of surprise, and he took another drag of his smoke as she sashayed off.

At this point, she wasn't concerned about any hurt feelings on his part.

Things were getting way too intense.

Why couldn't he just leave them as they were?

If he forced her to choose, she wasn't certain what she'd do.

She loved both men–each in their own way.

And her little boy was stuck right in the middle. His face swum before her, the light brown eyes and the small cleft developing in his chin–just like his father's.

Her face paled, and she kept her face hidden.

Didn't want him suspecting she'd been keeping secrets from him he didn't need to know.

Not now.

Not ever.

Chapter 45

Nathan gave a spluttered cough, trying to clear the smoke from his lungs but there was something over his face. Not the usual breathing apparatus, he could tell. This was lighter and smaller.

His eyes were closed, and he seemed to have trouble getting the lids to obey his command to open.

What's going on?

Did I go on a bender last night?

After what seemed like a hell of an effort, his lids fluttered and opened, and his sense of panic eased slightly as they revealed a room full of monitors, wires and faded maroon coloured draw curtains.

A hospital.

He was in a hospital bed.

But why?

He lifted his head, only to realise it was a big mistake-the dull *thump thump* sending a short sharp burst of lightning fast pain that left him groaning.

He dropped his head down on the pillow and let out a long breath. Placing a hand to his brow, he felt the bandage wrapped tight, lifting it to ease the pressure, if only for a second.

His throat felt parched, like dry sandpaper scraping his windpipe, and the smell of acrid smoke seemed to fill the room. *Funny*. It appeared clean and airy, yet he couldn't get the sensation out of his head as he racked his brain once again.

What's going on?

Is Evie here somewhere?

Or Mason? Where is the big lump?

He heard muted voices nearby, no doubt from the staff outside, yet no one entered.

Maybe they think I'm still asleep.

Nathan saw another shape in his periphery and tried raising a hand to grab their attention, yet the restriction of the attached wires had him give up that idea and it flopped back to his side, useless.

So much for that idea, genius!

Just have to wait for someone to show up, I guess.

He tried to slow his racing mind and think of the last memory he had. An image of Evie crept in, laying asleep in his bed, and he smiled. He saw Coops eating from his bowl, then he was at the front door, looking for someone.

What the hell was that about?

Nathan rubbed at his temple, trying to make sense of it all but for the life of him, the reason he'd gotten himself stuck here, attached to God knows how many machines, continued to elude him.

Realising his desperate need for water, he knew he couldn't wait any longer, the burning razor scraping his throat teasing in its intensity.

Looking to his left, he spied what appeared to be a buzzer on the wall and prepped his mind to make the effort.

Raising himself on both elbows, the constriction of a second tightly wound bandage around his chest caused the breath to catch in his throat. With his face still covered by the oxygen mask, the thought crossed his mind of feeling like an animal caught in a trap, unable to escape the confines it'd fallen into yet desperate to fight its way to freedom.

Just sitting upright for him right now was a fight he was prepared to take on—and win.

He waited another few seconds before shifting the weight to his left, at the same time moving his right arm over towards the red button. A sharp pain shot down his entire side, but he pushed through it, straining forward another few inches.

So close, dammit!

The pain intensified, and he began to feel nausea rise in his gut, yet he kept going.

Closer, almost there.

Got it! His finger touched the buzzer, and a loud "Errrrrrrrrrrrr" noise broke the silence, hopefully sending its signal to someone outside.

"Aaaarghhhhh," Nathan muttered through the mask, as he fell back into the mattress, his chest heaving with the effort.

Shit. It hurts like hell.

It seemed like ages later when a nurse entered the room, a smile lighting her round face as she approached his bedside.

"My goodness, you're finally awake." She spoke with what sounded like an Irish brogue, her words difficult to understand, yet he sensed her enthusiasm for her job.

"Now, don't you move a thing, Mister, not until we get one of the doctors to give you the once over. Don't want you getting any more hurt than what you already are." Nurse McCafferty leaned towards one monitor, checking the readout before turning back to face him. "You gave us all a scare, you know. Weren't sure whether you were comin' or going' but it's good that you're back now."

Nathan knew nothing about scaring anyone or where he'd been going, just wanted to tell her about his throat and the fact that it was bloody torturing him. "Wa.... ter," he croaked, pointing weakly to his mouth and her eyes widened with awareness.

"Oh, I'm sorry, love. You want water. I'll get you some." She made to exit the room and turned. "I'll contact the doctor first then bring you a glass. Be as quick as I can". With that, she was gone.

Nathan hoped she'd be quick but since she was of a rather large build-he guessed over 120 kilos and aged well into her fifties-it could be a while before she reappeared.

Still, someone had answered the call, and soon he'd be able to find out what had happened.

He hoped it wasn't anything too serious.

* * * * *

Moira returned to the present as the waitress placed a coffee mug in front of her, smiling in amusement that she'd caught her customer napping.

In truth, the girl was mistaken. Moira had been transported back in time, not sleeping at all.

God help her-she'd tried over the years to erase the memories from her thoughts, but that never worked. Not if she was honest with herself.

With a sigh, Moira thanked the waitress and sipped the steamy brew.

This terrible fire that had everyone on edge.

Checking her watch, Moira decided to take a chance and check on Nathan once more before leaving. Her constant concern was no doubt becoming obvious, but she didn't care. She couldn't help herself.

As she exited the lift and walked down the passageway, Mavis McCafferty swept past her, a determined look set on her face as she entered Nathan's room.

Moira peered through the glass but wasn't able to see much, her view blocked by the burly woman busy at Nathan's side. Moira wasn't sure what had prompted the visit to his room—perhaps his meds needed checking?

Was it too much to hope that…

She stepped back as McCafferty flung the door wide before re-joining her in the corridor. "Excellent news, Moira. It looks as though the boy's awake." She beamed and patted the visitor's arm. "I'd best find the doctor and let him know. He'll want to give his patient the once over, just to be sure everything's as it should be." With that, she hurried off at a skip, her cheery demeanour infectious as she scurried down the hallway.

Moira couldn't keep the grin from her face at hearing the news.

He was awake.

Thank God. Her prayers had been answered.

See Jack, she whispered to herself. *I told you he'd be fine.*

Fighting the urge to run into the room and embrace Nathan, she remembered she didn't have the right to barge in unannounced.

Best to wait and let the staff get on with it.

She took a seat outside Nathan's room, her mind wandering once more as she waited for McCafferty's return.

* * * * *

Moira had made her way home after leaving Bill's place, careful to take the back streets to avoid any unnecessary gossip in case she was spotted in the rural district.

Bill's parents had been cane farmers going back generations, and although they'd passed on, he'd been lucky to score rent-free accommodation from his Uncle Jimmy, albeit a rudimentary shed with little in the way of mod cons.

Only a few people knew of their relationship-some local workers who saw Moira's comings and goings-and Uncle Jimmy, whom they both trusted enough to protect their little secret.

Moira couldn't deny the thrill of excitement ignited by their affair, although at other times, she experienced guilt and shame. The time spent with Bill brought some much-needed colour to her dreary days, usually occupied with keeping house, mothering her son or baking scones for the local fete.

She knew a lot of women could find purpose in those things, but she personally felt little inspiration in remaining a member of that particular club.

She arrived home after midday that particular day, making herself a mug of tea and sitting in the kitchen as she sipped the warm brew.

Snippets of her last conversation with Bill had wandered into her thoughts, yet she pushed them away.

It was all too hard. Why can't he go on with things just the way they are? Everyone's happy, aren't they? Jack has no idea and...

The ringing of the telephone interrupted her and placing her mug down, she reached for it from the cradle on the wall as the harried voice of the local school principal came over the line.

"Mrs Barrett. It's Mr Harkness here. I'm just ringing about…"

"Oh dear, is everything alright, Mr Harkness? I hope nothing's wrong." Moira's heart rate had risen on hearing the principal's voice, knowing he'd only call during school hours if it was something bad.

The older man's voice assumed a calming tone. "No, it's not too serious, I believe. It's just, well, your son have broken his arm after falling off one of the monkey bars. We've called—"

"Oh, my goodness, no," Moira said, as her mind conjured up grotesque images of tiny bones exposed through bloodied skin as her little man crumpled over in pain. *The cheeky monkey*, she thought. *Always climbing up trees and anything he could. Jack was always encouraging him to get out and get exploring, never sitting still.*

"It's alright, Mrs Barrett. We've called the ambulance and they've just arrived and are checking him over. If you're able to come down to the school as soon as you can, we'd appreciate it. I think having a parent here for support would help."

The Principal's reassurance did little to ease her anxiety. *She needed to be there. Now.* "I'll come straight away," Moira said, grabbing the car keys and her handbag while she talked. "Tell him I'm coming please. He should know." She hung up before the principal had a chance to reply as she bolted out the door, the half-drunk cup of tea left cooling on the tabletop.

Her thoughts scattered, it had only been when she spied the ambulance parked out the front of the school that her sense of dread intensified. *Surely it couldn't be him? There's more than one ambulance in town. I mean, is he even working today?*

She'd done her best to keep Bill and her son apart, neither having set eyes on each other before and Moira intended to keep in that way.

Yet, it appeared fate had other plans in store.

As she approached the group gathered in the junior playground, Mr Harkness waved her over. Taking in the scene, Moira worst fears were realised.

She felt physically sick as she spied Bill's crouching form tending to a child, a female ambulance assisting. His attention was absorbed on providing aid yet as Moira knelt beside him, his steely eyes focused on hers with an intensity she hadn't seen before.

It frightened her to the core.

"Well, well. Look now little fella," he ruffled the boy's hair, "Mummy's here now. I told you it's all gonna be fine."

Moira wasn't certain if anyone else sensed the sharpness in his tone, but at that moment, she didn't care as she embraced her son, tears in her eyes. "Oh darling, what've you done to yourself? It must hurt something terrible."

"Oh, Mum. It's not that bad. They gave me a needle and now it doesn't hurt so much," the young boy said, a weak smile slightly undermining his words.

"Yep, he's been a real brave boy. Just like his *Dad* would want him to be, hey champ?" Bill said, looking at her with daggers, and Moira's eyes widened, shaking her head in response.

Later, he mouthed in her direction, leaving little doubt in her mind that a huge can of worms had just been opened that had little chance of being closed again.

* * * * *

Hours later, with her son safely ensconced in the children's ward at the local hospital, Moira stepped outside and walked around the rear towards the Ambulance bay. Bill had said he'd meet her there once his shift ended, and as she turned the corner, he stood leaning against his car, cigarette in hand.

He threw it on the ground as she approached, stomping it down before striding towards her.

"What the hell was that?" he said, stopping in front of her.

She knew full well what he was talking about.

"Bill, calm down for a minute. I—"

"Calm down! Why the hell should I? It's bleedin' obvious he's mine and you tell me to *calm down*! Jesus Moira—"

She turned to check that no-one was within earshot. Thankfully, the area was deserted. She grabbed his hands, attempting to ease the tension with her touch, but he pushed her away.

"Were you ever going to tell me? About the boy, I mean?" Bill said, hurt reflected in his gaze. Moira realised she had to be honest with him now. She didn't want to lose him. Wasn't ready to give him up. She loved him. This was too important to be fabricating lies and stories.

"No, I wasn't, Bill. You claimed you never wanted kids—"

"Yeah, but even so—"

"So, I didn't see why it should matter to you. As far as everyone's concerned, he's Jack's son. Why not leave it that way?" She took his hand, and this time, he gripped hers firmly. "It's best to forget about it. To leave things as they are. You don't have to feel responsible or that you owe me anything. I never expected that. I love you and—"

"Moira, I could do that but…," he hesitated before continuing. "I've had a job offer. In Brisbane. To head up the Ambulance department there." He released her, running a hand through his sandy hair. He avoided her gaze for a moment before staring at her. "We could go–you and me,… and the boy. If that's what you want."

Her mind began racing in a hundred different directions at his news, and she looked at him, confusion in her eyes. "What?… I don't… I can't—"

"Why not?" he returned to her, pulling her closer. "We can. Just leave this dump. It's what you've always wanted to do. You hate the small-town life." He tilted her chin towards him. "I thought you said you loved me."

"I… I do. You know I do. But…"

"No buts, Moira. Not after today. You need to choose." He cupped her face and kissed her lips before turning towards his car. "I'm sorry but I can't wait anymore. It's either Jackie boy, or me. With or without the kid. It's your decision." With a wave, he got inside the car and drove from the carpark, leaving her standing with tears running down her face as she touched a hand to her mouth.

It was some time later before she composed herself, walking in a daze towards the front entrance of the Hospital. She'd go back in and visit her boy, making sure he was comfortable for the night before returning home.

Home.

Images of its tidy neat appearance danced before her yet didn't bring the sense of comfort she'd hoped for. Instead, it felt like a prison, caging her to a life for the next twenty or thirty years to an existence of boredom and routine.

Choose, he'd said.

By the time she re-entered the Hospital entrance, she'd made up her mind.

Ten days later, she drove out of town, leaving most of her possessions behind and a note to Jack propped against the sugar bowl on the kitchen table.

She drove off alone.

Chapter 46

Evie stood at the food counter, contemplating whether she'd be able to stomach the bland chicken toastie she'd ordered even though she knew she needed to eat something.

After several days and nights of waiting for news of Nathan's condition, she'd about exhausted the somewhat limited menu this place offered. For all she cared, they may have been serving the very best cordon bleu cuisine, yet it still would have tasted like cardboard.

She'd felt sick to the stomach for days-from the time she'd received the call from Rylee, during the excruciating flight back, to meeting Mason here at the hospital and spending time with Moira and Kenny as he recovered from his injuries.

She was nice. A real motherly figure, fussing around everyone. She seemed as worried about Nathan as Evie was. A little odd perhaps, but understandable. She knew Moira's son was a fireman too. Maybe Nathan reminded her of him?

Dammit. Why didn't he wake up?

She felt as if she'd been swept up in a gigantic whirlwind, not unlike one of the cyclones that often raged through the region this time of year.

Cyclone Olivia. That's what it was.

Damn her for putting everyone through this.

Yet, as the thought crossed her mind, Evie berated herself.

Don't be such a bitch.

Nathan wouldn't blame her like that.

And he'd be right.

She'd been mixed up, dealing with issues that obviously got too much for her to handle. But to end up like that…, well, it didn't seem fair, somehow.

People lost their way sometimes-she could see that now.

Life gets complicated and bad decisions get made. Sometimes decisions that can cost your life.

Evie stifled back a sob and hoped no one noticed. Thankfully, the café was empty of customers, not yet time for the mid-morning rush.

She thanked the attendant for her order and left, dodging the hospital cleaner as she shuffled a bedraggled mop around the tiled floor. The woman appeared unfazed by the water and suds slopping around her booted feet and for a moment, Evie envied her almost casual regard for the world.

What she wouldn't give to have none of this drama, none of…

Shut up, Evie. Just stop!

There'd been a lot of self-talk over the last few days and it was becoming exhausting.

"It is what it is—let's move on," her father would say.

Memories of him filled her head, especially of the last time they'd talked.

At least she'd had some resolution in that part of her life.

Proud of what she'd done, the relief she'd experienced after seeing him, had been like a huge weight had lifted off her shoulders.

She couldn't wait to tell Nathan about it.

Evie returned to the foyer, pressing the *UP* button to take her back to resume her vigil. She briefly considered returning to the Chapel where she'd sat last night for an age, praying for him to wake up or give some sign of life. *Anything.*

But she'd been away for too long now and felt an urgency to get back to his side and just sit.

And wait.

* * * * *

As the metal doors clanged open, Evie sensed something had changed.

There was more noise, for one thing, and it seemed like there were twice as many staff, as several white-coated doctors stood in deep discussion at the nurses' station.

Evie thought she spied McCafferty someway down the corridor, her guess proved correct when the woman waved a hand in the air, motioning Evie forward.

"He's awake, Missy," she said as Evie scurried towards her, resisting the temptation to break into a sprint. "Your boy's woken up. 'bout time, too." They both stood outside Nathan's room. "Just getting the doctor to check him out first, then you can see him."

Evie couldn't stop tears of happiness from falling as she embraced the friendly nurse in heartfelt thanks. "Oh, McCafferty, that's the best news. Thank God." She craned her neck, trying to grab a glimpse of what was happening inside but as usual, the blinds were drawn, and she couldn't see a thing. "Did he seem… I mean, do you think he's okay?" She failed to control the fear in her voice, knowing there were never any guarantees when it came to brain injuries. She'd be naïve to think there may be no complications.

"Well, from his grunting and carrying on for water, he seemed pretty '*with it*' but let's just see, shall we? Dr Smithers is with him now and he's one of our best." McCafferty wandered off, leaving Evie no choice but to wait it out once more.

It was then Evie noted Moira's presence as the older woman approached. "Isn't it wonderful news, dear?" She embraced Evie briefly before stepping back. I bet you can't wait to see him for yourself."

Evie found herself lost for words, the stress of the last days and weeks suddenly overwhelming. Yet what she most felt now was relief.

What seemed like an age later, the medical team departed and Nathan's surgeon approached her wearing a large grin. "Seems like your fella has come through his ordeal pretty well." Dr Smithers gave her arm a light pat. "He'll need observing for a few days and strong painkillers for the other injuries, but as far as the clot is concerned, that seems to have gone. He should be back to normal following an amount of rest and recuperation." The doctor was passed a chart by another nurse and perused it as he spoke. "You can go in now. I believe he's waiting to see you. All the best to you both," he offered, walking off.

"Thanks Dr Smithers. Thanks for everything," Evie said, unable to keep the huge smile from her face as she entered the room.

* * * * *

Nathan was becoming annoyed with the fussing and fretting over his condition, even though he knew the staff had a job to do. It was obvious he was being well looked after and so needed to curb his patience, yet it was just about to run out. Big time.

From the time he'd woken up till now, the events of recent times had drifted back into his consciousness in bits and pieces.

He'd remembered Evie's leaving without a word, and how empty he'd felt in the days since. The stress of not being able to contact her; him racking his brain to try and work out what he'd done to make her leave like that.

He remembered too the callout to the fire, and the panic he'd felt when realising it was Olivia's house burning, along with his dash into the building to get her out.

He still knew nothing about her fate, having no recall of anything after that.

Nathan had been asking to see Evie since he'd taken that first delicious sip of water from the nurse with the accent. "In time, laddie, in time," she'd said, frustrating the hell out of him. Evie had been haunting his mind for ages now, yet he wasn't even sure if she'd been contacted, let alone cared about what happened to him.

After running out like she had, he'd had no clue what the reason was, but he didn't care. He knew now, beyond any doubt, that he wanted her in his world. She'd brought a light into his life that hadn't been there before, one that had given him real hope that he'd found someone to share his life with.

He'd never been more sure…

His prayers were answered when the door opened, and *she* walked in.

He wasn't sure if he was dreaming at first, the bright glow of the fluorescent light illuminating her silhouette in a white halo effect as she stood unmoving. He held out a hand and croaked, "Evie? Is that you?" his throat still scratchy and parched.

Her soft voice confirmed his vision wasn't his imagination going crazy.

"Yes, it's me, Nathan. They finally let me in," she said, rushing forward and leaning close, touching a soft hand to his face. "Thank God you're awake. I'm so happy." She lowered her lips to his, the featherlight touch filling his heart. "I've been so scared." She dragged a chair close to the bed and sat, resting her head on his uninjured arm.

"I know babe. I'm sorry." He ran his hand over her hair, its softness familiar as he breathed in her scent, the light fragrance of vanilla she was so fond of using. "Don't cry, now," he said, noticing the tears welling in her eyes. "I'm not worth it."

She gently punched his good arm. "Don't you dare say that, you pig," she laughed then. "You're more than worth it. You know you are."

He made to move closer to her, wincing as the pain of his shoulder made its presence known. He ignored the pain.

"Am I?" he laid intense eyes upon her. "Worth it, I mean?"

She said nothing for a moment, her eyes glowing with determined focus as she bent forward, placing her lips on his. His mouth rejoiced with her touch, as she teased and tempted him, stirring parts of him into action that had lay dormant for days.

She eased away, touching fingers to his forehead, playing with the hair that fell onto his brow.

"I love you Nathan. I realise that now. Even before I left…"

"I know, Evie."

"I made the biggest mistake and was such an idiot. Thinking the worst when you were only—"

He raised a hand to cup her face. "Shh. Don't worry about it anymore. It doesn't matter. It—"

"But it does matter. I ran away, not giving you a chance. Mason told me. About the call and that you were talking about Olivia and…"

"The call?" Nathan dropped his hand and gave his head a thump, startling her. He shook his head. "The morning I spoke to Mason about the promotion and… Jesus. What an idiot I am! I should have realised you'd heard it. It just didn't register." He touched her face lightly. "But you should know, Evie, I'd never say things about you like that, would never think that of you." He gave her the full extent of his smile. "How could I? You're the girl I love. More than anything."

* * * * *

Mason chose that moment to enter the room, having been informed moments before of his friend's recovery. "Hey bro, 'bout time you woke up and joined the party. I'm gonna kick…"

He smiled as he realised both Nathan and Evie were too preoccupied to notice his presence. Locked in each other's arms, it appeared the happy couple had made up and were back on track in the romance game.

Good for them, he thought, not without a touch of envy.

With a smile, he backed up towards the door, waving a hand to no one in particular. "Guess I'll come back later, bro."

Chapter 47

Several weeks later and the middle of May brought with it cooler weather, a timely reprieve from the heat of the summer months.

Evie smiled to herself, standing in the holding yard of the Fire Station currently adorned with streamers and balloons for the *Welcome Home, Boys!* party.

Nathan and Kenny had recovered well from their injuries and although he was yet to return to work, Nathan was hopeful he'd receive the all-clear from his doctor soon.

Spying him now as he chatted to Mason and another colleague, Evie's heart swelled as she thought of just how close she'd come to losing him-not only through the threat of the fire but also her stubborn lack of trust which had seen her flee to Melbourne.

In hindsight, it hadn't been such a bad thing. Being able to make peace and reconnect with her father had her believing she was the luckiest girl in town.

She'd learned a lot about herself these past weeks, no thanks in part to poor Olivia. She'd been buried without fuss in the cemetery next to Ambulance Headquarters and Evie and Nathan laid flowers at the plot last week when they'd visited the site. Nathan had arranged for a plaque to be laid for her. "It's the right thing to do," he'd said.

Pauline interrupted her thoughts as she came to place an arm around her daughter's waist. "Darling, you look lovely in that dress. I love the sunflower design, so happy and bright.

Evie laughed, placing a kiss on Pauline's cheek. "Thanks, Mum. You look great too. I'm glad you came up to meet Nathan and check out our life here."

Pauline and Cameron had arrived earlier in the week and were staying at her place, much to Evie's delight. Eileen had even given Evie extra time off to catch up with her family before they returned home the day after tomorrow. "What do you think of Nathan, anyway?" Evie asked her mother. "You haven't said much yet."

Pauline squeezed Evie around the waist in a supportive gesture. "Oh, darling. He's wonderful. Seems like the nicest man. So handsome too. I'm sure your father would love to meet him."

Evie nodded in agreement. "Yeah, I reckon you're right. Dad would get on with Nathan for sure. Hopefully, they can meet one day soon, when Dad gets home."

Her mother had updated Evie on Eric's cancer treatment which had finished, the results due any day now. According to the doctors, his prognosis was positive. "I'm sure Eric would love that too, darling," Pauline said as Oscar approached the pair, skilfully balancing a tray full of drinks.

Adopting the role of waiter, he smiled. "Ladies, can I tempt you with a beverage?"

"Why thank you. Don't mind if I do," Pauline and Evie accepted a glass, and Oscar sauntered off, his cheeky grin on full display.

Pauline took a sip and turned to Evie. "I'm hopeful your father will be home before Christmas. If the parole hearing goes okay, that is. I'm so excited, I'm counting the days."

Evie cheered at the news. "Mum, that's fantastic. I hope so too." She spied Kenny and Moira chatting and took her mother's arm. "Why don't you come and meet Moira. She's nice. I think you two will get on," and they moved towards the older couple.

Minutes later, leaving her mother in the couple's company, Evie continued to do the rounds, acting as hostess while chatting with colleagues and crew. Rylee and Caroline were there, as well as Eileen and several other operators only too happy to join in the festivities.

The Fire Service had been supportive of their officers and staff following the publicised incident which had helped to ease some of the physical and mental stress it had caused.

So far, Nathan appeared to be coping well yet Evie knew that there may be days ahead where he'd need her support and she fully intended to be around to offer it.

Evie spied Nicola at the station entrance, although she didn't recognise the tall hunk standing alongside. Evie waved as she approached in greeting, her mind spinning with curiosity at the mystery guy her friend had obviously been keeping secret.

"Nic, hi. Glad you made it," she gave her trainer a hug, feeling a slight tension in the air as she did so.

"Evie. I'm so happy to see you. You look amazing."

Nicola appeared nervous, which seemed out of character for her. She gestured towards the male standing close by. "This is my… friend, Owen." She turned towards him but didn't meet his eyes. "Owen, this is Evie, Nathan's partner." Nicola turned back to Evie. "Owen's in the Police Force. He knows Nathan through work." Her voice was husky. "We met recently at… ahh, well, I'll tell you later."

Strange introduction, Evie thought. No doubt, Nicola would fill her in on the details. She held out a hand to Owen, and he took it with a firm grip. "Welcome, Owen. Glad you could make it."

"Thanks for asking us," he said. He nodded towards the wall where the *Welcome Back Heroes* banner was displayed. "Love the sign."

Evie couldn't help but laugh at the efforts of Nathans' crew. "Yeah, impressive, isn't it? Meant a lot to the boys. They're both doing well and Nathan can't wait to get back to work." Evie pointed to where a group of men stood talking further inside the station bay. "He's over there if you want to say Hi."

"Thanks, I will." He turned towards Nicola. "Will you be okay for a minute while I go over?" he asked, to which she nodded.

"Sure. I'll be fine. Go ahead." She gave him a gentle nudge, and he sauntered off.

"He's cute. Is he a client of yours?" Evie teased her friend, who she knew hadn't dated a guy in ages. In fact, Nicola had sworn to Evie she was off men for good.

"It's a long story. I promise I'll fill you in later." Nicola took Evie's arm and led her inside. "For now, let's find a drink."

* * * * *

Nathan offered Evie a wave as she and Nicola headed towards the makeshift bar, manned by Oscar. The party was all the young firefighters idea, and he'd reluctantly agreed to it even though he hated being the centre of any attention. It was a nice gesture from his crew that both he and Kenny were greatly appreciative of.

Nathan still experienced regret whenever he thought about how Olivia had ended up, wondering if he could've done anything more to help. But, like many had told him, she'd been a troubled soul who hadn't wanted to accept any help. Not from him, or anyone else.

Still, it didn't lessen the feelings of guilt he held. Something he needed to work through in his own time.

"Hey Boss, good to be back?" Will patted Nathan on the back, the young man raising a drink. "We should have parties like this more often. Glad you've decided to stay with the crew. Couldn't do this…," he gestured to the crowd, "… if you were one of the big bosses, sitting in a glass office all day. Not your style at all."

Nathan smiled at Will's remark. "Yeah, buddy. Glad to be staying on the trucks with you guys, that's for sure. Can't let you have all the fun, can I?"

As Will wandered off, Nathan surveyed the area with a sense of pride. After much soul searching, he'd decided against applying for the inspector position. With all that had happened, he realised his heart wasn't into pen pushing and creating policies. Not when he preferred to be out making a real difference in the community.

Evie had supported his decision one hundred percent, which was one of the things he loved about her.

He chuckled to himself.

Love.

Who would have thought he'd have fallen head over heels?

The thing he'd wanted for so long had finally arrived-finding a woman he could trust and respect. He felt so grateful that she was in his life.

He spotted her talking to Kenny and guessing she may need rescuing from his countless stories, strode over.

She smiled as he approached, and raised her face for a kiss, to which he happily obliged. Feeling his heart swell with love and pride, he placed an arm around her, holding her close.

As she nestled her head against his shoulder, thoughts of his father entered his mind.

Yeah, Dad. I finally found the one.
Took me a while, but I found her.

THE END

Epilogue

Moira gazed around the station bay, amazed at how events had worked out in her favour for a change.

Asked along as Kenny's date, she'd decided to commit to him and give their relationship a chance. After so many failed attempts in the past, Moira realised that living life alone wasn't something she fancied.

Kenny had a lot of redeeming qualities underneath his rough exterior, and treated her with respect and caring whenever they were together.

Who could complain about that?

She felt for the locket around her neck and for the first time in a long time, undid the clasp, gripping it in her hand. Memories swamped her as she opened the fastening and felt the usual surge of love upon gazing on the faded image inside.

The black-and-white picture of the little boy playing with his red fire truck was as clear today as it had been all those years ago.

The dimple in his chin was less prominent these days but the light brown eyes never failed to remind her of his father, the man she'd given everything up for.

The man who'd dumped her, leaving her bereft.

Regrets?

Sure. If she had her time over–who knows what may have happened?

Looking up, she spotted Nathan and Evie deep in conversation with Kenny, the older man laughing out loud at something she'd said.

Moira couldn't stop the tears of emotion that began to form in her eyes.

Tears of happiness and joy.

"Yes, my boy…," she whispered, her gaze fixed on the confident man as he placed a protective arm around his partner. "…you're just as amazing now as you were back then.

"I'm so proud of you-my beautiful son."

The End

Acknowledgments

Everyone knows that although I'm the one writing the words to the story, no journey is taken alone.

In fact, there are many involved who deserve my thanks. Apologies to those I've forgotten.

Firstly, I'd like to thank the on-line Indie community (short for independently published authors).

Thanks to Joanna Penn, whose website was the first I discovered aimed at how to successfully self-publish, and who continues to inspire me today.

Joanna, your chirpy presence echoed in your podcasts, webinars and courses is an amazing source of inspiration to me. I'm so grateful to have found your body of work. It's encouraged me to keep going.

Thanks to Mark, James and the team at the Self Publishing Show. Your content and encouragement has provided me with such a wealth of knowledge, I'm forever grateful. May you keep it going for as long as you're willing and able.

Lastly, for the online community bit, much appreciation to the two Marks, Stay and Deveaux, of the Bestseller Experiment. I've spent many hours commuting in laughter at your entertaining interviews, information and knowledge.

Love, Reignited

A big thanks also to the BXP Facebook community - your encouragement and advice has been a great inspiration to me.

To Lindsey Alexander, my editor. Thanks so much for your help and guidance through this first time process for me.

You've helped in so many ways and I look forward to working together on future projects.

To my Firecom buddies, KD and Katie, thanks for the laughter and support. You guys keep me sane in the job.

KD - sorry I couldn't use the prawn trawler idea - maybe next time!

To my family - love you all.

To Bradd, words can't express how much I love you.

Thanks for your belief and support over the many months. It means more than I can say.

Coming Soon…

Return to the tropical paradise of Far North Queensland as we follow the story of Nicola and Owen as they search for love, in the second instalment from my <u>Love in the Tropics</u> series:

<u>Love, to the Rescue</u>

Due for release 2020

Love, Reignited

JOIN MY EMAIL LIST TO RECEIVE YOUR FREE NOVELLA

A Love Betrayed-

telling the background story of the Meriwether family and the truth behind Evie's escape from Melbourne to begin her new life in Cairns.

You'll also receive regular offers including gifts and discounts for upcoming books.

It's absolutely free to sign up and I guarantee you'll never be spammed by me and can opt out at any time

Sign up today at https://www.wendytipping.com

<u>Review Request</u>

If you have enjoyed this book, it would be wonderful if you would consider leaving a review.

Reviews help me gain greater visibility as an independently published author, as well as bringing my book to the attention of others who may enjoy it.

To leave a review, please go to your favourite on line bookseller, search for my author page and follow the prompts.

Thanks so much!